To my family.
Your support has been my inspiration.
All my love to you.
Royal (Dad)

Earth Portals

Cover Art and Illustration by Stacy Shofner Williams

ISBN 978-0-9912537-0-8

For information address:
Earth Portals
827 Hickory Stick
Chickasha, OK 73018

Earth

Portals

Earth Portals

Chanel could smell soil. She could *really* smell soil. The damp musk with its bitters and tannins wafted through her senses. The collage of the diverse mix of odors invigorated her. The cool aromatics relaxed the muscles in her face and her neck and shoulders. She could discern the clays from the earthworms and the decaying grasses. She had never felt this sense of oneness with the earth.

Opening her eyes, she found herself crouching in dew glistened grass. The tendons in her hands and feet were alive with kinetic energy. She could spring forth in an instant. The hair on her face sensed every whisper of breeze, every puff of... *THE HAIR ON HER FACE!* There is hair on her face? This is not some fine baby hair; there a fur coat of hair on her face! She ran her finger through it! She was mortified!

She smelled water. Creeping forward to a pool of water at the edge of the knoll, peering slowly through the tall asparagus plants and into the water; she saw her reflection. It was not *her* reflection. The reflection was that of an animal. She recoiled backward from the water's edge. What is going ...?

Crash! The impact of wood against brick rattled the porch. Chains that had heretofore supported her in the swing now flailed in pendulum as aftershocks.

The fall and subsequent bang on her forehead from the life-of-its-own glider awoke Chanel from her vision. She was sprawled on the porch with one arm shielding the chaise from further retaliations.

She felt of her face for reassurance. What a dream! What a nightmare.

Honk, honk, honk!

The noise brought her back to reality. Instinctively she tried to jump up before her spectacle was noticed. It was her father's horn tooting down the street. His pickup truck was just a house away and coming to the driveway.

As her father reached his parking spot he stopped and put his battered carriage in gear, he jumped out laughing.

"It is futile to look so innocent, I saw that," he announced. "You can't sleep *under* the porch-swing! That's where Pepper sleeps when we let her out in the front yard!"

Chanel tried to regain more poise and lost her balance.

His calloused hands were quick but gentle to stop her fall.

Chanel's father doted over his kids. Chanel was the youngest of five. She had a brother and a sister and a new set of stepsisters. They were all at least ten years older than her. Chanel and her brother and sister knew him as *Dad*. He was hoping soon the new stepsisters would also.

Dad did light construction and landscaping work around the county. He loved working with his hands.

"I fell asleep waiting on you and I had a weird dream." Chanel touched the scuffed spot on her forehead.

"A weird dream about me?" He asked as he brushed the porch debris from the side of her jeans and arm.

"No, it was about me or maybe about me," Chanel got her feet under her. "I dreamed I was a wolf or dog or something."

"That's it! No more *Animal Planet* after eleven," Dad chided mockingly. His attention switched to her forehead. "That looks like a knot forming. Are you going to be okay for our walk or do I need to call the paramedics for a medi-flight to Oklahoma City?"

"Dad! Of course I'm okay. It was just that swing you

6

built. I probably hurt it more with my head." Chanel said as she turned to enter the house. "Let me get my jacket and some breakfast bars. Do you want a bottled-water?"

"Sure, make fun of my little chair." Dad answered as he followed behind her setting a large sack on the counter as Chanel rummaged through the cabinets. "I will take a bottled-water."

He dialed his cell phone and after a moment, he spoke into the receiver.

"Hi. Honey, Chanel and I are going into the woods. I brought some of Roy's Bar BQ home and we'll eat when we get in… Yes… Okay… Well, don't wait on us. You go ahead and eat while it is warm. We should be in by dark… Okay... We love you. Bye."

"Mom on her way?" Chanel asked.

Mom, is Steph. She and Chanel's dad Rick had been married for four years now. Steph and Chanel had bonded quickly as Steph also did with her sister and brother. But Chanel was the first to refer to her as Mom. When her dad had introduced Chanel to Steph when they first started dating, he knew it would be so.

"Yeah, a mile or so out," Dad said as he filled a glass with tap water.

"Want to wait on her?" Chanel asked out of politeness.

"Nope, it's just me and you kid," Dad answered after gulping down the whole glass of water. "Unless you want to wait?"

"I'll bet she is hungry so we better not interfere with her digestive system," Chanel smiled as she headed toward the front door. With a bound and a quick step to avoid the closing screen door she was out into the front yard and headed to the woods. Her dream was behind her but not far

7

gone.

It was cold and blustery that Thursday afternoon, but Chanel and her father were soon knee deep in their adventure. They loved their excursions into the "Hunnert Acre Wood" as they called it after *Christopher Robin's* adventurous playground. Each trip into these wooded acres brought discovery, though not all discoveries were of a physical nature. Many were emotional. Each trip was an opportunity to re-enforce the bonds that had been stressed through Chanel's parents' recent divorce and subsequent remarriages. Not only did the constant growth of wild vines and brush change the scenery for them to explore; but, time away from each other also dictated new paths for them to examine. The woods were a wonderful place to create and mime adventurous tales. And, it was a therapeutic place to keep a father and daughter's relationship solid.

"Dad, can I ask you something?" Chanel interrupted the crows off in the distance.

"Sure, Sweetheart, what's up?"

Slowing her pace but just a little, Chanel asked, "I know you and Mom, my mom, not really *my* mom but my real mom, not that Steph isn't my real mom now also but…"

"Sweetheart, I know who you are talking about." Dad grinned and tugged softly at a wisp of her golden brown hair.

"Sorry." She started again. "I know you guys said I wasn't or we weren't the cause of your splitting up, but, wasn't I or were we not enough to keep you two together?"

Rick stopped and put his hand on her shoulder to stop her also. Her eyes swept the ground before looking up at his.

"Chanel, you guys were the reason we tried to put aside differences to stay together for so many years. We tried very hard to keep our family as one unit but it was not a fair representation for you guys to model your future family life after. We had quit fighting at night after you were sleep but the alternative silence between us was deafening. Your sister told me she had rather us argue and yell than to walk past each other like we didn't exist."

"I don't remember all that," Chanel confessed.

"I know you don't and that is such a blessing." He pulled her close and hugged her tight.

"Sweetheart, your mom and Jay are so happy and Steph and I are so happy, it is our hope that that is more of a blessing to you, Chelsea, Cody and now Jaimie and Jordan. There is so much more love to spread around."

Chanel pulled back and smiled. "And I feel it. We feel it. I just wonder sometimes when I think too much."

"Well, you don't have to wonder." He assured, "We feel that a guiding hand directed us to this place for a reason. We are on a good path now. Good for all of us."

"I think so, too." Chanel confirmed.

Come on, I'll race you to the plum thicket." He pulled her by the hand as he exaggerated his pace.

Breathing hard, they reached the plum thicket which marked the edge of the woods. Catching their breath, they entered.

As a hobby, Chanel's dad researched history and geography so every walk became a lesson within itself. They actually bored Chanel much of the time but his talking always set a rhythm to the walk. He had her imagine they were the first persons to see this bend in the creek, or to see the way the hill fell away to a nestling grove of eastern red cedars. He wanted her to love her imagination and the power it provided to embellish a sometimes disappointing life.

Dad told her that she had a sight gift. As early as four years old, Chanel could see shapes and details on blank paper which allowed her to sketch with great precision. He wanted her to pursue this gift and nurture the opportunity it afforded her. If, indeed, that is what she wanted.

His lessons while walking were both comforting and comical. He once said of the cedar groves, "These God-made shelters were both a refuge in a strong wind and a great place to hunker under if you were one of the travelers in the tragic Donner party of 1847."

Of course, he was referring to the tragic story of stranded pioneers resorting to cannibalism to stay alive in a blizzard while crossing the Rocky Mountains.

"It was possible they drew straws to see who got eaten," he went on. "They rarely ate the ugly pioneers because of the indigestion that comes from eating *ugly* people."

Chanel, wide eyed to this point, relaxed and grinned. He was interjecting *his* historical perspective.

"I am most certain, Chanel, you would have been the first eaten and I would have been the last." All this said most matter-of-factly.

Chanel was in town visiting with her dad and step-mother for two weeks during the Thanksgiving holiday break and on this particular adventure in the woods, the vines had closed most of the paths normally taken. In fact, instead of following the creek as they often did, they were being herded by the extra undergrowth onto a flat table of unfamiliar property. Large bark-less oaks stood sentinel over the slight mesa like old Indians in a sweat lodge. A trepid gathering of dead limbs was centered among them as if in cowered answer to the 'council' of the ancient oaks looming over them. Mist hung low over the buffalo grass and clouded some of the ground around the pile, yet Chanel and her dad never stumbled. It was as if their steps were being guided.

Upon reaching the pile of broken and twisted deadfall, a faint outline of stacked red rocks in the middle of the heap caught their attention. Chanel's dad pulled the limbs away and uncovered a circular well. It was three feet tall and some five feet across. The well was mortared by time and some long-ago hands, the smooth red stones looked firm as if just laid. The plaster between the rocks was smooth and free of rough edges.

"This is not regular concrete mortar," Her dad observed and commented. "It has a porcelain feel like log cabin chinking. It must be very old."

"What is chinking," Chanel asked.

"Chinking was like riverbed clay. It dried hard and was fairly waterproof. The settlers used it to fill the gaps between logs to keep wind and rain from entering the house," he explained.

They were both fascinated by the discovery, not because of what it was, but more so by the fact that neither had seen it before. For years, the two of them had walked here nearly every weekend that Chanel came to visit. Hours had been spent hiking and talking in these woods. There were the favorite places and landmarks each searched for during their outings. But now, even the towering circle of dead oak trees was unfamiliar.

Missing this site was some great oversight on their part and both were a little embarrassed. They had adopted these woods as their sanctuary but this new discovery was evidence they have been negligent in their observations and embrace.

The well was full of splintered limbs and debris that

appeared to be only a few feet deep. Instinct demanded investigation. Her dad pulled some of the deadfall and leaves out to find it was obviously deeper than the initial assessment. He stopped at a thick log pockmarked with the holes of carpenter ants.

"Sweetheart, most of these are rotten and will probably just crumble in my hands if I pull on them," he said holding on to the largest limb. "After being unattended for so long, it's probably full of accumulated branches, grasses, and who knows what else."

Undeterred, Chanel reached in and grabbed that very same log wedged diagonal across the inside of the well. She tugged hard, encouraging her dad to work harder on breaking it loose.

"Pull a little harder, Dad."

After much loosening of decayed pieces, he finally found a solid piece of the thick limb to grasp. Letting out a ferocious roar for dramatic effect, he broke the jam free. It was no longer lodged in the well. Some debris fell into the chasm below where the jam had been. He let the massive branch fall from his grasp and much of the debris fell with it, deep into the darkness. His roar echoed from the well and faded into the woods.

They looked wide-eyed at each other. It was no less a feeling of accomplishment than had they discovered a treasure.

"Too bad we don't have a flashlight," Chanel said. "I would sure like to see how deep it is."

"I don't think it is very deep," Dad started, "I heard the big log hit bottom fairly quick."

Her mind raced with the possibilities.

"This could be a mine shaft not a well." Chanel wished

aloud.

Chanel's dad confirmed the log had hit bottom, not splashed! They possibly could find gold or silver or precious jewels and become the only prospectors in the state of Oklahoma.

Dad looked up at the tops of the trees and then at the fading orange glow to the west. "It could be, though the closest mining to Chickasha would have been in the Wichita Mountains thirty miles south of us. I think it is an old water well."

"Really?" Chanel wasn't accepting the dismissal. "It could be a mine someone abandoned."

"Could be," he placated. "We can check it out with flashlights later, but it is getting late and the shadows will make it a harder hike home."

"Could we come back with a flashlight," she begged? Chanel knew her dad's curiosity was also piqued.

He thought for a time, peering deep into the well opening. He glanced again at the horizon. His adventure bug was working overtime on his sense of reason.

Finally, after much consternation, he said, "Not tonight, Sweetheart, maybe tomorrow when I get off work." He hesitated again before turning away from the well. He knew his was the right call because it was getting dark in the woods and a cold November breeze trickled through the trees. Fog could roll in to make things worse.

Chanel knew tomorrow's anticipation would make for a long night.

Once home, they shared their discovery with "Mom." She was excited for the discovery but also disappointed not to have been there with them. She, too, loved walking the woods.

Steph and Chanel's dad had married four years ago and now the family consists of dad and mom, mom's two girls Jaimie and Jordan and dad's three children Cody, Chelsea and Chanel. Cody is married to Kenzie and lives in Pampa, Texas. Jaimie lives and works in Chickasha. Chelsea is a college student at the University of Science and Arts of Oklahoma in Chickasha. Jordan is a student at Oklahoma City Community College and Chanel is in Junior High School in Elk City, Oklahoma. Chanel spends nearly every weekend in Chickasha; at least every other.

She is now trying to decide who she calls first to announce that she and her dad had discovered a treasure in Chickasha, Oklahoma!

It would have to be Chelsea. Her sister was a romantic just like

Chanel. They talked frequently about the divorce and school and boys. Her explanations further exemplified that love amidst turmoil could and does thrive.

She tried Chelsea's cell phone. Straight to voicemail! Chanel knew was going to be a long night of anticipating tomorrow!

Chapter Two

Morning came to an exhausted state. Chanel, drifting in and out of consciousness, could hear voices outside her window. She felt that she had slept five minutes. Dreaming about the treasure at the bottom of the well kept the possibilities racing all night.

Steph and Chanel's cousin Jessie were on the back porch cleaning up after Pepper, Steph's ten year-old Schnauzer mix she had rescued as a puppy. Pepper had pulled the charcoal grill cover down and had slept in it, as she often does at night when the wind blows hard.

"Aunt Steph," Jessie asked, "why does Pepper sleep in this grill cover? I know I have found her in it a thousand times."

Steph laughed and looked at Pepper resting on her belly in the doorway to her igloo dog house. "Her dog-house whistles when the wind gets up," she started. "I think she thinks someone is whistling for her. We have watched her all but exhaust herself running in and out of her house to see who it might be. I think she finally gets tired of it all and just pulls the grill cover down to wrap up in."

Jessie is Chanel's new cousin since Dad married Steph. She has also become her best friend when Chanel comes to stay in Chickasha. Jessie and Chanel are just a year apart in age but Chanel naturally feels she is much more mature at thirteen years then Jessie is at her twelve years. The *one year* difference has been debated between the two of them many times with various winners.

Jessie's dad, Steve, and Chanel's new mom, Stephanie, are brother and sister. Uncle Steve is a bit off the beaten path

15

like Dad, so that gives Jessie and Chanel an excuse for the way they approach life. Steve's wife, Rebekah, balances Steve's world much as Steph balances Dad's.

Jessie peered through the window and saw that Chanel was now awake. She entered via the den and roller-bladed through the house and into Chanel's bedroom.

"Why are you still in bed?" she teased, "We are skating to the park, aren't we?"

"No! We can't cross the overpass on skates," Chanel argued as she rubbed the sleep from her eyes.

"What then?"

Chanel smiled and touched her finger to her lips. She eased out of bed and shut the door softly in case Mom was in the house also. Jessie picked up on her effort to conceal something and a big grin released the twinkle in her eye.

"Whaaat?" She whispered this time.

"We are going treasure hunting," Chanel whispered back. "No one can know."

"Where?"

"In the woods," Chanel answered. "Dad and I found a secret passage or a mine shaft or something." She was slipping into her clothes over her pajamas.

She was so anxious to get started that she tried putting her boots on over her house slippers. She started the process again with no slippers.

Jessie laughed at her aloofness and asked, "What about Aunt Steph? What will you tell her we are going to do?'

"I thought we'd try the 'we'll-be-at-each-other's-house' thing," Chanel explained. "Your mom already knows you are at my house, all we have to do now is tell my mom that we'll be at yours. They won't miss us for a while anyway."

"How far is it?" Jessie was trying to figure how long "a

16

while" might end up being. She'd already been grounded from the phone for not being in on time once before. It was cruel and unusual punishment that she would rather avoid repeating.

"It is just at the edge of the woods and it won't take long to look down it with our flashlight Chanel explained." Even as she heard words coming out of her mouth, Chanel was amazed again at how they had never noticed the well before. Her saying '*Just at the edge of the woods*' aloud to Jessie reinforced that it should have been discovered on some previous walk.

After making her bed and brushing her teeth, they stopped out back long enough to tell Mom they were going to Jessie's house. "We might stop by to see Kelsey, so it may take a little bit for us to get there," Chanel explained. The guilt at lying made her avoid looking Steph in the eyes. A knot tightened her stomach. She had never lied to her parents. But it wasn't a malicious lie, she justified in her mind. Burdened with it, she and Jessie went quickly on. She so wanted to look into the well.

Once out of her Aunt Steph's earshot, Jessie gave Chanel a high five. "That was smart thinking, girlfriend. Now we have more time."

"Just a little more," Chanel said, "All I want to do is look down into the well. Dad says we can check it out more when he gets home."

"Okay, then are we going skating?" Jessie was laying her skates by the front porch and slipping on her shoes that she had carried in her backpack.

"Sure," answered Chanel. "You know, it's kind of cold, I'm going to get something warmer on before we go."

Chanel went in the house and saw Mom's old Chickasha

High School Senior jacket on a storage box in her stepsister Jordy's old room. Mom was sorting and putting away some of hers and Jordy's clothes since Jordy was off at college. Thinking it was going to the attic anyway, she decided it was probably all right for her to wear it. On her way out, she also grabbed Dad's flashlight from the cabinet and joined Jessie out in the front yard.

"Ready?" she asked Jessie, who was busy putting her roller blades behind the porch swing.

"I guess so," Jessie answered. "Hey, what happened to this swing? The arm is cracked?"

"I'm embarrassed to tell you," Chanel quipped

"Okay, "Jessie accepted. "Chanel, I don't remember seeing a well when we went out there last time."

"We didn't either. It was covered with a bunch of dead limbs and stuff. We probably walked by it a million times," Chanel explained exasperatedly.

"Yeah, it probably was there all along." Jessie kicked a rock in front of Chanel. Chanel kicked it farther ahead for Jessie to kick next. Jessie kicked it a little ahead of Chanel again. This understood rock-soccer way of traveling went on for a few more yards. As the woods became more definitive and less a horizon, Chanel missed her turn and Jessie had to kick it twice. At the second skip of her turn, Chanel slowed her pace way down. She was looking off at the woods.

"What's up?" Jessie asked.

Chanel couldn't get the well's sudden appearance off her mind.

"Jessie, we probably walked by it maybe even a *billion* times but we should have seen it before... had it been there before," Chanel interjected as they walked.

"Maybe," Jessie agreed. She kicked the rock far ahead

and out of their path.

They walked in silence. Soon enough, they arrived at the edge of the woods. Up to now, they had never explored into the woods without an adult, so now they slowed their steps a little bit.

"Okay where is it? I don't see it," Jessie said.

"Just inside that thicket by those forked trees," Chanel directed.

The girls quietly stepped into the woods. Both knew they were on the edge of being irresponsible. Inside the thickets that formed a natural border to the woods they stood and looked around. Chanel couldn't find the circle of oaks or the flat table that brought their attention to their well yesterday. After a slow search for something familiar, Jessie looked at her as if to say *'your time is up'*.

"Jessie, it was covered in dead limbs and kind of hard to see…" Chanel was trying to explain about how hard it was to remember exactly where they had stumbled upon the well, suddenly a shrill screech broke her train of thought.

"Did you hear that?" Chanel asked.

"Hear what?"

For a brief moment they listened to the empty sounds of the woods.

"I thought I heard a bird or something." Chanel explained.

"Well, I didn't. You are hearing things." Jessie laughed at Chanel's seriousness.

Chanel cocked her head to listen, forcing Jessie to rethink her accusations.

Finally, Chanel gave in and resumed her search. Just as Jessie turned to join her the shrill screech echoed in their ears and the ruffle of feathers dangerously close to their

19

heads caused them to instinctively duck. The call echoed through the woods. They turned simultaneously. A hawk swooped down through the trees and landed on top of the same jumble of limbs that had covered the well yesterday. The pile was twenty feet away but if it hadn't been for the hawk, they wouldn't have seen it.

Chanel looked up from the debris and her eyes met the hawk's eyes. As if to confirm their connection, the hawk momentarily locked its gaze with Chanel's. Then, as suddenly as it appeared, the majestic bird left his perch over the well and again swooping close to the girl's heads; arched it's flight back into the woods.

"Jessie, he is showing me the well." Chanel was incredulous.

Jessie just followed the hawk's flight into the woods until it disappeared.

"He," Jessie started, "I think it was a *she*. That thing looked intense!"

"No, it was a he," Chanel said softly.

She reached over and slipped Jessie's hand into hers and they stepped away from the thickets and headed to the well.

Chapter Three

Jessie broke free from Chanel's hand and ran the last few steps to the well.

"Cu-wull!" Jessie exclaimed. She had her head and shoulders deep into the well before Chanel could catch up.

"Can you say 'cool' as if it had one syllable please?" Chanel couldn't help mimicking her other big sister Chelsea who was studying to be a teacher and thought it okay to practice language critiquing on Chanel.

"Whatever!" Jessie laughed, "You talk like you want and I'll talk like I mean what I'm saying."

"I told you it was cool," she said as she stepped up to the well's edge with Jessie. "There's no water in it, listen." Picking up a rock from the ground beside the well, Chanel dropped it over the opening. Instinctively, they both leaned forward to hear the rock hit. Jessie almost lost her balance and Chanel had to restrain her from tumbling into the well. Neither took their eyes off the darkness within the well.

All the while, Chanel was counting aloud: "One-Mississippi…" Before two-Mississippi had completed its voice, they heard a dull thud somewhere below.

"I don't know how far a Mississippi is, but it can't be too deep," Chanel said. She shone her dad's flashlight down the hole, but the beam barely reached the bottom. "I think I can see the outlines of limbs and stuff, but I'm not sure. What do you think?"

Jessie stared long and hard at the end of the beam. "I think those are limbs but I'm not sure. If we could just get a little closer to the bottom we'd know."

"I got an idea!" Chanel offered. "I have this long shoestring in my pants pocket. We'll tie the flashlight to a long branch and hold it down closer to the bottom."

"Okay. I'll go find a long stick," Jessie said. She went to the edge of the circle and came back with a six-foot limb.

"Will this work?" Jessie was pulling loose bark off her new-found extension tool.

"Perfect, Jess, hold it there while I tie it," Chanel said. She tied the flashlight on as best she could. The long flashlight was shaped like a smooth tube with no appendages to tie to. Chanel wrapped the string around the tube and stick and made the knot as tight as possible.

Poking it down the well, they both tried to look at once, causing their heads to hit. Laughing aloud, they their voices echoed in the well. The violent head banging and subsequent laughing caused the flashlight to slip out of the string. The laughter stopped.

"See what you made me do!" Chanel snapped at Jessie. "Now how are we going to get that flashlight before dad knows we came out here?"

"It wasn't my fault, you were holding it," Jessie defended.

"I know, my bad." Chanel apologized.

Looking back over the edge, they discovered the light was shining up the walls of the well. It had lodged in a branch somewhere below and was shining back up at them.

"Look," Jessie said, "it is like a ladder is carved into the walls."

Chanel leaned over to reach down to touch the rock wall. Sure enough, there was a handhold about two feet down from the rim and several more in succession as you looked directly below the first.

"Maybe, I could crawl down and get the flashlight," Chanel offered, hoping Jessie would volunteer.

"Okay," Jessie said.

"Okay?" Chanel asked.

"Okay. Yeah, why?" Jessie asked.

"I just can't believe you'd let me go down there after that flashlight!" Chanel pulled the limb with the now empty shoestring out of the hole. "You would just let me go down into that dungeon of a well all by myself, wouldn't you?"

"Did you want me to go?" Jessie asked.

"Only if you want to."

Jessie raised her hands to the sky. "Here you are mad at me for letting you go without an argument and when I say 'I will' you say 'only if you want to'. What's up with that?"

Chanel was busted. She thought how she really did want to go down the hole, just not alone.

"Alright." Chanel reasoned. "There's nothing down there. So, I'll go and you stay here and watch me."

Chanel looked down the artificially lit passageway. "Don't go anywhere. I want to be able to see your face all the time," she instructed sternly.

"I won't!" Jessie confirmed.

Chanel swung her leg over the edge of the rocks.

"Snakes, what about snakes?" Jessie interjected still looking into the darkness.

Chanel stumbled back onto her backside trying to pull her leg out of the well.

"Where?"

"I didn't say I saw a snake. I was just asking about snakes." She offered her hand to help Chanel up off the dead leaves and twigs.

Waving off her assistance Chanel got to her feet. She brushed her backside clean and looked down into the well.

"I don't think there would be snakes, it is too cold," she

24

offered weakly. "And, don't just blurt out *snakes*, like that!"

After gathering her composure, she pinched Jessie on the shoulder. They both laughed at their seriousness.

"Here I go." Chanel announced.

Starting down the wall she found the steps and handholds were surprisingly easy. She never slipped or struggled but just as yesterday, when they first found the well, she felt as if someone were guiding each hand and foot placement. As she reached the pile of dead limbs and the flashlight, she noticed a slight warm breeze coming from behind her. Turning the flashlight towards the source she found a tunnel. With careful placement of her steps on the loose branches and debris, Chanel moved down towards the tunnel. She shone the light down the tunnel's path to check the length.

"What are you doing down there? I can't see you or the light anymore!" Jessie cried out with angry anticipation.

"Jessie, come down here!" Chanel wanted her to see this. She was a bit scared to be so far into the well; yet almost comforted by the warm breeze blowing in her face. It was inviting, like puppy breath.

"Duh, do you think I'm a bat? I can't see the hand holds!" Jessie's sarcasm hid her fear.

"Sorry!" Chanel answered as she shone the light up the shaft for Jessie. Jessie searched the wall for assuring support and then crawled over the ledge and climbed down using the handholds. When she finally got down to where Chanel was standing, the light was directed down through the tunnel for both to see. It was surprisingly dry and free of any debris. The floor was rippled sand. Maybe the breeze had kept the forest litter out of the tunnel and in the main shaft of the well.

"Let's go to the end. It is not very far because I can see

some light when I turn the flash light off," Chanel said.

"I'm with you. That is, I'm with you as long as you have the flashlight. If you lose it, I'm going back outta here," Jessie warned.

Chanel's boldness surprised even herself. She was usually the "scaredy cat". In fact, Chanel was almost wishing Jessie would take the lead and let her think about each movement on. Since starting her trips to Chickasha when her dad was still just dating Steph, Chanel had put on this front to be seen as confident and in charge. It had kept her bravado up when she had wondered so many times why her real mom and dad were apart and what was she doing in another town visiting her dad's girlfriend anyway. But that was years ago now and here she is: Chanel in charge. Through all the adventure, she felt responsible. She just didn't know who she felt responsibility for.

The girls crept the length of the tunnel and found the light to get brighter as they walked. The light was their comfort. The walls were dry but cool like those you would find under a bridge crossing an empty stream.

The tunnel opened into a glade of sorts, but both recognized the layout of the trees and creek bed of the Shannoan Springs Park. The park was almost a mile north of the house but Jessie and Chanel had reached it in less than a hundred steps walking.

The park was as it should be. There were people walking down by the big pond and geese begging bread from the kids on the bridge.

"How did we get here?" Jessie asked. "My Dad says it is at least a full mile to the park from here and we didn't walk that far. Plus, I know we didn't go under the turnpike." She was noticeably concerned about the time and distance disparity.

A boy came by running by with long hair and thick sideburns covering his entire jaw-line. He was wearing a Doobie Brothers T-shirt, tight denim jeans cut short to his upper thighs and long white socks pulled up to his knees. A Frisbee landed by Jessie's feet and she threw it back to a girl who was wearing a shirt that was tied around her neck *and* tied behind her back. Her jeans had bell-bottoms that covered almost all of her ugly shoes. The shoes had heels that were lower than the front sole. They reminded her of the wooden clogs from Holland. "You talk about some dorks!" Jessie murmured to Chanel.

Banners announcing an upcoming "Bicentennial Celebration" flapped in the breeze near the entrance of the park. Chanel also noticed the big "Christmas in the Park" sculpture was missing. The sculpture was made out of thirty-five foot steel bars that spanned the whole entrance, but now it was gone. Something more than just the clothing that the kids were wearing and the park entrance was different.

"Chanel, we need to get back," Jessie warned. "I bet Aunt Steph or my mom is looking for us."

"Alright, but let's look around on the way back and we can tell them we started back as soon as we realized the time."

Jessie looked at Chanel with furrowed brow, "Duh, seeing as how we are supposed to be at each other's house, that made a lot of sense."

"Well, you know what I mean." Chanel defended.

As they turned around to head back into the tunnel, Chanel heard her name whispered. It was soft as a distant moan in the breeze.

"Did you hear that?" Chanel stopped in her tracks and

cocked her ear to hear more.

Jessie stopped and looked around slowly. "Hear what? All I hear is Led Zeppelin's *Kashmir* coming from that guy's pick-up over there." Jessie pointed at a guy waxing a lime-green truck. "Look how wide his tires are!"

"How do you know it is Led Zeppelin?" Chanel questioned.

"My Dad has that CD. It's old music from when he was in school. Your Dad has it also. I have heard it in his pickup," Jessie defended.

"Yeah, I know but…shhh…!" Chanel was straining to hear it again. "I heard someone say my name," she explained.

They both listened for a moment and then Jessie gave it up.

"It was probably Aunt Steph and we are both in t-r-o-u-b-l-e, let's go!"

"Yeah. You're probably right." Chanel conceded.

Just as they entered the tunnel she heard it again but chose not to mention it to Jessie. Deep inside, she knew it was someone else besides Steph calling her name. She also took mental note that she could smell her house. She could smell the familiar odors of walking through her front door. She and Jessie were still a quarter mile away from the house.

Chapter Four

The girls climbed quietly from the well. Once they had their feet on the ground and were walking towards Chanel's house; Jessie asked again about skating when they got home. It was as if the strangeness of the place and events hadn't registered with her. Chanel was preoccupied with all that had unfolded in the well and in the park. Skating was far from a concern. She couldn't wait for her dad to get home, although she knew she couldn't tell him about going into the well.

"Jessie, did you not notice how dorky those guys looked at the park?" Chanel asked.

Jessie laughed, "Yeah, it looked like Mom's high school yearbook pictures."

"Yeah, but did you notice they were wearing shorts and it was warm in the park?" Chanel asked.

"Hmm…crack-heads probably," Jessie offered. "My dad said people on drugs sometimes couldn't feel their faces much less this cold wind. I know they were sure dressed like crack-heads!"

They both laughed aloud at that. "They sure were," Chanel agreed.

"But, now that you mention it," Jessie stopped Chanel with her hand on Chanel's arm, "I was warm also."

After a look of agreement and nothing else, they continued on their way. They didn't speak until they got to the house. Mom was inside the front room and waved from the window.

They grabbed their roller blades and offered them up as if they had forgotten them. Then they skated down to Kelsey's house where they skated and talked the rest of the afternoon.

Finally, Chanel saw dad's truck go past. He was headed home.

"Hey guys, I am going to catch my dad. I'll call you later tonight."

"I thought you were going to ask if I could stay the night," Jessie looked hurt.

"I will, but let me talk to him first. You know what I mean?" Chanel rolled her eyes to indicate the secret.

"Oh, yeah." Jessie rolled her eyes towards Kelsey.

"Whaaat?" Kelsey pleaded. "I hate it when you do that."

Chanel locked her jaw and looked stern at Jessie.

"Nothing!" Jessie explained, desperate to come up with a "*Whaaat?*" for Kelsey.

"Okay then. I'll call tonight. Kelsey, do you want me to see if you can spend the night also?" Chanel asked.

"No, we have to go to *Big Daddy's Burgers* to eat. My aunt is coming in with her nose-picking kids. It is so hard to eat while they're around. Everyone in *Big Daddy's* gets sick just watching them."

"Too much information, Kelsey," Chanel said. "How about next time, then?"

"Sure." Kelsey replied and then turned to confront Jessie about the "*Whaaat?*"

"Jessie, I'll call after I visit with my dad." Chanel called over her shoulder as she skated away.

Skating hard and fast, Chanel caught her dad as he was unloading his tools from the pickup. He smiled as she tried to jump the curb and rolled in the grass.

"Smooth landing. Maybe we should get you shoulder pads to go with the helmet." He bent to help her up and gave her a kiss on the nose. "If I take you home all black and blue, your mother might hesitate to let you come stay with

30

me. And then she'd have a fight on her hands."

"Yeah, you and me both," Chanel added as she looked down at the pressed green grass on her kneecap. "Ow, look!" Chanel gestured to her knee.

Her dad gingerly cleaned the "yard" from her jeans. Blood started spotting through the denim. He pulled his dew rag from his head and exaggerated making a tourniquet for her leg.

"DAD!" Chanel pulled her leg away from his playing doctor.

His thinning hair and wedge nose reminded Chanel of the *Ichabod Crane* illustrations from Washington Irving's Legend of Sleepy Hollow story. His laughing blue eyes gleamed with how much he loved her.

"Let's go get cleaned up or we are going to be late for the nursing home."

"Nursing home!" Chanel pressed her palm to her forehead, "I forgot all about the nursing home!"

She wrestled with her rollerblade plastic and velcro latches. "Dad, you said we could go to check out the well when you got home and I wanted to ask if Jessie could spend the night." Her pleading was more a matter-of-fact reminder than a plea.

"Well, I did, but I also forgot about the nursing home when I offered. We won't be there very long and Jessie can still spend the night if it is all right by Mom. But, afterward, it will be too dark to go to the well." He thought for a moment and added, "I will take off early tomorrow so we can go to the well. Is that alright? I really need to finish Mrs. Adams fence before Thanksgiving Day."

Chanel's shoulders sagged but she really did like going to the nursing home and reading. The snacks were always good and the "girls" really enjoyed hearing the stories. Not wanting to appear to give in so easy she held up her pinkie.

"Alright, pinkie-promise you won't find something else to do."

Dad locked pinkies with her, "pinkie-promise."

Chanel rushed inside and cleaned her leg. She found some fresh jeans and put Mom's jacket back on the box where she had found it. She stopped to run her fingers across the Senior '76 embroidered on the pocket in purple and gold. Mom and Dad had graduated from Chickasha High School in 1976. Chanel thought about their yearbook photos that she had looked at so often. The people she and Jessie had spotted in the park were dressed in the same fashions. Her dad interrupted her thoughts with "You ready, sweetheart?"

"Coming!" she answered.

"Steph we are going to the nursing home to read to the residents, did you need anything on our way back?" Dad asked.

"I remembered." She said as she handed him the sandwiches and chips she had put together for her two volunteers. "I can't think of anything that I need. You'll have your cell phone?"

"Yes, ma'am," he offered.

"And eat these sandwiches, you two can't just eat cookies all the time." She teased.

She kissed Dad on the cheek leaving soft pink lipstick marks.

"You better wipe that off," Steph warned as she walked away.

"Nope. Those marks keep the lonely-hearts club at bay," Dad defended while leaving the lipstick in place.

Chanel and her dad got into Dad's work truck and backed

32

out of the driveway. They drove to the park.

Pulling into the WPA built rock entrance Chanel was very alert to the existing features. The park was now as she knew it. The arched entryway was there and no banners announcing a bicentennial celebration existed. Chanel's mind raced with the possibilities of the well.

Shanoan Springs Nursing Center was home to some of Chickasha's first residents. It sat on a hill overlooking the Shanoan Springs Park that had at one time, long ago, been the watering hole for the many teams of mule-skinning freighters that came up the Chisholm Trail moving cattle to Abilene, Kansas.

The Chisholm Trail was a route used in 1867 through the early 1890's. The trail stretched from San Antonio in southern Texas across the Red River and the Arkansas River to Abilene, Kansas, and before a north-south railway existed, was used to drive cattle north to the railhead of the Kansas Pacific Railway. It had originally been a trading path for Native Americans but it soon grew to be one of the main routes for shipping agricultural products, horses and cattle overland due to the ease of crossing the many rivers that stretched ahead of it. At Abilene, these products and cattle were then loaded on rail cars and shipped east to the great slaughterhouses in Chicago where they brought as much as ten times their value in Texas. Oklahoma was just Indian Territory and no real infrastructure existed to handle the commodities.

The trail is named for Jesse Chisholm who had built several trading posts in what is now western Oklahoma before the Civil War. Though he never drove cattle on the trail he was influential in laying it out for his own trading ventures.

The Indian Territory route of the Chisholm Trail ran about three miles east of the current city of Chickasha, Oklahoma where the Washita River afforded a low water crossing on hard sandstone. Originally the town of Fred grew here on these banks to service the many trail drives that slowed to cross. Pensee was the original name of Chickasha on the north side of the Washita River. In 1892, when the Rock Island Railroad moved south from El Reno, Oklahoma and built a bridge across the Washita River, a group of businessmen convinced James and Annie Speed to donate land off their Swinging Ring Ranch for a new town. Anne had been an Indian allotment owner, as she was a Chickasaw Indian by birth. Without this connection, no people of white ancestry could own property in Oklahoma Indian Territory. Many convenient marriages existed for the business aspect of land ownership prior to Oklahoma becoming a state in 1907.

The new town was named Chickasha after its Chickasaw heritage. Soon, Pensee and Fred closed and moved their entire towns, board by board, to join in Chickasha's location and prosperity.

That was in 1892. Now, every Friday night at the current nursing home overlooking the park, volunteer readers would meet and read aloud from books, journals and letters that the residents had chosen regarding the history of the area. Some wanted specific things read; others just liked to hear the children's voices. Some were in groups and some just in their room alone. Chanel liked the groups best because there were always interruptions and that meant she didn't have to read as much. She loved to hear them comment on the story or argue an event. Sometimes she'd throw them a loop by adding something to the story they knew to be out of place.

That move always got someone correcting her and another defending her.

Tonight, though, after their arrival, she noticed Ms. Ireland was missing from the circle. Chanel was *her* favorite and therefore *she* was Chanel's.

"Where is Ms. Ireland?" Chanel asked the aid as he passed out the snacks.

"Ms. Ireland is in her room. She is really down in the dumps today," one of the aides mumbled over his shoulder, "She has been kinda down for about a month."

Blair Ireland was the nursing home's oldest resident. She had been a school teacher in Chickasha most of her life and had never married. Her father had come over from County Donegal, Ireland to Ellis Island in New York City and had found his way to Oklahoma in 1935 when the Works Progress Administration was looking for stone masons to build a capital in Oklahoma City. Her father's real name wasn't Ireland, it was O'Halley, but he had misunderstood the questionnaire at the Ellis Island immigration center in New York harbor and so, therefore, Ireland's Sean O'Halley became America's Sean Ireland. The immigration from Ireland had been so tedious and difficult he was afraid to attempt to correct the record.

Ms. Ireland's stories fascinated Chanel, but the sadness in her constant moving about and the way people treated Catholic foreigners was sometimes overwhelming for Ms. Ireland to discuss. Her mother had died years before the move to Chickasha and she had never mentioned a family beyond her father. Chanel thought that this was the reason for the periods of melancholy that prevailed in her mood.

Chanel came to her doorway and peered in. Ms. Ireland was awake but still in her nightgown. This was a bad sign.

Even during her bouts of sadness, Ms. Ireland was always fastidious about being dressed proper. Here she sat in bed with her knees up with a book perched on them. Her face was turned toward the window; her eyes, unblinking on some long ago memory; and her thoughts, a thousand miles away.

"Ms. Ireland." Chanel stepped only far enough into the room to be framed by the doorway, waiting for an invitation before proceeding.

"Hello, Miss Chanel. Please come in," Miss. Ireland spoke and turned her head toward Chanel in one fluid motion. Chanel was her only frequent visitor most days and she knew her voice. Given that Chanel was only in Chickasha every month or so, made that a sad commentary. When Chanel reached her bedside, Ms. Ireland sighed softly.

"Now, don't lecture me for not being in the reading circle. I am old and sometimes I need to rest longer," she defended in her soft Irish brogue. She didn't always have the accent. She only used it when fishing for sympathy or when it was advantageous to win a debate.

"I won't," Chanel responded. "But I would rather you be in the circle when I read. Are you feeling sick?"

"No, child. I am feeling... unfinished." She looked back at the window as she said the word.

"What does that mean? Unfinished?" Chanel rested her leg and hip against the bed.

Ms. Ireland sat up a little to gain composure.

"I feel like there is something that I haven't done and that I must do it before..." She paused and peered into Chanel's eyes.

Chanel knew why she had stopped her sentence but she had to ask so she could coax Ms. Ireland to speak more,

"Before what?"

"Before it is time for me to go." Ms. Ireland was suddenly somber.

"Ms. Ireland, it is a long time before time for you to go," Chanel tried to sound like an adult but she felt a squeak in her voice. She knew Ms. Ireland heard it also.

From their private discourses, Ms. Ireland understood how Chanel felt about the people she loved leaving her daily life, so she tried to change the tone of the conversation.

"Yes, you are probably correct, but I can't do squaddle from this nursing home. I could still have years before time to go, but all that is unfinished, will remain so."

"Oh." Chanel scooted up on the bed. "What do you have to do?"

Ms. Ireland took Chanel's hand in hers. "I'm not sure."

"Not sure?" Chanel asked. "Then, how do you know it is unfinished?"

Ms. Ireland sighed again. She glanced out the window again and then pulled herself to sitting erect as if preparing for a task.

"Miss Chanel, I am going to tell you a story about two little girls. It happened so long ago that some of the story is lost in my wandering thoughts, but I think you might help me to understand what is unfinished better than I can do alone. Do you have time for a story such as that?"

"Yes, no one has missed me from the circle and Dad knows I came to talk to you." Chanel made herself more comfortable on the foot of her bed.

"Very well, then. I am counting on you to give sound advice when it is done," Ms. Ireland smiled, "is that a bargain?"

"Yes, ma'am," Chanel smiled back.

37

"Chanel, we came to Chickasha from Oklahoma City when word came of a need for builders with the Works Progress Authority. My father was a stonemason and he knew he could find work. A stonemason is a person that lays bricks and large rocks. He had been a stonemason in the old land just as his father had been. My mother had died from the pox there and he was ready to start afresh." She wiped the corners of her mouth with her silk handkerchief and when she saw Chanel wasn't looking at her, she dabbed the corner of her eyes.

"What is the pox?" Chanel asked.

"Smallpox, honey, it is called smallpox by the doctors. Now days, children are vaccinated for it and so you don't hear much about it. But there was a time when it wiped out entire communities." She settled back into her pillows to continue with the story.

"I was about your age then and was left alone to care for the house quite often. Father would be working on the bridges at the park nearby and it was not uncommon for me to put together a lunch for him and deliver it to the worksite. I liked doing that because I got to be with him and the other workers. All the men had their stories and while they laid stones they told them. I loved hearing them."

"Me too," Chanel agreed. "I like going to work with my dad."

"And that's a good thing, Chanel. Sometimes, like in the case of this story, my dad would be working near other children or around a place where people gathered and I could see and sometimes play with the children that were there. Grownups were fine, but I missed playing with my friends from Oklahoma City."

At this moment Chanel's dad came to the door.

38

"I hate to interrupt, but they need us in the reading room. Are you sure you don't want to come join us, Ms. Ireland? They do miss you." He tried working on her sympathy by exaggerating a frown and blinking puppy-dog eyes.

She smiled at his sincerity. "No, thank you."

She took Chanel's hand in hers, "You should get down there because I *know* they miss you."

"They miss you also," Chanel softly pleaded.

"Maybe so, child," she let go of Chanel's hand. "You go on down to the group and you and I will finish next time."

"Alright." Chanel got down from the edge of her bed and started toward the door.

"Oh, wait!" Ms. Ireland said, "I have something for you."

On the windowsill she had laid a silver and turquoise brooch. She motioned for Chanel to bring it to her.

"I found this in my jewelry box and I wanted you to have it. It was given to me a long time ago. You are the smartest twelve year-old reader that I know and I think people should see that you are worthy of accolades."

She pinned it on Chanel's lapel.

"Thank you very much," Chanel beamed. "I will take good care of it and if you need it back, I will have it."

"I won't need it back, dear. It's yours to keep and to someday pass on to one of your own beautiful children."

Chanel got up on the bed and hugged her tight. She knew something was wrong for Ms. Ireland to be so down and she felt sad that she could not help.

"Till next time, then," Chanel added.

"Yes, next time."

Chanel and her dad left her room and joined the reading circle. After they had read, talked, and ate cookies, Chanel and her dad went back to check on Ms. Ireland. She was asleep and so they exited quietly and drove home.

Chanel was worried about Ms. Ireland, but she was also anxious to investigate the well. Thoughts of the well were stealing her attention. She called Jessie on her dad's cell phone to confirm the sleep-over plans and within minutes, they were at Jessie's house loading her and her bicycle in his pickup. It was just four blocks to Chanel's house but the Oklahoma winds in November were cold once the orange sunset faded from the skies.

Tomorrow was another opportunity to explore the well. Chanel knew she and Jessie would not wait for dad to get home. She was giddy with the thought of the adventure and even with the possibility of getting caught. Chanel wasn't a bad girl, just overwhelmed with this new adventure in her life. With her parents divorce and her dad moving to Chickasha; the last five years were like living in limbo with the world and this new sense of purpose empowered her. She was hoping to discover something that would have been worth all the heartache.

Chapter Five

Morning came with little fanfare. The girls had talked all night long about the well and the odd circumstances in the park. As they discussed the people's dress, the warmer temperature and the missing archway, Chanel and Jessie knew something was special about the well and tunnel. Normally after an "up-all-night" episode, they would sleep until wrestled from the bed. This morning, however, anticipation overmatched their fatigue. They were up, dressed and making their bed when Steph stuck her head in the doorway.

"Girls, are you hungry?" She asked. "I have cereal or we can go for donuts."

"Donu…" Jessie started but caught the look in Chanel's face, "…no, cereal will be fine Aunt Steph."

"Yeah, me too!" Chanel chimed in. She really wasn't hungry but thought it best to present a reasonable sense of normalcy. She couldn't wait to get to the woods.

"I heard your voices almost all night long, I thought you two would be racked out till noon. It is very cold out, what's going on?" Steph asked as she set out bowls and boxes of Cocoa Pebbles and Honey Nut Cheerios.

"Nothing," Chanel answered quickly. "We just thought we'd go ride bikes or something. We talked about it last night and decided we stay in the house *way* too much."

"Yeah, *way*," Jessie agreed as she poured milk over a mound of brown cereal.

"You did hear me say it was cold?" Steph said as she came to Chanel's bedroom door.

"We know. We might go by Mrs. Keevert's to see her garage sale stuff or we might end up at Kelsey's," Chanel stated trying to sound nonchalant. "If we get cold we'll come home. I'll wear my coat I wore to the nursing home last night and the cool scarf you gave me."

"Yeah, I brought a warm coat and my gloves. If we get out of the wind on a side street, we will stay warm," Jessie added.

"Okay, but remember to keep me informed as to where you go to get out of the cold. Also, don't take any money down to Mrs. Keevert's garage sale. We have enough stuffed animals and costume jewelry for two garage sales already."

"Okay," they said in unison.

"By the way, I saw that brooch Ms. Ireland gave you. It is really pretty," Mom said.

"Yeah, isn't it?" Chanel agreed. "She said I could give it to my daughter one of these days."

"It looks like real hand-made Indian Jewelry, not costume. Do you think it might be too valuable to wear on your coat while hanging out?" Mom questioned.

"I'll be real careful," Chanel promised. "We're just hanging out."

"Yeah, Austin and Jarrett won't play football with us after we smoked them last time," Jessie laughed.

"*SMOKED* them!" Chanel emphasized with a high five.

"Okay, well if you get cold, I have some cocoa and marshmallows," Mom offered as she went back to her housecleaning.

"We'll be back," Chanel confirmed.

After inhaling their cereal and watching Mom go down the hall, they put their bowls in the dishwasher and headed out the door stealthily. Pausing briefly to see if the creak in the front door brought a word from her, they slipped out and softly closed it behind.

"The round hay bales are on the way to the woods. Let's stash our bikes behind them so mom won't see them and wonder what's going on," Chanel directed. "We can pick them up after we come out of the woods."

"Okay, but I really don't like sneaking around." Jessie kicked her bike-stand back out of the way of her pedals. "I just got ungrounded you know. Besides, you never sneak around. What's up with this well?"

Chanel wasn't sure what was up with this well. It had all of her attention.

"I don't know Jessie. I haven't been thinking about something this hard since the divorce. Anyway, you know they would say no to us going to the woods by ourselves," Chanel justified. "Besides, Dad is going to take us later, so it must be safe."

At the hay bales, Jessie expressed her doubts about going into the well. "Chanel, I'm not sure we should go back into the well without your dad."

"Why?" Chanel asked.

"Because you said you heard voices calling your name. I didn't hear that and it kinda creeped me out," Jessie explained. "Why don't we wait for your dad?" She held onto her handle-bars even after Chanel had dropped her bike next to the bale.

"Why?" Chanel asked again. She needed Jessie's support to continue on this quest so she kept walking towards the woods so Jessie wouldn't dig her heels in and make her go by herself. At this point, she would go by herself if she had to.

"I just think it might be better," Jessie repeated.

"I don't."

"Well…I do." Jessie stammered.

"Because I heard something that you didn't?" Chanel asked to make the argument seem trivial.

"Not just that, you got all weird when we were in the park. You said you heard things and you said the park looked different. I know about the park looking different but I don't know about the voices. Like I said, it seems scary now," Jessie explained.

Chanel knew in her mind these were creepy things, but somehow these creepy things got her heart to race. She was usually the hesitant one of the two girls but there was something pulling her to check out the well further.

At the edge of the woods, they entered through the thickets that formed a perimeter around the actual trees within. She looked fruitlessly for the well. Worried that Jessie might take this as a sign to give up the endeavor she started to make a compromise.

"Jessie, how about if we…" Chanel was interrupted by a ear piercing whistle that echoed through the trees.

It was the hawk's cry. Jessie obviously didn't hear it again as she waited for Chanel to finish her question.

He swooped in and landed on the brush pile that had been unseen heretofore.

Jessie was a few steps behind her and didn't look up at the hawk. Chanel wondered why Jessie hadn't heard it or acknowledged seeing it.

"How about if we what?" Jessie asked Chanel to continue her question.

Chanel thought for a moment as they arrived at the well. She was determined to follow her instincts.

She then offered this: "I'm going in and if you don't want to, that will be fine. But you can't leave because then someone will know I went in because you'll be by yourself." Chanel had a pleading look on her face.

"So, what am I supposed to do while you are in the well?" Jessie demanded.

Chanel thought for an instant, "Just wait for me."

"I'm not standing out here in the woods with all this wind blowing and everything!" Jessie's voice rose.

"Fifteen minutes," Chanel offered.

Jessie glared at Chanel and thought for a moment. "Five," she countered.

"Ten and I'll give you the rest of my cookies from the nursing home."

"I don't want your cookies," Jessie huffed, "but, I will stay here for ten minutes by *my* watch. If you don't come back by then, I'm going after Aunt Steph."

The thought of Jessie being scared, allowed fear to invade Chanel's anticipation. She felt safe but if Jessie didn't, maybe it was not being smart for Chanel to go in. Still, it was as if she was *supposed* to go, she *had* to go.

Dad said sometimes people did things because it was for them to do and they had no control over it. He said God gave us wonderment for us to expand on and this wonderment was what made the modern world. She reached her hand into her pocket and felt the cell phone that her mother had given her for her birthday. It was there and she could use it if needed. She felt safer.

"Okay, ten," she agreed. "Let me see your watch and make sure it is the same as mine. Now don't start until I go into the well."

"Okay, but as soon as I see your head disappear into the tunnel, I'm watching the time," Jessie confirmed.

"Okay," Chanel agreed. This time it was easier to agree

45

with Jessie's logic.

Chanel climbed down the well and all but ran through the tunnel. She didn't know what she was hoping to find but felt as if she were racing another clock besides Jessie's. As she ran, she noticed that she could smell the park. It was still far away yet she knew those odors.

Chapter Six

Chanel came out of the tunnel and into the park
expecting at least to see the weird dressed people she and
Jessie had seen before if not the people she sees every day in
the park. Instead, she saw a group of men gathering at a
large stone fountain with big horses. There were many old-
timey cars and trucks with skinny tires and wagon wheels as
well as more than a few horse-drawn freight wagons loaded
with stone. She stayed back from the crowd of men as she
had been taught. She edged around to where she heard
children's voices.

Near a small stream, she saw children playing with sticks
and large steel hoops. They were dressed as if in a formal
program. All the girls wore long dresses and lace-up black
leather shoes. The boys were in white shirts and black pants
with suspenders. Most all of the girls wore small bonnets
and there were wool hats with bills for the boys. They all
looked the very similar.

Her dad had explained some traditions of the local
Mennonite communities and their dress, so Chanel wasn't
too confused about the children. But the men at the fountain
looked out of place. They were holding the reins of horses
being watered at the large fountain. All the horses were big
horses like you see on the beer commercials. None were the
quarter-horses or thoroughbreds her grandfather in Elk City
raised. And the stone fountain was just like the one at the
museum downtown.

"Hello," came a voice from behind her.

The voice didn't startle her nor was she surprised to hear
it. She turned to meet the eyes of a girl about her age and
size.

"Hi." Chanel answered.

For a few seconds the girls sized each other up. A sense of happiness and familiarity enveloped them. It was as if they were repeating an encounter from before. The question was, before what?

"Want to go walking?" The girl held out her hand and Chanel took it.

"Yeah, let's go walking."

They walked a few steps in silence but the sound of the men talking in their groups brought Chanel back to her inquisitive self.

"Who are those men?"

"Freighters, of course. They are here every Saturday, haven't you seen them?" The girl asked.

"Every Saturday?" Chanel was skeptical in her tone.

"Yes," The girl stopped walking. She looked closer at Chanel and then her clothes. "You haven't seen them every Saturday because you haven't been here before, have you?"

Chanel shook her head. "*You* have been here *every* Saturday?"

"Only since my father started selling leather and vegetables to the townspeople. We don't live here. We camp outside of town, so there is no trouble."

It was only then that Chanel noticed the clothes she wore. Under a woolen brown waistcoat, she had on a blue print dress that came down to her ankles. Soft brown moccasins beaded in vibrant colors disappeared under the hem of the dress. A woven leather necklace ornamented with white and red beads and supporting an octagon of flaxen quills hung down to her waist. A bird formed by tiny feathers wrapped in red string filled the center of the quill-framed medallion. Silver slender bracelets covered her wrists and smaller

48

versions held her pigtails in place. Her head was not covered like the other children and her pigtails draped softly over her shoulders. She was Indian. On her jacket, she had a brooch just like the one Miss Ireland gave Chanel. Chanel reached to her chest to feel the brooch and discovered it to be gone. She must have lost it in the well, she thought to herself.

Chanel had gone to school with African-Americans, Mexicans, Asians and many Native Americans, but for some reason this Indian girl seemed out of place with all of Chanel's previous associations. She definitely was out of place with the current activities in the park.

"Are you full blood Indian?" Chanel asked.

"I don't know how '*full*' I am but I am Kiowa." She laughed.

Chanel was embarrassed but laughed also.

"Are you full blood white-girl?" she tried to say with a straight face.

"I suppose, just to my knees," Chanel answered. "Dad's grandmother was part Chickasaw, I think."

Both laughed at the absurdity of the terms.

When they had calmed, the girl spoke sincerely, "My name is Cynthia Tallchief, what is yours?"

Chanel tried to say her name as Chanel Lane but it came out *Blair Ireland.* "Blair Ireland is my name." She heard it and knew it wasn't right but sensed she was supposed to be known to this person as Blair. Oddly, though, she was satisfied with saying it.

Suddenly, she looked at her watch. It had stopped. She knew she had passed ten minutes. Panic overwhelmed her.

"Cynthia, I have to go, but I will be back. Are you here all day?"

"Yes, but…"

"I'll explain later but right now I have to be somewhere. I want to see you again so don't give up on me. Okay?" Chanel started back to the tunnel that lay hidden in the grove of bushes. "Just don't give up on me!"

"Okay but I will have to go when my father takes us back to our camp so don't be gone too long."

Chanel yelled over her shoulder, "I will try to hurry."

She ran through the tunnel and crawled quickly up the well wall. Jessie was standing there still holding the handlebars to both bicycles.

"Oh, Jessie, I'm sorry. Thanks for waiting. I think my watch stopped."

"Waiting. What do you mean?" she looked at her watch. "Did you get scared? It has not been two minutes."

Chanel looked at her watch. Two minutes had passed since she started into the tunnel. Her watch hadn't stopped … but time had.

"Uh. No," she said absentmindedly. She had an idea. "Jessie, I left my, uh, my scarf in the tunnel. I will be right back."

"Scarf?" Jessie asked.

"I mean my glove," Chanel corrected hurriedly. She was already headed down the well. "I will be right back!" She hollered loud enough for Jessie to hear.

"Your gloves are on your hands!" Jessie called down the tunnel.

"I will be right back!" trailed Chanel's answer from deep within the tunnel.

Chanel knew she could go back and Jessie would not be left for any time. Something was strange, but it was a good strange. The tunnel was magic. Fear never entered her thoughts because she was also very comfortable being with

50

Cynthia. She didn't understand why, but she had a greater sense of purpose with being there.

Once she arrived at the park again, she looked out over the crowd to find her new or old friend whatever the case might really be.

Finding Cynthia collecting stones near the creek, Chanel slipped up behind her.

"Boo!"

Cynthia didn't jump.

"I knew you were behind me," She said not looking up. "I could hear you a mile away."

"Because you are an Indian?" Chanel asked.

"No, because you have big feet and you kicked everything you stepped on," Cynthia added sarcastically, "or maybe it was the White Buffalo that whispered in my ear, *look out! Here comes the Full-Blooded White-Girl sneaking up on you!*"

Chanel was embarrassed. "I'm sorry. I really am not this dorky usually but something is different here than where I live and I haven't figured out what yet."

"Where you live?" Cynthia asked. "Do you not live here?"

Chanel started to answer but paused and thought. I kind of live here when I am with my dad, but here is not here when I come through the tunnel.

"Never mind." It was too confusing to explain. "Tell me about where you live."

"We camp about five miles to the southeast on the Little Washita where the river widens."

"And where do you live?" Chanel probed.

"We live on Medicine Creek, near Saddle Mountain." Cynthia turned to make eye contact. "I have answered your questions. You can't just say never-mind when I ask questions, alright?"

"Alright."

"Where do you live? Is it near here?" Cynthia asked.

"I live with my mother and step-father in Elk City. On weekends I come to my father and step-mother's house here in Chickasha."

"What is a step-father and a step-mother?" Cynthia asked. "Why do you not live with your father and mother together?"

Chanel was taken aback by the question. Cynthia doesn't know about step-parents. Does she know about divorce?

"My real parents are divorced. They both remarried and the people they married are my step-parents." Chanel explained softly while looking at the ground. She knew more questions would follow.

But Cynthia was wise enough to get the full picture. From the tone in Chanel's voice and the fact that she had lowered her eyes to the ground as if in shame, she understood that this had hurt Chanel so she was not going to make her relive the hurt.

"You seem to be happy with both sets. I hope so. Where is Elk City?" Cynthia asked as she took Chanel's hand in hers.

"It's about two hours from here," Chanel explained.

"Two hours? That is no farther than where we camp!" Cynthia said almost protesting.

Chanel started to defend herself, but remembered how different the world is through the tunnel. "It takes you two hours to drive your car five miles?"

"We have a car but we come here by wagon to haul the leather and wooden furniture that my father makes and sells

52

on Saturdays and Sundays." Cynthia answered.

"Wag…" Chanel stopped herself. That would explain the men and the horses. Not only does this place feel different so does the time.

"Oh," she said, "my dad has a car and it is about two hours to Elk City, if you go by car."

"A car is nice. "Cynthia added. "But only a few of our people have them where we live. Your dad must be a rich man."

Chanel shook her head and said, "No, we are not rich." It dawned on her then that the time was surely different. Cars were around but not in the numbers as she knew. Chanel needed to know what the time this side of the tunnel was. She decided to be direct.

"Cynthia, when were you born?" Chanel asked hoping to find out the date.

"Well, I'm thirteen years if that's what you mean," Cynthia answered. Cynthia was now getting suspicious of the questions.

"No, what date?" Chanel dug deeper.

"Well, if you can't subtract, it was thirteen years before now. Let's see," she laughed, "thirty-six minus thirteen is twenty-three. I was born July thirteenth nineteen twenty-three. Do you want to see that on my fingers?" She laughed even more.

Chanel let out her breath and almost forgot to inhale. Nineteen thirty-six? She must be dreaming all this.

Cynthia sensed the confusion, "What?" She released Chanel's hand. "What is the matter?"

Chanel sat down on a rock near where they stood. She was shocked.

"What is it, Blair? Tell me because you are scaring me."

"Sit by me, Cynthia," she started, "I want to tell you something and I know you will think that I am lying."

Cynthia sat down next to Chanel.

Chanel told her of the well and where she was from and about Jessie and that it all seemed like a crazy dream when she explained it. Cynthia listened and said nothing.

"So, do you think that I am making this up?" Chanel asked after minutes of silence between them.

Cynthia smiled softly. "No, look how you are dressed. Look at the way you talk to me. What is 'dorky'? I never heard of 'dorky' until you said it. But it is something you say often so it means something normally said where you come from."

"I know. But when I say it here it is almost foreign, even to me. Why didn't you ask me about my clothes when we first met?"

Cynthia smiled again. "Full blooded white girls always dress funny to me."

They both laughed.

"Show me the well," Cynthia said.

"It is not a well here." Chanel explained, "it is a tunnel from the well."

"Show me the tunnel, then."

Chanel thought for a moment. What if things were not supposed to be this way? What if things would change by what she showed Cynthia?

"I don't know, Cynthia," Chanel looked at the ground intently.

"You don't know about what?" Cynthia stood. "Is this not true what you told me?"

Chanel could see where this was leading. *Prove it!*

"Okay, but we can't go through it together," She stated.

"Why not?" Cynthia demanded.

"Because, I'm scared that I am undoing history or something and my stomach tells me to slow down."

Cynthia backed off. She crossed her arms in a defensive posture. Her head was tilted to one side and her eyebrows were arched. She is thinking hard about what Chanel has told her.

"Alright then. You are probably right. You must go before something happens," Cynthia turns her back on Chanel. "You are probably not even here. I must be dreaming *you* also."

Chanel stood and walked to Cynthia's side. She put her hand in Cynthia's. "I don't think we are dreaming this. I think we were suppose to meet to finish something." Chanel was remembering Ms. Ireland's concerns from yesterday.

"Finish what?" Cynthia asked.

"I don't know. I only know all this is familiar to me and comfortable. I don't know why because it is also all strange at the same time."

The girls looked at each other for a moment. Finally Chanel asked, "Cynthia, how long had we been together before I left a while ago?"

"I don't know maybe half of an hour," she answered. "why?"

Chanel took Cynthia's other hand, "because when I returned to Jessie at the well, time had not passed at all."

"What do you mean, time had not passed?" Cynthia asked.

"I mean when I looked at my watch, it was only two minutes later than when I first came down here," Chanel explained.

"You have a watch?" Cynthia asked. "My father has a

55

watch. Why would you carry a watch?"

Chanel pulled up her sleeve to show Cynthia her wristwatch.

"Oh! It is beautiful!" Cynthia turned Chanel's wrist to examine the details. "My father's hangs from a chain on his vest. I have never seen a bracelet with a watch. And, who is the boy with the glasses?"

Chanel looked at her Harry Potter watch that she had been given for her thirteenth birthday. She wanted to laugh, but the thought occurred to her again that everything about her dress and vocabulary would be new to Cynthia. If Cynthia knew this and questioned more, Chanel would seem like an alien to her.

"It is nothing. Just something my stepfather gave to me," She tried to fend off the amazement.

"It is wonderful. This man must be a very great artist." Cynthia looked at her own bracelets and necklace, "Would you be willing to trade for something that I have?"

Chanel would have loved to but she wondered if she should. What was she doing in this time and how were her actions going to affect Cynthia. How would her actions affect history?

"You know what? I would love to give this to you but I am afraid that the man who gave it to me would be sad that I didn't keep his gift," Chanel explained.

Cynthia was disappointed but extended her hand for Chanel to take. "It is well that you care for his feelings. I believe that you would give it to me if you could. This necklace is my *tai-me* that my grandmother gave to me to protect me from harm. I could give it to no one but my own daughter."

"What is a *tai-me*?" Chanel asked.

"*Tai-me* represents the animal spirit that watches over a family. When my great-great grandfather was a boy, as is Kiowa custom, he went to his fasting and prayer place to find his medicine. He went for four days without eating and prayed to find the true source of his strength. It is said that a red-tailed hawk brought a rabbit on the fifth day to satisfy his hunger. This kept him from being too weak and therefore it was his spirit animal."

Cynthia removed the brooch from her waistcoat. "I do want to give this to you, though." She pinned the brooch on Chanel's coat. "It was a trade from a nice woman who taught us at Riverside School for Indians," she smiled. "Come, I want to show you my favorite place."

Before Chanel could protest about the brooch, Cynthia took off running. The girls ran through the buffalo grass towards a wooded section of the pasture. A small creek flowed back towards the watering fountain. Chanel could almost picture where she would now be standing in the park as she knew it. There is a housing addition called Mandeville Estates on the southwest side of the park. Steph's sister's house was part of that addition, now at this same time in the year 2009. The original Mandeville house still stood there and Chanel reasoned this would be the area to where they were running.

As they ran, the sounds of people swimming in the small lake beyond the fountain faded behind them. Chanel thought about the concrete pool and bathhouse that now opens every summer up on the hill east of this very lake. Would Cynthia believe her if she told about how this place would change in seventy-three years?

"Seventy-three years!" Chanel exclaimed aloud and stopped in her tracks. Cynthia almost fell trying to stop with

57

her.

"Seventy-three years? What?" Cynthia asked.

"Cynthia, I want to talk about who I am and ..." Chanel started.

"Wait!" Cynthia cut her off, "My secret place is right over here. We can sit and talk there."

As they walked on, Chanel stared at the ground trying to plan what she was going to say as Cynthia led her by the hand.

"Here, we can sit here," Cynthia stopped.

Chanel looked up to see what 'here' was. Her eyes were wide and her mouth fell open. It was the rock well!

Chapter 7

It was the same smooth round rock well that Jessie stood sentinel over in 2009. It was now four feet higher than the ground around it. A wooden hoist and roof were attached to two columns sunk into the ground beside it. Chanel sat down next to it with her back against a column.

Cynthia slumped down next to Chanel.

"Blair, what is wrong?"

"Cynthia, this is the well. This is how I got here and this is maybe why I am here."

"I don't understand," Cynthia sat in the grass at Chanel's feet. "You came down this well and through a tunnel to the watering fountain?"

"No!" Chanel looked into Cynthia's eyes. "I came through this well seventy-three years in the future and through a tunnel to find you. I don't know why but I came to find *you*!"

"Blair, you are like my grandfather," Cynthia said.

"How?" Chanel asked.

"He tells stories of the future and the past also," Cynthia explained.

"So does my dad!" Chanel laughed.

"The stories are many and I have heard them over and over," Cynthia said as she rolled her eyes skyward.

"Ditto," Chanel agreed.

"Ditto?" Cynthia asked.

"It means 'just like me'. What is your favorite story from your grandfather?"

"The story he tells of why the Kiowa people are so few is my favorite," Cynthia said.

"Tell me this story," Chanel requested.

59

"First, let me tell you that Kiowa is a white-man's term. We call ourselves *kwuda*, which means 'those who came out'. My grandfather says our ancestors came out from the underworld by climbing through a hollow log to the upper earth. During that journey a pregnant woman got stuck in the log, preventing the others from joining. This kept us from being as strong as the Sioux, or the *nadouessioux* as they call themselves."

"Sioux is much easier," Chanel politely interrupted.

"Even for us," Cynthia agreed.

"Why did it matter if the Sioux were stronger? Weren't they from Little Bighorn or somewhere up north like that?" Chanel asked.

"Grandfather told me that we were from up north also. The *kwuda* lived as far north as the sacred Black Hills as did the Cheyenne and Arapaho. The Sioux were a strong and large nation that drove every other tribe south into Kansas, Colorado and Texas. We are *here*, now, because the government of the United States settled us here in 1867 when it was still Indian Territory. Grandfather was the first of our family to actually be born in Oklahoma. His family was moved here at the end of the white man's civil war. They shared the 'allotment' with the Comanche and Apache near Fort Cobb. Fort Cobb was where the federal government kept an Indian Bureau."

"Fort Cobb is a tiny town with a big lake!" Chanel said, "my new mom's family has a cabin there."

"A lake?" Cynthia asked.

"Yeah," Chanel then explained, "there is a spot-in-the-road town there but there is also a lake called Fort Cobb Lake." She was incredulous. "Was there a real fort there, a fort like in the westerns?"

60

"I guess?" Cynthia was puzzled. "I only know what my grandfather and grandmother tell me. Where do *your* white people come from?"

"Well, my dad says we are part German and part Chickasaw and my mom says were are part Irish and part something else." Chanel was lost as far as specific details.

"But where do *you* come from?" Cynthia asked. "You said you come from seventy years in the future but from where? Is it not important to know where you came from in your family?"

Chanel thought for a moment. How important was it? It was important that her dad told her about it, but really, how important was it to Chanel?

"My dad says two brothers came to New York from Germany in the early eighteen-hundreds and they are thought to have separated somewhere in Illinois. One is supposed to be my dad's great-great-great grandfather. My part Chickasaw grandmother's family came from Tennessee after the Civil War. My other grandparents were from Arkansas and Texas, I think."

Cynthia used her fingers to figure. "How could your dad have great-great-great grandfathers in just one hundred years?"

Chanel was confused by the question until she remembered where she was. In this park today, it is 1936 not the year 2009. Cynthia was too smart and Chanel was only confusing her. It was then that she realized she hadn't told Cynthia more about how she found the well.

"Cynthia, listen to how I got here to be with you." Chanel took Cynthia's hand in hers.

"My father and I always walked in these woods beside his house when I would come to visit. It is where we are able to be alone and to talk." Chanel began. "It was our place and we were there often. We knew every inch of the woods by memory."

"What did you talk about?" Cynthia interrupted.

"Everything, but mostly, we talked about the divorce and how he and mom still loved me and my sister and brother the same as they had when together. He even said they were not angry with each other but could not be together because of their great differences." Chanel detailed.

"How did that make you feel, Chanel. I think I would be too sad." Cynthia squeezed Chanel's hand.

Chanel fought back a tear.

"I was so sad," She confessed. "I knew there had to be something that I could have done. I really thought it was all my fault since I was the last to be born. But my father said their differences existed long before I was born and that it was their love for me that prolonged the decision to separate. He even hinted that they thought my birth would work out those differences. But it didn't."

"I'm sorry, Chanel." Cynthia leaned over and hugged her.

Chanel hugged her back but then put her hands on Cynthia's shoulders and pushed her to arm's length.

"I'm sorry, Cynthia, I didn't mean to go off on that," she apologized. "My father and I walked and talked all over those woods. When we saw the well under a pile of deadfall we were amazed. We should have seen it before and neither of us had.

"My cousin Jessie and I came back the next day to investigate and found that we could go down into the well and a tunnel existed. The first time we were in another time not so far in the past and this time I came to find you!" Chanel knew the story was sounding crazy but it was what it

62

was. Then suddenly: "Jessie!"

"What?" Cynthia asked.

"I left my cousin Jessie to wait for me. I need to check on her!" Chanel leaned forward to rise.

"But wait…" Cynthia began.

Suddenly, from the woods west of the well, the girls heard voices. People were coming. The sound was ominous. Chanel smelled alchohol.

"Did you see how those old coots looked when my father pulled his trucks up next to their ancient horses and wagons?" boasted a drunken voice. "I believe…"

Cynthia stood up.

"Well," the drunken braggart asked as he stopped the procession, "what do we have here?"

Chanel tried to rise but Cynthia's hand pushed her back to the ground.

"It looks like an Indian Princess," another of the voices chimed in.

Cynthia stood firm and glared at the directions of the voices. Chanel could not see who or how many were behind her and the well.

"And her face looks all dirty red," came the first voice again. "What fortune, we have a well right here and therefore we'll have water to clean the dirty red off her face and arms and legs."

"And we can wash the Indian smell from those rags she is wearing," echoed a second voice.

Cynthia moved around the well to shelter Chanel from the drunken gathering. There were three of them. Not quite men but older than most of the boys she had been around.

"What do you want?" she asked firmly.

"What do we want?" The tall one handed an almost

empty liquor bottle to the fat, grinning boy beside him. "We want to be rid of vermin. We want our water and our air and our land to be free of the dirty red pests that are squatting here on *our* land. I think that is all we want. Isn't that all that we want, Jacob."

"I.. I.. d..don't…wa..want… I..don't want…anything, Zeke," spoke the stammering voice that had been silent up to this time.

"Sure you do, Jacob." Zeke stepped quickly and grabbed Cynthia by her upper arms. "We need to wash the dirty red off the Indian Princess and send her back to her people with a clear message."

The fat boy dropped the bottle and pushed the well bucket off the edge of the well into the water below.

"Here, Zeke, I'll fetch some wash water."

"There you go, Edward," Zeke responded. "You see, Jacob, we just needed some clean water."

Chanel was frozen with fear.

Zeke pushed Cynthia back to the well. He tried to pin her with one arm, but she brought her leg and foot up to his midsection. Kicking with all her might, she attempted to free herself. But losing her balance, she plummeted over the edge backwards. Her arm hit the full bucket of water that was being hoisted up on the pulley. It tumbled along beside her as she fells.

Chanel stood when she heard Cynthia's gasp.

"Cynthia!!!" She screamed as she looked over the edge into the darkness. A sharp thud and then a loud splash were heard from the well.

"D..damnit, Ze..Zeke," the stuttering boy cried out, "wh..what…are ...y..you doing!"

They all looked into the well and then Zeke realized the

worst.

"Grab her!" he yelled at the two boys.

The boys circled the well. Zeke and Edward trapped Chanel. Zeke held his hand over her mouth and gripped her to his chest. He searched the horizon around him to see if anyone might have seen what happened.

"What are we gonna do?" the fat boy, Edward, asked frantically. "Zeke, what are we gonna do!"

Zeke thought but for a moment. "We are leaving."

"But what about this girl and the Indian in the well?" the fat boy was almost in tears.

Zeke picked up Chanel around the waist still holding her mouth with his left hand. He scooted over to the well and tried to sling her feet over the edge.

"Help me you two idiots. Don't just stand there! Help me reunite this white trash with her friend."

Jacob stuttered, "W-wait Zeke. Y-y-you can't…!"

Reacting without thinking, the fat boy helped Zeke center Chanel over the well opening. Without a word and with her desperately trying to spread her legs and arms to the well rim, he dropped her.

Chanel hit her head and shoulder against the side of the well as she fell but in only a brief instant she was in the water beside a motionless Cynthia.

"C'mon you two. Let's go!" was the last words Chanel heard from above. She raised Cynthia's head and face from the water and brought it to her chest. Then, looking up at the almost insurmountable depth of the well, the blackness overwhelmed her. Cynthia's labored breathing faded from her ears as the world seemed to cease its being.

"Jessie," Chanel whispered as a deep sleep overwhelmed her.

Chapter Eight

Warm sunlight bathed her face. Raspy, labored breaths were faint in the background of her thoughts. A familiar, comforting dream began. She was in her bed and her dad was wrestling with her to wake up for breakfast. He had thrown all her pillows on top of her and was shaking the whole mattress. The shaking made it hard to sleep. The shaking and someone's erratic breathing were waking her. The shaking…

"Blair, I'm so cold," a voice spoke from far away. "Where are we? Blair, where are we?"

Chanel opened her eyes to mere slits. The sun was bright and focused in her eyes. She blinked to stop the glare but it wouldn't go away. She realized she was looking up through a tunnel at a bright light but no other thoughts were coherent.

Then she remembered the boys and Cynthia. It was Cynthia's shaking that had aroused her. The weight on Chanel's body was not thrown pillows. It was Cynthia's head and shoulders on Chanel's chest. Cold water rippled away with each quiver of Cynthia's tremors.

"Cynthia, are you alright?" Chanel asked through closed eyes and trembling lips. She was on her elbow and leaning against wet rock.

"I don't know. My head hurts and I can't move my arm," Cynthia replied.

"Can you sit up? I need to move my back and legs. We need to see if we can stand up," Chanel explained through half gasps.

Cynthia rolled down Chanel's stomach to get her good hand under her. She then put her weight to her knees and

Chanel felt the burden off her body.

Chanel pushed down with her right hand and back with her left elbow to free herself from the rocks that she'd been leaning on. She blinked again and stared ahead instead of upward. She knew then that they were in the well. She became conscious that the light was moving across the walls and that soon it would be gone altogether.

"Cynthia, we have to get up. I think it will start getting dark and no one will know where we are."

"I am trying, but I can't move my other arm," Cynthia explained through gritted teeth.

Chanel was gaining more focus and she looked towards Cynthia to evaluate of where they lay. Cynthia's left hand dangled limp and the contour of her forearm was distorted above the wrist. Cynthia saw Chanel almost gag at the sight. In dread, Cynthia closed her eyes. She turned her head towards her left arm and reopened them to see what she done. Numbness surrounded her like a thick fog and she stared unbelieving at the sight of the deformed arm. It seemed foreign to her because of the lack of feeling and response.

"Blair, I can't feel anything so don't get upset. I think I can stand up," Cynthia tried to get her feet under her before waiting for Chanel to respond.

Soon she was on her feet and squatting on her heels. She rubbed her forehead with her right hand trying to clear the cobwebs from her thoughts. The efforts had brought some muscle warmth back to her body and she felt stronger with the lapse of trembling.

Chanel tried to follow suit but her head was spinning and her balance was absent. She brought a hand to her forehead and found a knot the size of an egg above her right eye. Her legs were tingling as feeling came to them completely and the scrape on her back was burning against her clothes. She hurt all over. But, after looking again at Cynthia's arm, she thought her pain a welcome affliction.

She was able to stand and stooped to get her hands under Cynthia's right arm for support. The water was up to her thighs. She straightened and Cynthia came up with her. They steadied themselves against the wet rocks behind them.

"We need to yell for someone to find us," Chanel said at last.

"What if it is the boys?" Cynthia worried aloud.

Chanel looked up the irregular rock wall. The sunlight was already half way up the wall and leaving quickly. Chanel was able to make out irregular gaps that resembled a ladder in the face of the formation. It was familiar to her.

"This is the well, Cynthia. Remember, this is the well I came through to find you." She was relieved and excited knowing that they could climb out.

Cynthia looked up at the wall and soon found the hand and footholds that Chanel had seen. Then the realization that she would need both hands soon deflated her.

"Blair, I don't think I can climb out with one hand."

Chanel looked from Cynthia to the wall and back. "Maybe if I am right behind you, I can help keep your balance." She suggested.

Cynthia looked up the shaft of the well one more time. "Alright," she agreed, "let's try before it gets dark."

She placed her foot in the highest outcropping of rock she could, leaving one for Chanel to use. Chanel got behind her and lifted her up to the next. With her strong hand, Cynthia tried to pull herself up. Chanel placed a foot in a small ledge and tried to hold Cynthia close to the face of the well walls

68

as she climbed. There were no extra handholds or ledges than had been placed when designed for one person to use. Chanel had no place to set her own feet and hands. She tried to wedge her fingers in between the mortar-set rocks and to use her head and shoulders behind Cynthia's legs for support.

As Cynthia relinquished the first foothold, Chanel tried to place her foot in it to keep the support behind Cynthia's lower body.

"I am going to let go now to get the next handhold. Can you hold me pressed to the wall?" Cynthia asked.

Chanel dug her fingers in as deep as she could and put weight on the foot that now occupied the foothold.

"Okay, go," she said through gritted teeth.

Cynthia released the handhold and tried to grab upward to the next but the lack of available support made her lean back slightly and she and Chanel tumbled backward into the water.

"Ahh!" came a scream as her left arm splashed beneath the water.

A trickle of blood flowed from Chanel's lip as Cynthia's heel popped it.

She shook her head and face clear of well water and rose to help Cynthia to her feet.

"No!" Cynthia cried out loudly. 'Don't move me!"

Chanel waited still squatted over her agonizing friend.

"I can't do it, Blair. It hurts badly now and I am afraid to hurt it more. Maybe even hurt it too much to heal." Tears mixed with the well water on Cynthia's face. Cynthia's clenched teeth allowed no whimpering to escape.

Chanel looked up the well wall. As she did, a dizzy sick feeling almost overwhelmed her. Resolute, she shook it away.

"I am going to go get help, Cynthia. I want you to stand against the wall and to try not to sit in the cold water."

"Alright, you go get help but I'm staying down here because I think this water helps with the throbbing in my arm," Cynthia explained without looking up.

"Okay. I'm going but I will be back so don't think I won't. I will be back with some of those men to lift you out." Chanel tried to comfort Cynthia with her hands on her back and shoulder. She felt as if she was abandoning Cynthia, but she knew it had to be done to get help to her fast. "Are your parents closer than those men? Would it be better for me to find them?"

"Just anyone, Blair," Cynthia gasped, "Get the first person you find."

Chanel started her climb up the wall and had made it about ten feet when, in her haste, she lost her grip and fell back into the well. Anger beset her and she stumbled back to her feet.

"My bad, Cynthia. I was hurrying and lost my grip." Chanel explained over her shoulder.

"Your bad, Blair?" Cynthia asked behind her.

This time with utter concentration and determined desire, Chanel pulled herself up the wet wall. With a few feet left she knew she had it and said as much to Cynthia over her shoulder. Upon reaching the edge she pulled a leg up and over to be free of the well completely.

The sun had passed to the west and shadows hid Cynthia in the abyss below. Chanel leaned far over the edge trying to make out Cynthia's figure in the water.

"Cynthia, I'll be back. Can you hear me? I'll be back."

No sound came back to Chanel.

70

"Cynthia, I'm going for help so don't give up on me. I'll be right back."

Chanel tore herself away from the rocks and started to run back to where she remembered the men to be working. As she ran she fought the dizziness that challenged her.

At a small depression in the grass, she stumbled to her knees and threw up. She coughed once and got to her feet again.

"I'll be right back, Cynthia." She said aloud to reassure both herself and Cynthia. "I'll be right back."

She ran forever but found no one. She heard machines running to her left away from the setting sun and followed the noises.

A group of men hauling used lumber to a truck saw her running towards them and then fall into the tall grasses that separated them.

Very soon a man scooped her up and carried her to a truck bed.

"What's the matter, girl? Where are your folks?" Chanel could only hear the voice. It seemed so distant. "Who are your folks?"

Suddenly it became relevant to answer, "Cynthia...

"The well, she's in the well." Silence and darkness came over Chanel.

Chapter Nine

Chanel awoke leaning against a large sack of grain. A quilt had been thrown over her lap and a wet towel was draped across her forehead. Except for an oil lantern on the tailgate of the truck, it was almost dark. Chanel had slept past dusk.

"Cynthia!" she screamed aloud and tried to get up.

A woman came rushing to her side and tried to comfort her. "It's alright, dear. My name is Mrs. Johnson. The men are looking for your folks. You just lay still till they get here."

"But Cynthia, needs help," Chanel tried to explain. She started crying with the realization that Cynthia was still alone in the well.

The woman just pushed her back down to the makeshift bed and patted her on the arms. "Hold still, little one. We'll go find your mother. Cynthia is her name?" She asked.

"No!" Chanel tried to explain through sobs. "I'm talking about my friend. She fell in the well and hurt her arm. She needs help, now!"

"Child, what on earth are you talking about?" The woman stood to get help. "Jim," she yelled towards the darkness, "where are you, Jim? This girl needs a doctor!"

Chanel knew that it was up to her to find Cynthia and the well. She got to her feet when the woman turned to find her husband, Jim. Walking away backwards at first and then at a slow run she went to where she thought the well was. Near a grove of shrubs and short saplings she heard the hawk cry. Bursting through the edge of the bushes she found the tunnel to the well.

"Chanel," a soft murmur whispered in the wind.

Chanel walked hesitantly towards the voice.

"Chanel," whispered the voice again.

The tunnel came into view.

"I need to find the well not the tunnel!" Chanel cried to the hawk.

There was nothing but silence.

"Jessie!" Chanel said aloud, "Jessie can help us!"

She ran into the tunnel and fought the dizziness once more. She found the well's wall and the footholds and struggled resolutely to make her way to the top.

Jessie was sitting on a log with her back to the well when Chanel called out to her.

"Jessie!"

Jessie turned to see Chanel running from the well. Jessie's mouth fell open, as Chanel got closer. A large knot and several scratches marred her face.

Chanel fell face first to the ground at Jessie's feet.

"Chanel!" Jessie cried as she turned her over. "What happened to you?"

Chanel lay motionless and Jessie knew she needed assistance.

She ran through the thickets that separated the woods from the pasture. Running hard across the pasture she saw Chelsea's white car turn the corner headed home.

"Chelsea! Hey! Chelsea!" She yelled, waving her arms. "Chelsea!"

Chelsea never heard Jessie's yell but a hawk flew just feet above her hood across her windshield and she followed its flight west towards the woods. There was Jessie waving at her and running towards her. Chelsea rolled down her window and stopped.

"Chelsea! Chanel's hurt! Come help me!" Jessie's hands

grabbed her knees as she bent to catch her breath.

Chelsea put her car in gear, jumped out and ran to Jessie's side.

"Over to the woods!" Jessie gasped.

Chelsea ran through the thickets and to the edge of the woods and looked around.

"Where, Jessie?" she yelled. "Where is Chanel?"

Suddenly, the shrill whistle of the swooping hawk caused Chelsea to duck. It landed on the branch of a dead oak. Beneath the branch lay Chanel!

Chapter Ten

Chanel awoke in the backseat of Chelsea's car. They were headed home from the pasture. Jessie was trying to explain to Chelsea about the well and about going into it and that Chanel was just gone about two minutes when she came out with the bruises and scratches.

"Maybe she fell from the well and I didn't hear her!" Jessie reasoned. "I don't know! She just freakin' told me to wait for her and I did!"

"Calm down Jessie, it wasn't your fault," Chelsea tried to relax Jessie.

Pulling up into the driveway Chelsea honked the horn and yelled for someone to come help. Jessie ran into the house to hasten whoever was there.

Steph came running out clearing the storm door from her path with the sweep of her right arm and in three steps was at the side of Chelsea's car.

Chanel was cradled in Chelsea's lap in the backseat. Chelsea's left leg and foot were on the door threshold.

"Scoot all the way in and I'll drive," Steph took charge and slid behind the wheel. "Jessie, get in the car and let's go."

Steph backed out of the drive and listened as Jessie and Chanel tried to explain the day's events. Mixed in with Jessie's two-minute theory was Chanel's story of a girl named Cynthia and a gang of boys. Sequences of children in old clothes and oil lanterns led Steph to believe Chanel had dreamed while unconscious. She probably had a concussion.

At the hospital, Chanel's dad and a nurse awaited their arrival. Chelsea had gotten hold of Chanel's dad at his work-sight via her cell phone. After an exasperating two-hour insurance verification and check in and a brief ten minute examination, Chanel was released to go back home. She had a slight concussion and should be fine with bed rest and quiet.

Mom and Dad took her home to bed and Chelsea took Jessie to her house. Jessie's mom and dad were updated as to the story. It was emphasized that the events were led by Chanel's desire to explore and that Jessie shouldn't be held accountable.

"I did kinda save her life, you know," Jessie offered as exoneration.

"Well, let's hope someone saves yours." Jessie's mom offered in mock earnest. She walked into the house.

"Bye, Jessie," Chelsea said as she crawled back into the car.

"Bye." Jessie replied. "Chelsea," Jessie interrupted the door being shut, "Chanel and I were in the tunnel before and it was weird. The whole park was different. She even said she heard someone call her name and all."

"Really?" Chelsea asked. "When?"

Jessie related all that had transpired within the well and tunnel to Chelsea. She detailed the strange dress of the frisbie players and the unusually warm temperature during their initial visit to the park. She was sketchy on the second trip because she hadn't gone in but she wanted Chelsea to know there was something greater happening than just the girls crawling through a tunnel.

She stopped and looked at the ground. "I know we are in trouble and all, but when she feels better ask her what happened. It was spooky weird."

"I will," Chelsea promised. "And Jessie, thanks for being there for her."

Jessie smiled as Chelsea pulled out of her driveway. She knew she should have protested more, but Chanel was almost possessed with going into the well; maybe by the voices she heard.

Chapter Eleven

At home Chanel slept fitfully. The uncertainty regarding the possibility of it all having been a dream was wrestling with the fear that she had abandoned Cynthia to die. Her dad entered the room when he realized that she was tossing in her sleep.

She felt his presence by her bed. He sat down and stroked her light brown hair from the bandage on her forehead.

"How do you feel, sweetheart?" he asked when her eyes were open and focused.

"I don't know," she said. "Mom thinks I was dreaming but I don't think I was."

Dad smiled. "I know." He sat closer to her. "Once I had a bike wreck and it was days before what really happened was clear. It is expected for your thoughts and dreams to be cloudy when you have had such blow to your noggin."

"I know dad, but it wasn't the first time I went into the well. It was a different park then also." She tried to sit up on her pillows but gave up when her head throbbed. "Dad I really think I am going to another time when I go into the well. In fact, this last time, I came out of the well after talking to the Indian girl and Jessie said I had only been gone two minutes when I know the girl and I had walked around and talked for a long time. We had checked our watches before I went in and then again after I had met the girl!"

"Okay, okay," her dad started, "let's say that when you went into the well, you fell. You dreamed that you came back out and then the rest of the dreams happened. It could possibly be that everything that happened after you started climbing into the well the first time was a dream because

78

you fell immediately."

"No, Dad!" Chanel protested. And I can prove it." She tried to rise up off the bed. "If you call Jessie she'll tell you about the first time and then about the second time."

He put his hands on her arms to guide her back down to the pillows. "Okay, sweetheart, we will talk to Jessie some more. But, I think you need to rest and let things sort a little. I called your mom in Elk City and she thinks you need to come home. She's probably right, I should have been watching over you more."

"No, Dad," she pleaded. "It was my fault and I'll tell mom that. But I know that there is a Cynthia and she needs my help. I was chosen to get it for her."

Her dad rose to leave. "Alright, but right now, I want you to rest. After you are wide awake, we'll call Jessie."

"I'm awake now, Dad!" Chanel pleaded.

"I tell you what," he offered. "I'll drive down to Jessie's to see if she can come over to talk. But I'll only do it if you will rest right now."

"Pinky promise?"

He held his little finger out to her to confer, "Pinky promise."

Chanel lay back into her mound of pillows. Their cushiony comfort did feel better now but she knew she wouldn't sleep.

Her dad left the room and walked down the hallway into the kitchen. Chelsea and Stephanie were sitting at the bar talking about what Jessie had said. Chelsea gathered her books and headed to her room.

"I am going to see if Jessie can come down to help ease Chanel's worries," he said. "Then, I'm going down to the well."

79

"Want some company?" Steph asked.

"I would love it, but you had better stay here with Chanel. Chelsea is probably capable but I *know* you are," he replied out of Chelsea's hearing and kissed her on the cheek. "Honey, I'm glad you took off work to be here for the girls."

"Remember, they are *my* girls also," Steph admonished.

"What about me going with you to the well, Dad?" Chelsea asked from down the hall.

He rolled his eyes at Steph over being not quiet enough. "If you want," he answered as he dug his flashlight out of the hall closet. "It'll be dark soon so we have to hurry."

They got into his pickup and drove to Jessie's. No one was home.

They then drove across the pasture and parked as close to the woods as possible. The headlamps of the pickup truck showed eerie shadow figures on the edge of the woods. He turned off his truck and walked into the woods.

For an hour, they walked in circles trying to find the well. Full darkness came and it became apparent that it wouldn't be found tonight. They loaded up and headed back to Jessie's. Still, no one was home, so the two amateur detectives went home.

He went into Chanel's room to explain and found her sitting up in bed.

"Dad, who do we know named Blair?" She asked.

"I don't know, sweetheart." He thought for a while. "No one comes to mind."

Chanel stared at the floor and then as if a light had come on. "Dad I know someone."

"Who?"

"Ms. Ireland," she announced.

"What has that got to do with anything?" he asked, sitting

down at her side.

"When Cynthia asked me my name, I said Chanel but it came out 'Blair'. She called me that the whole time I was with her."

"Honey," he cautioned, "you had just seen Ms. Ireland the night before. In this circumstance, that probably made you incorporate her into your dreams."

Chanel slumped in despondence.

"Dad, I know there is more to it," she defended. "Did you bring Jessie? You promised."

"No, but I did go by there as I promised and they were gone. They probably went out to eat or something. Chelsea and I actually tried twice."

"Dad, this is making me crazy," Chanel started to sob. "I know it all happened and I am doing nothing to help Cynthia. I promised her I would be back to help her and now I am sitting in my bed, in my dry and warm house not doing anything."

Her dad pulled her onto his lap. Wrapping his arms gently around her he attempted to soothe her fears.

"Sweetheart, I know it was all so real. I don't know what else to say to make you realize that it had to have been a dream."

"Dad, it was not a dream. I know it sounds so dumb and outta this world, but it was not a dream." Chanel was sobbing softly and slowly going limp in his arms. The concussion was taking its toll on her consciousness. Her breathing went from labored, to regular, to soft. "Cynthia, I am coming back with help," Chanel murmured as she slept.

Chelsea stood in the doorway listening. As Chanel drifted to sleep and her dad was making her comfortable, Chelsea grabbed her cell phone and left the house. "I'll be back in a little bit!" she announced to Steph who was straightening up the kitchen.

From the front porch, she called her stepsister Jordan. Jordan was over at Jaimie's house visiting. Chelsea told her to stay there and she jumped into her car. As she drove by the woods she had an eerie feeling that the trees were closer to her than the quarter-mile that separated them from the road. With her window down in the cold night air she heard the echoed scream of a red tail hawk. She slowed as if to listen for instructions and then as none were exposed, she accelerated to get to her destination.

At Jaimie's house she found Jordan and Jaimie going through some old yearbooks and laughing at the clothes and hairstyles that had been popular in their junior high years.

"Hey, girlfriend, whassup!" Jordan asked as Chelsea entered the living room where they were perched.

"Did you guys hear about Chanel and Jessie?" Chelsea asked as she plopped down next to Jaimie.

"No, what?" Their voices were in unison.

"She and Jessie went down into the well that Chanel and dad found in the woods. She has a humongous knot on her head and an even bigger story about how it got there."

"What well are you talking about?" Jaimie asked closing the book they had been looking into.

Chelsea told about Chanel and dad finding the well and then told what she knew about the incident with Chanel.

"She says that the girl she met is lying in the well with a broken arm and that it was her destiny to find her and save her or something like that."

"Okay, you lost me," Jordan said. "She used the word destiny? Dang! She did have a blow to the head."

"Well she didn't say destiny," Chelsea corrected.

82

"Well, you lost me also," Jaimie added. "When did all this happen?"

"Just this afternoon. We took her to the emergency room and brought her home and then dad and I went to find the well," Chelsea started. "We couldn't find it. Dad said it was hard to find and we'd have to wait until morning to try again."

"So," Jaimie asked, "how is Chanel doing?"

"She is sleeping now but before she went to sleep she mentioned that Ms. Ireland. You know the lady from the nursing home that she reads to," Chelsea tried to explain, "I think that Chanel believes she went back in time as Ms. Ireland."

"Dude! That is so deep!" Jordan offered. "She must have taken such a lump that she's thinking like her dad now."

They all laughed at the reference to Chanel's dad's imagination.

"Yeah, we all are infected with it," Chelsea laughed.

After a moment of watching Chelsea stare blankly at the coffee table, Jordan asked in her best ghetto, "Chelsea, what is on wit-choo. Girl, I can hear the Rolex running in your head."

"Jordan, do you have to always talk in Ebonics?" Jaimie chastised her younger sister.

"Can't help it. I'm Jordan from the block. My sista," she laughed.

Jaimie rolled her eyes and left for the kitchen. Chelsea was staring out the window quietly. Jaimie returned with bottled water for all of them

"What is wrong, Chelsea?" Jaimie asked.

Embarrassingly, Chelsea looked at both of them and offered, "I want to go talk with Chanel's Ms. Ireland."

Jaimie and Jordan looked at each other and laughed again.

"Chelsea, you *are* infected with it," Jaimie said.

"I know, but Chanel was so adamant and if nothing else we will be able to put her at ease with what we find out. Plus, Jessie told me they went into the well the first time together!"

"We!" they said in unison.

"Yes, I don't want to go by myself," Chelsea pleaded.

Jordan jumped up and grabbed her cell phone. "Road trip!" she announced.

"Well, I can't," Jaimie said. "I told the girls that I would pick them up to meet some other friends for dinner. We are planning our ten year reunion."

"Alright then. Jordan you'll go with me and we can call Jaimie if ghosts get us at the nursing home," Chelsea said, trying to sound cocky but still burdened by the eerie feeling in her chest.

"Ayight, den," Jordan started out the door. "Who ya gonna call? Ghostbusters!" she sang as she strolled past Chelsea in the doorway.

Chelsea looked at Jaimie and shook her head. "I think we may need you to keep us on track."

"I'll stay here. You two are embarrassing," Jaimie defended as she cleared the books from the coffee table.

"Okay." Chelsea started out the door. "Hey, if dad or Steph calls to tell you what's going on, act surprised. I don't think dad would want me encouraging Chanel by following up on Ms. Ireland."

"Okay," Jaimie assured her.

Once in the car Chelsea and Jordan discussed what to ask Ms. Ireland.

"I think we need to confirm her first name and to ask her if she knows Cynthia," Chelsea suggested.

"Yeah, and we need to know if Chanel had mentioned the well to her," Jordan offered.

They drove the last six blocks to the nursing home discussing Chanel's imagination.

"That girl is crazy brave for going down into that dark well," Jordan announced.

"Yeah," Chelsea began, "that is so not like her. She was always so passive and reluctant. I remember how she worried about meeting your mom that first time. She wanted to make sure that I was with her and dad when they came to Chickasha."

"I'll tell you now," Chelsea added, "I would not have gone into the well alone."

"Ditto!" Jordan emphasized.

At the nursing home they parked in the small lot in front of the building. Inside, Chelsea asked the front desk if Ms. Ireland was awake and if she had time to talk with them.

"I can check for you," the receptionist warned, 'but not being family, it is out of the ordinary for late visitors to be accepted."

"Thank you," Chelsea offered.

After a short time waiting, an employee came for Chelsea and Jordan.

"I wheeled Ms. Ireland into the visitation room," he explained, "if you will follow me, I'll take you to see her."

He turned on his heels and started down a long corridor with Chelsea and Jordan close behind him. The man was lanky and older. Chelsea thought he may even be a resident.

"Ms. Ireland has been feeling poorly," he explained as he walked down the hallway, "so she can only visit for a moment."

At the entry to the visitation room, he backed away to let Chelsea and Jordan meet with Ms. Ireland. He stood close by in an almost protected posture. Chelsea looked at him and smiled. He left.

"Ms. Ireland," Chelsea said while extending her hand to introduce herself and Jordan, "my name is Chelsea and this is Jordan. We are Chanel's sisters."

"Well, she told me about you, but isn't there a third?" Ms. Ireland asked.

"Yes, my older sister, Jaimie, is at home," Jordan answered.

"I see," Ms. Ireland acknowledged. Her brows were furrowed with worry. "Is there something wrong with Chanel?"

Chelsea explained that Chanel had fallen and hurt her head. She deliberately left out the well and the Indian girl from the details.

"She has a knot on her head and is a bit confused about how it happened," Chelsea ended the relating of the events.

"Oh, I can surely understand that." Ms. Ireland said as she brought her hand up to her right eye. A small scar was there among the age lines.

Jordan stole a glance at Chelsea upon seeing Ms. Ireland rubbing the point above her right eyebrow.

"Why is that, Ms. Ireland?" Chelsea asked as she sat down in the chair opposite Ms. Ireland's wheel chair. Jordan slowly sank down to sit on the arm of Chelsea's chair.

"Many years ago, I fell and hit my forehead. It was a bad fall and I even lost consciousness for a while." Ms. Ireland stared blankly at the floor after she explained the fall. She was quiet for a time as she reminisced.

"How did you fall?" Jordan could stand it no longer.

"Why, child?" Ms. Ireland asked as she came out of her thoughts.

"Ms. Ireland," Chelsea started, "we are kind of worried about Chanel's fall and injury. How did you fall and how long did it take you to feel better?"

Ms. Ireland was feeling uncomfortable with her memory of the incident and hesitated to talk more. She could feel the tenseness in the Chelsea's question and worried that Chanel might be seriously hurt.

Finally she explained, "I fell in a well. It was probably about twenty feet. I came out of it all right and in a few days, I was fine. You girls shouldn't worry, I am sure that Chanel will be fine also."

Chelsea looked up at Jordan whose mouth had fallen open at Ms. Ireland's story. Chelsea brought her left hand up from her lap with finger raised to push up on Jordan's chin to get her to close her mouth.

"Ms. Ireland," Chelsea said as Jordan stared, "did you ever tell Chanel about that event?"

"No. Not that I recall, why?" Ms. Ireland asked.

"Do you know Cynthia?" Jordan interrupted.

Ms. Ireland gasped and tried to catch her breath at the question. Her eyes fixed upon Jordan's face, but it was not Jordan she was focusing on.

"Ms. Ireland." Chelsea tried to help her with her loss of composure.

Ms. Ireland's hands started to tremble and then to shake. She raised one hand and was grasping in the air for help and gasping for air at the same time.

"Chelsea!" Jordan stood quickly. "Go get the orderly, she can't breathe!"

Jordan took Ms. Ireland's hand and her other hand locked onto Jordan's wrist as she did. Jordan tried to assist by helping her sit up straighter in the wheel chair.

"Chelsea, hurry!" Jordan shouted as Chelsea rushed down the hall to the nurses' station. "Hurry!"

Soon an orderly appeared at the door with an oxygen bottle and placed the mask over Ms. Ireland's nose and mouth. He pushed Jordan to the side to get better positioning.

Another orderly came and they started the wheel chair down the hall.

Ms. Ireland called out in the hallway as the orderlies hurried her off, "I *am* coming back! Cynthia, I *am* coming back!"

Chelsea and Jordan stared in disbelief.

A nurse came and interrogated Chelsea and Jordan about what had happened to Ms. Ireland. They apologized for having said anything to upset her. They wrote down a phone number for her if they might be needed.

"Needed for what?" The nurse asked.

"We don't know," Chelsea said, "but Chanel and dad would want to know if they could help."

With that, they left the nursing home. They drove in silence back to Jaimie's house. Jordan's car was there and she got into it to follow Chelsea back home. Jaimie was already gone to her planning committee.

They stopped on the front porch to talk. They decided not to tell anyone yet. It was too unbelievable.

Chapter Twelve

Morning came and Chanel awoke to the doorbell ringing. She found Chelsea and Jordan in chairs beside her bed.

Soon, Steph and Jaimie walked into the room to survey the patient and her sentinels.

"Hey, Chanel, how are you feeling?" Jaimie asked.

"Fine, I guess."

Jordan and Chelsea stretched and yawned. As if in synch, they both remembered what had transpired at the nursing home. They sat up straighter and looked at each other to confirm neither had discussed the nursing home events.

"Hey, girlfriend," Jordan scooted over to hug Chanel. "You scared us."

Chanel smiled but she was still worried about Cynthia. She didn't know if she should bring it up again. She looked at Chelsea who had her hand on Chanel's lower leg and was a bit more comforted. Chelsea had this look of knowing on her face. She wanted to talk to her. She wanted to talk to her alone.

"Mom?" Chanel said aloud still looking at Chelsea.

"Yes, honey," Steph replied.

"Do we have any orange juice?"

"I believe so. Are you hungry?" Steph moved closer to her bedside.

Chanel turned to look up at Steph, "No, just thirsty."

"Okay. Coming right up," Steph left the girls and headed for the kitchen.

While she was gone, Jaimie whispered to Jordan, "What happened last night?"

Jordan started to talk, but heard her mom coming. "In a minute," she whispered.

After Steph returned to the room with the glass of orange juice, Chanel sat up to drink. Her head was still woozy and she gingerly touched the knot above her right eye.

At that, Jordan looked at Chelsea and subtly raised her eyebrows.

"Why don't I go get some donuts?" Steph asked. "You might be hungry in a little while."

"Jaimie, you want to ride with me?" Steph asked.

"Uh, no, I'll stay with Chanel," Jaimie answered. She knew something was learned at the nursing home and she didn't want to miss any of it.

"Jordan?"

"Uh, no, Mom. I'm going to jump into the shower," Jordan said.

"Okay," Steph said suspiciously, "I'll leave you girls to take care of Chanel."

Once Steph's car was heard backing out of the driveway, Chelsea moved over to the side of the bed to talk to Chanel.

"How do you feel?" she asked.

"I feel okay but my head hurts and I have a bad feeling in my stomach," Chanel explained.

"You aren't going to hurl, are you?" Jordan asked as she backed away from the bed.

Chanel smiled and shook her head no.

"Chanel," Chelsea started, "Jordan and I went to see Ms. Ireland last night."

"Really?" Chanel sat up some more.

"Chanel, did she ever tell you about hitting her head?"

"No, she didn't."

"Did she ever mention...?" Chelsea paused.

"Cynthia?" Chanel interrupted when Chelsea paused.

"She said something about Cynthia didn't she?" Chanel

said not waiting for Chelsea to answer. "I met Cynthia in the well, Chelsea, Ms. Ireland never mentioned Cynthia to me."

Chelsea looked at Jordan.

"This is too weird," Jaimie added sitting down on the edge of the bed.

"No, she didn't say Cynthia's name but she got upset when Jordan mentioned it. In fact she got real upset and couldn't catch her breath. The orderlies had to come to her with oxygen," Chelsea explained.

"Chanel are you sure she never mentioned Cynthia or falling into the well to you?" Jordan asked.

"The well also?" Chanel asked. "Chelsea, I never mentioned the well to *her*!"

"You guys are jacking with me aren't you?" Jaimie asked. She thought they were now trying to punk her.

"Jaimie," Jordan explained, "we went to Ms. Ireland at the nursing home. We told her Chanel had hit her head and she started rubbing a spot over *her* right eyebrow where Chanel's knot is. We never mentioned where Chanel had been hit. Chelsea asked her how she had been hurt and she said *she* had fallen in a *well*! We asked her if she knew of a Cynthia and she started having a panic attack. I'm serious!"

"Huh-uh," Jaimie said in disbelief.

"Seriously, Jaimie," Chelsea assured.

Jaimie took Chanel's hand in hers. "Chanel, what happened to Cynthia?"

Chanel related the story again starting from the first time she and Jessie had entered the well. She told of the park's different entrance on the first visit and then about the men in the park on the second. She told of the big stones and the men building the bridge and the short walls around the road.

"Chelsea, I need to talk with Ms. Ireland. Can you take

me?" Chanel asked after her explanation was over.

"Take you where?" came a voice at the door.

The girls all jumped and Jordan grabbed at Jaimie's arm in a startle.

"What is going on?" Steph asked quietly as she entered the room with donuts in hand.

"Nothing," Jaimie defended guiltily.

"Chanel?" Steph asked.

"I told them about my fall. They wanted to know what happened and I told them about it." Chanel continued, "Mom, I don't think it was a dream."

"We don't either," Jordan announced.

Steph looked about the room at the faces of each girl. She knew they were sincere, but logic and reason told her it had been a dream. She decided not to upset Chanel further by arguing.

"Okay. Let's say something might have happened. Regardless, Chanel has had a blow to her head, is sick and should be resting to get better. If you girls are going to keep her excited and jumpy, you're doing more harm than good," Steph admonished. "Now, Jordan you go take your shower and Chelsea and Jaimie, do you not have class or something you guys need to be doing?"

"Yes," Chelsea answered. She got up to leave and bent over to hug Chanel. "We'll talk more," She whispered in Chanel's ear.

"Bye, Chanel," Jaimie said as she went into the kitchen, "I'll see you a little later."

"Bye Jaimie, love you." Chanel said as she slunk back into her pillow. "Bye Chels, love you also."

"And me?" Jordan asked. "You love me?" She grabbed at the bag of donuts. "You love me enough to share your donuts?"

Chanel smiled, "Yeah. Love you enough to share my donuts."

Steph went into the kitchen to get a plate for Chanel and more orange juice. "Girls, there are plenty of donuts and I will throw away all that is left, so you better eat them all!" she called over her shoulder.

The phone rang on the cordless next to Chanel's bed. It was her dad.

Chanel reached over to answer it.

"Hi, sweetheart," he said, "how are you feeling?"

"Better," Chanel replied. "When are you coming home?"

"Well, I'm trying to finish up so I can be off Thanksgiving *and* Friday. So, I will probably be a little late. Do you need me to come home sooner?" he asked.

"No, mom's here. And the girls are just leaving," Chanel explained. "I just thought you might get to talk to Jessie."

"I can. I won't be too late to swing by and talk to Jessie. Promise."

"Okay," Chanel yawned. "I'll see you tonight."

"Alright, honey," Dad said. "I love you."

"Love you too, Dad." And with that Chanel sank into her pillow and her breath was soon steady and soft. Steph came in with the donuts and juice but saw that she was asleep. She closed her door and left her to rest and to heal.

Chanel fell into a deep sleep. Her dreams brought a repeat of the previous events. Then the dream took a different turn.

A voice was speaking. It was a woman's voice but not Cynthia's or Blair's. It was a harsh demanding voice.

"*Leave her!*" the cold breathy whisper filled Chanel's sinus and drifted across her eyes, moving her lashes. "*Leave her to us!*"

Chanel turned her head, though still asleep, to avoid the unwanted intrusion of the cold, lifeless breath across her face.

"*Leave her to us,*" came the breath again. Now it was not a voice, but a raspy breeze.

"Cynthia?" Chanel spoke aloud.

"*Leave her,*" answered the wind.

"Cynthia! Blair!" Chanel's mind corrected what she was hearing, as if a mistake was being made. Instinctively she pulled her sheet over her chin and up to her forehead to stop the breeze from waking her.

On its own, the sheet pulled slowly down her face and proceeded to drag slowly off her chest, down her stomach to her waist. Her hands were still framing her head as the sensation brought clarity to her mind.

"*Leave her to us.*" The voice was clear and no longer the wind. It was a woman's voice. It was a raspy, cruel woman's voice.

Chanel opened her eyes and found a face silhouetted against the ceiling leaning over her. She could see her ceiling fan though the vacant eyes. She reached forward with her hands to repel and found icy space in front of her. Pushing forward through it, she found a warm air behind the face as she reached upward. A dark globe of stagnant frost was inches from Chanel's face.

Slinking into her bed to get away from the 'being' and pulling her covers back up to shield herself, Chanel cried out, "Dad!"

"Dad! Mom!" she screamed again.

At that, she heard once more, "Y*ou must leave her to us.*"

"I'm coming, Chanel!"Steph called out from the hallway

94

beyond the bedroom door. She was pushing hard with her hands to get it opened, but it resisted. It resisted not against the door jamb but as if someone was holding it closed. She leaned more into the door and pushed with her shoulder and legs.

"Chanel!" She cried out louder.

The curtains at the bedroom window billowed out and the window vibrated noisily within the pane. Her stereo lights and her television screen came to life and the alarm started a loud monotone buzz. The vibration intensified.

Then, a flutter of wings and a moment of conflicting breezes brushed across Chanel's shaking body. Someone or some things were in her room. A conflict was being waged above her. Exaggerated heartbeats filled her ears. She brought her hands to her face and screamed!

And then, her scream faded as an echo in a canyon. The conflict and commotion stopped. The breezes were gone and the curtains went limp. Chanel knew her room had just been vacated.

At that instant, the door swung free into the room and Steph was soon at her side. Lifting her up with her hand under her shoulders to comfort her, Steph leaned to look behind the bottom of the door to see what had restricted the opening of it. Nothing was there. No clothes were piled at the base and there is not a lock on it. She reasoned then that maybe she'd been over anxious and hadn't turned the knob all the way. Quickly her attention was back to Chanel.

Chanel had her arms wrapped around Steph but she was not weeping. She was trying to reassure herself it was a dream.

"What is it, honey?" Steph asked with her chin against the top of Chanel's head.

"I don't know. I thought someone was talking to me. Someone was in my room, I think."

Steph got up to turn the blaring stereo, television and alarm off. She walked to the window and inspected the latches. Then she jerked open the closet door prepared to attack whatever might be inside. Nothing but the rustling clothes from the vacuum she'd created by pulling it open so fast.

"Honey, it was a dream." She sat down on the bed again.

"I know," Chanel said. She knew that it had to be. She wanted it to be.

"What was it? Sometimes it helps to talk about it," Steph asked.

Chanel sat up against her headboard. She looked up at the ceiling fan above her and then to the window.

"I heard someone telling me to *leave her to them.* Someone wanted me to leave her to them. And then…someone was struggling above me. It was like a fight was above me."

"Oh?" Steph asked, "Was *her,* Cynthia, the girl in the well?"

Chanel thought for a moment.

"It was, or is. I don't know. *It* just said to leave her to them."

Chanel's brow furrowed and she closed her eyes. "I don't know anything now."

Steph pulled Chanel to her chest. "I know, honey. It is the head injury."

"No, Mom!" Chanel pulled away to see her face. "I know I went to Cynthia through the well. I know *that* is true!"

"Then, what is it that you don't know anymore?" Steph asked.

"I don't know *who* I am supposed to save," Chanel replied dismally.

Chapter Thirteen

After leaving the house, Chelsea went to the university library. She found books on Chickasha's city history and one on the history of the springs at Shanoan Springs Park.

It seems that Shanoan Springs had been part of the Chickasaw-Choctaw allotment of W.T Shanoan and his wife Nora Mayes. The original property was a full section of land as all allotted parcels were. The springs were located on the west edge of the allotment and flowed 250 gallons of water per hour. It was sweet and cold.

During the days of horse drawn freight wagons, it was known far and away to be the best water around. A large swimming pond was constructed to the east of the springs and the townspeople used it for recreation and assemblies. Bathhouses and floating platforms were built to accommodate the hot summers of central Oklahoma.

The Shanoans sold the property to W.A. Hopkins and their original Victorian style house was torn down to build the present Shanoan Springs Nursing Home.

The Hopkins added concrete and a gazebo over the springs and water was bottled, sold and delivered by wagon throughout Chickasha.

During 1936, as an extension of the Works Progress Administration aid, a native stone bridge was built over a creek to replace an old footbridge. An amphitheater on the south side of the park was built along with hundreds of feet of rock wall. Paving on both sides of the existing roads and a zoo were also built using native rock believed to have been quarried from the Mollet family farm near the community of Norge, some ten miles to the southwest of Chickasha. Chanel had told Chelsea that Blair Ireland's father had been a stonemason following the WPA projects across the United States.

From the library, Chelsea drove to the Shanoan Springs Nursing Home to check on Ms. Ireland. The nurses at the nursing station again chastised her for upsetting Ms. Ireland the night before. They inquired as to what was said and why had Ms. Ireland been brought into the situation with Chanel.

Chelsea told them that Chanel had fallen and was asking about events that would otherwise be foreign to her. Chelsea thought Ms. Ireland might have said some of these things to Chanel since Chanel had dreams about Ms. Ireland after the concussion. She left out specifics of the time period and also about the parallel to the well injury. She did mention Cynthia.

"Did Ms. Ireland ever have a visitor named Cynthia?"

One of the nurses pulled her file and opened it to check the visitor log.

"Melba, wait," a woman's voice was heard from behind Chelsea.

"Miss...?"

Chelsea turned to find she was facing a woman in a business suit. She had a deep raspy voice like someone who had smoked cigarettes all her life. Her demeanor was all business. There were no laugh-lines on her face though she looked to be in her late sixties.

"My name is Chelsea Lane. I am the sister of Chanel Lane who reads to the residents on Fridays," Chelsea answered.

"I see, Miss Lane, but why do you need to know about Ms. Ireland's visitors?" the rigid lady in the suit asked.

"Chanel had a dream about Ms. Ireland and about a girl named Cynthia," Chelsea explained. "We were just wondering if she had met her here."

"I understand," the woman took a step towards the nurses' station. She took the file from the nurse's hand. "But you have to understand, Miss Lane, about the privacy of the patients and residents."

"But Miss Cross," came the nurse with the file in her hand, "Ms. Ireland has had no visitors but Chanel. I thought…"

With just a glaring squint of her eyes, the suited woman cut the nurse off in mid-sentence. "Betty!" she stepped menacingly toward the nurse. "My name is *Huffman*-Cross and it is not your place to discuss private and confidential information about our residents with non-family or non-medical personnel! You have read the privacy policy of this establishment?"

"Yes ma'am," Betty acknowledged and turned away to return to her duties.

"Miss Huffman-Cross," Chelsea started, "I don't mean to overstep my bounds or to get anyone in trouble. I was only trying to find out what might be upsetting Chanel."

"I'm sure you were." Miss Huffman-Cross straightened her jacket to regaining her composure. "But you must respect our obligation to the residents."

"I do respect the policy." Chelsea looked at Betty who in turn smiled and winked at her round-about way of answering Chelsea's question. "I hope Ms. Ireland is feeling better and I know Chanel is anxious to get back to the reading sessions."

Chelsea turned and walked towards the doors.

"Thank you again, Betty and you also Miss Huffman-Cross," she said as she exited.

Miss Huffman-Cross gave Betty a visual admonition and

walked down the hallway. Betty mimicked her nose-in-the-air composure, but only after knowing she was well out of range to catch her.

"Betty," Miss Huffman-Cross said down the hallway without turning, "please see me in my office after your rounds."

"Yes, ma'am," Betty answered with a touch of fear now in her voice.

Chelsea walked back to her car. She wanted to believe Chanel because there was something extraordinary about Ms. Ireland and Chanel's connection. It was, however, a bit far-out to believe in "supernatural well travel." She would have to talk to Jessie with Dad. Clouds were building and a few drops spattered on Chelsea's windshield.

At the same instant that Chelsea was leaving the nursing home, Dad was pulling up the driveway to Jessie's house. Jessie's dad was working in the garage. The light and steady drone of rain against his roof caused him to grab his jacket from the passenger seat.

"Hey, Steve, what's up?" he asked.

"Not much. I'm just getting the boys bikes in from the yard." Steve stopped moving bikes and came out into the driveway. He winced at the increasing rain. "Rick, come into the garage. I might melt out there."

Once inside, he wiped the water from his face and forehead. "How's our girl?"

"Well, I think she is fine but she is adamant about this wild story about going into the well and she thinks Jessie can confirm what she believes to have happened. Is Jessie here?"

"No. I thought she was down at the house with you guys," Steve responded.

"She could be there. I came here from the work site," Dad said. "I'll go there and check." He turned to go back to his truck. "I'll call you as soon as I get there."

"Sounds good," Steve said. "Send her home before it gets dark. Or better still, with this weather getting nasty, I'll come get her in my truck so I can check on Chanel." The rain drops picked up in frequency and size making it harder to hear Steve.

"Good enough, thanks." Dad got into his truck and drove the four blocks to his house.

After parking his truck and picking up the soaking wet newspaper from the driveway he entered the house.

Steph was still in Chanel's bedroom when Dad walked in.

"Whew, good thing you guys are in here, there is a storm building." He bent and took turns kissing them both. "How are my girls?"

Steph arched her brows and said, "I think we're fine overall but these dreams are wearing Chanel out." She stood up. "Here, you guys can visit and I'll get something put together to eat."

Dad sat on the edge of the bed, "That sounds good. I'm caving in. What about you?" He asked putting his hand on Chanel's knee.

"Yeah, I am kind of hungry. Did you talk to Jessie yet?" Chanel asked attempting to prop herself up on the headboard.

"Not yet." He looked around, "Is she not here?"

"No. She's probably at home," Chanel said smoothing out her covers.

"Well, I stopped by there and Steve thought she was here. Has she been here?" Dad asked as Steph entered the room.

"Not today," Steph said noticing a look of concern forming on Dad's face. "I'll call Steve to see if she has shown up yet."

Steph left the room and Dad asked Chanel, "Sweetheart, do you think that maybe, just maybe, all these thoughts have come to you while you were in a big daze after the fall? You remember about me telling you the story of my concussion as a kid. It was days before I remembered what had happened and even then it had come to me as a dream."

"I know dad, but listen," Chanel started, "this was the second time that I went into the well. Jessie was with me on the first and so I know I went into the well."

"Well, I haven't got to talk with Jessie yet and …"

"HONEY!" Steph called from the kitchen.

"YES!" he called back.

Steph walked into the room with the cordless phone in her hand.

"Can you talk to Steve? Jessie is not home and she has not been to Kelsey's either," Steph explained.

Dad stood and took the phone from Steph's hand. He walked down the hall to talk without Chanel hearing. Steph followed.

Chanel could hear, though, and she leaned toward the door to not miss anything.

"And you tried her other friends?" Dad asked on the phone.

"Did she say she was coming down here?" he asked.

"What time was that?"

"Okay, I'll walk that way and meet you near the edge."

He turned off the phone and turned to Steph.

"Steve says Jessie told Rebekah that she was coming down here, but, Kelsey saw her walking her bike towards the woods two hours ago."

He walked back into Chanel's room. "Honey, Jessie might have gone back to the woods. Do you think she would go to the well?"

"She might," Chanel offere., "I wouldn't think she would go by herself. The well kind of spooked her."

He looked at Steph. "Why don't you stay by the phone here and I'll go meet Steve. Call me on the cell phone if Rebekah calls with news."

"Well, you better take your rain coat. It is blowing harder and there are rain drops coming in under the porch," Steph said as she put the phone in its cradle. "And take the big flashlight. It will be dark soon."

Dad looked at Chanel and got down on one knee beside her bed. "Chanel, I'm going to ask again, do you think Jessie went back to the well?"

"Dad, I don't know. She argued with me when I went in alone, so, I think she would be against going into the well," Chanel explained.

Dad looked into her eyes. "You would tell me if you knew what she was doing?"

"Yes, dad, I don't know where Jessie is," Chanel huffed sincerely.

"Okay, sweetheart, I believe you," Dad said and hugged Chanel before getting up to leave. He left the house to join Steve and Rebekah in their search for Jessie. Chanel and Steph waited by the phone for word of her discovery.

Chanel was initially angry at her dad's accusing tone but she knew she had it coming to her for lying about the first time into the well.

For almost half an hour Steph was staring out the window towards the woods. She was wringing a kitchen towel in her hands and staring towards the dark silhouette of the woods a quarter mile to the west. Wind whipped the silver maple's branches in the front yard. Occasional debris flew by illuminated by the porch light, only to disappear into the darkness.

Steph's cell phone rang.

"Hello," Steph answered it.

Static and silence was on the other end.

"Hello, is that you Steve?" She asked.

"*Jess…by…the…Come, now,*" was all she heard.

"I can't hear what you are saying. Try me again," She spoke louder hoping she was being heard.

"*Jess…come…now. Come…now…*" the voice trailed away and the phone went dead.

Steph tried to dial Rick's cell phone but it would never connect. She tried Steve's house but it too would never ring.

She went to the closet and got her heavy coat.

"Chanel, I think they need me to come to Steve's house. I can't get them on the phone. Will you be alright here?" she asked Chanel as she buttoned her jacket.

"Yes, but call me as soon as you get there so I know what's going on." Chanel started to get out of bed.

"No, you stay in bed. Here is the cordless. I don't think you should be up and about just yet." Steph directed, "You stay right here, okay?"

"Yes ma'am." Chanel had an ominous feeling. A tightness was in her chest. She could feel her heart beats intensifying. She didn't know how to explain to Steph without sounding like a child. "Call me as soon as you get to Uncle Steve's. Okay?"

"Okay. And I have my phone with me so if you get a call from your dad, call me. And if any of your sisters come in, make them stay put! Alright?"

"Yes, ma'am," Chanel said. "Mom?"

"Yes?"

"Do you think Jessie is alright?"

"Yes, Chanel. I think she is all right. You don't worry, okay?" Steph bent down to kiss her forehead. "I'll lock the door behind me so listen for the doorbell, okay?"

"Yes, ma'am." Chanel was sitting up now. She was no longer leaning against the headboard. She knew she was going to be needed.

Steph got into her car and drove down to Jessie's house. Inside, Rebekah and the boys were watching the television to pass time and trying to stay calm. Rebekah had her phone in her hand.

"Hey guys," Aunt Stephanie called out as she entered the kitchen in route to the front room where they were sitting.

"Hey," Rebekah stood to hear news.

"Well, have the guys found her?" Steph asked as she unbuttoned her coat.

"No, I thought you might have been with them," Rebekah asked quietly suppressing her anxiety.

"No, but I got a call and I couldn't hear it very well," Steph explained. "It just said to come to Jessie's. I think."

"You think?" Rebekah asked.

"Well, I'm not sure. It was breaking up because of the storm, I guess, and all I heard was *Jessie* and *come*." Steph stopped unbuttoning her coat.

Rebekah sat down on the chair. The boys, oblivious to what was going on, continued to watch their movie.

"Rebekah, I'm sure it was Steve saying he had Jessie because…"

Steph was interrupted by the sound of the guys coming

106

into the kitchen.

"See," she said, trying to reassure Rebekah, "that must be them now."

They both turned the corner into the kitchen as Chanel's dad and Steve came into the kitchen brushing rainwater from their faces.

Steve saw Steph and made a face at her.

"Where was she?" he asked.

"She's not with you?" Rebekah asked before Steph could answer.

"No!" Steve said with his tone increasing. "Why did you call us then?"

"I didn't call you!"

"Why did you call me?" Steph asked quickly.

"We didn't call," Chanel's dad answered for the two of them.

He looked into the front room.

"Where's Chanel?" He asked.

"She is at home waiting for me to call her." Steph pulled her cell phone from her pocket and dialed home. The call would not connect. "Hand me your cordless, Rebekah, mine has been acting up all night."

She took the phone from Rebekah. As she dialed and hung up twice, the three other parents stood with bated breath.

"This one's not working either!" Steph dropped the phone on the table and started towards the front door.

"Where are you going?" Steve asked.

"I think Chanel needs me!" Steph said as pushed open the front door and ran to her car.

"Steve, you guys stay here and warm up for just a moment," Chanel's dad said. "We'll go get Chanel and then start looking for Jessie again. Go ahead and call the police for help."

Rebekah, dialing the other phone again, "I'm already doing that." When she got a clear ring and answer, she said to Chanel's dad, "This phone is working fine!"

Steph and Rick drove in silence to their house.

The storm door was flailing in the wind and the porch light was out.

Inside, the house was empty. The cordless lay on the bed. Chanel was gone.

Chapter Fourteen

Chanel knew she was near the well when she heard the red-tailed hawk cry out. She had a flashlight and Jordan's coat buttoned tight against the wind and rain.

"Jessie!" she cried out ahead of her, struggling through the briars and tall grass. "Jessie!"

Something angular and cold bit into her shin. Sharp waves of pain shot up her leg causing her to fall forward losing the flashlight. In the dark she found herself spread eagle over Jessie's bicycle. She fumbled for the flashlight with one hand.

Suddenly, a talon-like hand hooked the crook of her elbow lifting her to her feet. She looked up to the silhouette of a tall black figure. Lightning flashed behind him, as he gestured to a leafless tree at the edge of the briar patch. There Jessie sat with her chin to her chest. A coat of some sort was draped over her to shield her from the rain.

"Jessie!" Chanel cried as she rushed to her.

Jessie lay motionless. Chanel brushed Jessie's hair away from her forehead and felt a knot above her eye. She felt a chill as she reached up to touch the knot above her own.

"Go get my dad…" Chanel shouted over her shoulder. When she heard no reply, she turned. The figure was gone. Chanel's flashlight was shining in her face from where it had been propped against the bicycle tire.

She grabbed the flashlight and turned to get Jessie up to her feet. Jessie was coming to but was groggy from the injury. She pulled the soaked coat off Jessie and pulled her up by her wrists.

"Jessie, get your feet under you! I have to get you out of this storm!" Chanel struggled to get Jessie upright.

"Chanel!" voices echoed from the darkness behind her. "Jessie!"

In a flash of lightning, she made out two figures. It was her dad and Steph.

She stood up and waved the flashlight.

"Over here! Dad, we are over here!"

Within seconds they were wrapped up in their parents arms. Steph called Rebekah and Steve to let her know they were on their way home. The phones were working! Dad carried Jessie while Steph walked Jessie's damaged bicycle in front of her. Her head throbbing, Chanel looked over her shoulder back into the dark wet woods.

The bicycle was placed in the open trunk of Steph's car. They loaded up and headed to Jessie's house. No one said a word all the way back.

At the house, Rebekah and Steph put Jessie in bed and looked at her head-wound. Chanel sat in the kitchen with Dad and Steve. She was wrapped in a dry blanket drinking the hot chocolate that Austin had made in the microwave. Jarrett stood at Chanel's feet watching her sip the warm drink.

Steph came into the kitchen with Jessie's wet clothes and carried them to the washroom.

Breaking the silence, Steve instructed, "Put Chanel's in with them and we'll bring them down tomorrow."

Dad took the opportunity to quiz Chanel.

"Chanel, what's going on?" he asked sternly.

"Dad, I don't know anymore," Chanel sighed. "I did go into the well with Jessie and I did go back by myself. I don't know what happened to Jessie except her bike was broken. I don't know who the man was that was there with Jessie"

"This man that helped you up, did you see his face?"

110

Steve asked.

"No. All I saw was his shape against the sky. He was tall and thin and had hands like…like claws on an eagle."

"Chanel?" Dad asked as he cocked his head.

"Dad, I'm serious! I tripped over the bike and fell to my knees. Then, it felt first like a big hook had me by the elbow. Then I could feel a tight grip around my shoulder. It lifted me like it was nothing to pick me up." She put the cup down on the table. "Dad, I was just looking for Jessie on the edge of the woods when I heard the hawk again. Instantly, there was Jessie's bike and then Jessie."

"Chanel, why did you get out of the bed?" Steph asked.

"Jessie called me on her cell phone."

Rebekah interrupted as she entered the room, "Jessie's phone is here, Chanel."

"But she called me!"

"Did she call you on your cell phone?" Steve asked.

"No, I don't think so, because … because I don't know where my cell phone is," Chanel said, looking to the ground.

Chanel looked up at her dad. "I was going to tell you that I had dropped it in the well, but I thought I might could get it back before I had to."

A thought occurred to Dad. He turned to Steph. "Honey, check the call log on your cell. See what number made the broken call."

Steph checked her phone. "It was made from Chanel's phone."

Dad checked his. "Mine also."

"Rick, Chanel was beside me when I got the broken call," Steph explained.

He turned to talk to Chanel, then stopped and

asked Steph, "What time was the call made?"

"Five thirty," Steph answered.

"Mine also," Dad said and he sat on down on a chair next to Chanel.

"You mean about five thirty?" Steph asked.

"No, five thirty, exactly," he said emphatically.

He dialed Chanel's cell phone. "*Hi this is Chanel. Sorry I missed your call. Please leave a message at the beep.*" BEEEEEP.

He started to hang up when he heard breathing through his earpiece. "Hello," he said. "Hello! Whoever has the phone, please answer."

"*Save... Blair,*" whispered a voice.

"Say that again!" Dad stood to get focus. "Say that again!"

A girl's voice crying in the static was all he heard.

"Whoever you are, stop this game!" he demanded. Stop this game, now!"

It was silent. Chanel's phone stopped transmitting.

"That's it!" Dad stuffed the phone is his pocket. "Chanel, I want you to promise me that you'll not go looking for the well again."

Chanel turned to face him squarely. "Dad, I..."

He cut her off, "Promise me, Chanel, that you will not look for the well again! You're hurt and Jessie's hurt. Who else is to get hurt while we chase ghosts?"

Chanel's shoulders sagged and her chin fell. "Okay, Dad, I promise."

"Good." Dad started to gather their things. "Let's go home to warm up before we are all sick and we'll check on Jessie in the morning. Steve, Rebekah, thanks for your help and if you know of a good exorcist I'll split the cost with you." He smiled weakly at his joke. Steve laughed and made the sign of the cross in the air.

"We'll be alright, Dad," Steve said, "Their big adventure just got the best of them." He punched Dad in the arm. "Remember, dude, we had our share."

Everyone smiled and rolled their eyes at Steve's confession of their youthful adventures. Then the three of them started out the door to Steph's car.

"See you guys in the morning," Steph added as she shut the kitchen door behind her. The three of them crawled into her car.

Their trip home was quiet. The few blocks seemed like a mile.
At the house Chanel changed into dry pajamas and kissed Dad and Steph, goodnight.

"Dad, I'm sorry," She offered and then hugged her dad.

"Sweetheart, you don't owe an apology. We've all been through a lot today and we'll be able to talk clear about it after we've rested. Okay?"

"Okay," Chanel said as she crawled into bed. She rolled over in her bed to face away from the door. Her head was throbbing and she was sad for Jessie.

Steph and Dad checked all of the rooms and then checked to make sure the house was locked up tight. They didn't talk until they were in their own bedroom and out of Chanel's hearing distance.

"Steph, I think something is wrong here that doesn't make any sense," Dad said.

"Yeah, I know," Steph agreed. She told him of Chanel's dream and then reluctantly of her inability to open Chanel's bedroom door earlier today.

They both felt silly to some degree, but still worried about the night's events.

"What do you think Jessie was doing out there?" Steph asked.

"I'm not sure. What about you?"

"I think she was led there to be bait for Chanel." Steph waited for Rick to laugh at her.

He didn't laugh. "I think we are just tired and are thinking too hard about what the girls have been saying," Dad reasoned.

"I think maybe you are right," Steph agreed again.

They crawled into bed and kissed each other goodnight. Steph switched the light off and settled into her pillow. Dad did the same.

Both stared into the darkness. Sleep came *much* later.

Chapter Fifteen

Morning came and the house was quiet. Chelsea didn't have a class so she volunteered to stay with Chanel while Rick and Steph went to work. He gave strict instructions about the woods. No one was to venture near them.

Chanel wandered into the kitchen to find Chelsea reading from some books that she'd picked up at the USAO library.

"Good morning," Chanel offered. "Don't you have class?"

"Good morning. No we're out now just like you. How do you feel?" Chelsea asked as she got up and poured hot water from the tea kettle into a cup for Chanel. "Here's some cocoa."

"Thanks. I feel tired and sore and mad," Chanel answered.

"Mad about what?"

"I'm mad that I've caused so much trouble."

"Chanel, I don't think *you* caused the trouble," Chelsea said as she sat next to Chanel.

"What do you mean?" Chanel asked.

Chelsea hesitated to stoke the fire the might otherwise be going out altogether. She had found out more than she had anticipated. But, she also found more questions.

"Chelsea, what do you mean?" Chanel asked with a bit more demand in her voice.

Chelsea looked at Chanel and then just gave in.

"I think you might be telling the truth," she offered.

"Might be?" Chanel asked emphatically.

"Well, you know what I mean. I think maybe you did go into the well and that maybe you did go back into time. There, I said it out loud!" Chelsea knew how silly it sounded.

"Now, why do you think I went back in time?" Chanel asked.

Chelsea got up and poured more hot water into her own cup.

"I went to see Ms. Ireland. Jordan went with me. And she has a scar over her right eye where your knot is. She said she had fallen in a well as a little girl," Chelsea explained.

Chanel took a sip of her cocoa. "I know. You told me all this."

"Chanel, she knows Cynthia," Chelsea said.

"I know!" Chanel admonished.

"I know *you* know and *she* knows you know, but you claim not to have been told by her and she goes into cardiac arrest at the mention of the event. I don't know what is going on!" Chelsea calms herself with her palms on the table. "I'm sorry, Chanel, either Ms. Ireland told you and you then dreamed about it or…"

"Or what?" Chanel asked "Or I went into the well and back into time?"

Chelsea's eyes met Chanel's in agreement.

Chanel's hands began to shake. The finality of someone else admitting that she had gone back in time was overwhelming. The cup fell from her hand and broke on the white tile floor. Hot cocoa splattered on their legs and on the white cabinets beside them. Tears filled her eyes and she looked pleadingly to Chelsea. The kitchen was quiet after the porcelain crash. She began to sob uncontrollably.

Chelsea went to Chanel's chair to put her arms around her.

"Its okay, Chanel," Chelsea said, "whatever happened, it is still okay."

"No it isn't, Chelsea!" Chanel's voice rose. "If I *went* into the well, then I abandoned Cynthia to *die* in the well!"

Chelsea hugged tighter. Then, as if a light bulb had been turned on, it dawned on her.

"Then, that is why Ms. Ireland is so upset," she explained. She *also* left Cynthia to die in the well."

"What?" Chanel asked.

Chelsea stood to collect her thoughts.

"Maybe Ms. Ireland was you or you were Ms. Ireland."

"What?" Chanel asked as she wiped tears from her cheeks.

"Chanel maybe, back in time, you were Ms. Ireland. You said Cynthia called you Blair. Maybe she and Cynthia were dropped in the well and Ms. Ireland escaped as you did."

"And?" Chanel was catching on.

"Maybe Ms. Ireland is sending you back to save Cynthia," Chelsea offered.

Chanel thought for a moment. "Chelsea, Ms. Ireland doesn't know about the well or that I went back to see Cynthia. I never told her about it. How could she be sending me?"

"I don't know. Maybe..." Chelsea started but was interrupted by the phone ringing.

She answered the phone.

"Hello."

"Is this Chanel?" a voice on the other end of the line inquired.

"No, this is her sister. How can I help you?"

"Is this Chelsea?"

"Yes, it is, who is this?"

"This is Betty from the nursing home. Ms. Ireland took a bad turn last night. We found her crying in her room. She is being sent to the hospital. I thought you would want to know," Betty explained.

"Yes, Betty, I did want to be told," Chelsea said. "What is going on?"

"We don't know. She had packed all her belongings in a box and we found her on the floor along with an empty pill bottle," Betty continued. "I have to go now. You *know* that *I* can't have been the one who told you this, don't you?"

"Yes, Betty," Chelsea acknowledged, "I won't say a thing. Thank you for calling us."

Chelsea hung up the phone.

"What is it, Chelsea?" Chanel had regained composure and was starting to wipe up cocoa from the floor.

"It is Ms. Ireland. She is in the hospital and is very sick."

"Chelsea, take me to see her!" Chanel said.

"No, we had better stay here." Chelsea assisted in cleaning up the cocoa and the broken cup.

Chanel slumped back into her chair. Her head hurt and thoughts were swimming wildly in her mind. Suddenly, her eyes lit up and she straightened her posture as if a burden had been lifted

"Chelsea."

"What, Chanel?" Chelsea asked, not looking up from her cleaning.

"Chelsea, I know what is going on."

"What is going on with whom?" Chelsea asked as she rinsed the cocoa from the dishtowel.

"Chelsea, I am supposed to save Ms. Ireland," Chanel revealed.

"How are you supposed to save Ms. Ireland, Chanel?"

I have to save her from herself," Chanel went on. "She has given up on life. She told me in so many words one night in her room at the nursing home. I think she has this guilt over Cynthia. So, now, she has given up on her own life."

"Chanel, even if this is true, how are you supposed to save her?" Chelsea sat down next to Chanel.

"I think I have to save Cynthia to save Ms. Ireland, but I don't know how."

Chelsea sipped her cocoa and pondered what Chanel has proposed for a moment. Then, "Chanel, what is Cynthia's last name?"

Chanel thought long and hard to remember. Finally, "Tallchief. Her name was Cynthia Tallchief. Why?"

"Chanel, I need to do some checking on this name. Maybe she is in the archives," Chelsea tried to clarify her reasoning.

"What are archives?" Chanel asked.

"They are files and newspapers stored on a disc. These might tell us about Cynthia Tallchief." A solution was unfolding in her head.

"How? I don't get it." Chanel's frustration was almost to a breaking point.

"If she fell in a well that was used on a day to day basis somebody would have found her. Even if she was…" Chelsea stopped.

"Even if she was what, Chelsea?" Chanel knew the answer even as she asked the question.

"Even if she had died, Chanel," Chelsea responded somberly. "If she had been found, it would have made the newspaper and it would be in the archives."

Chanel protested more, "I still need to talk to Ms. Ireland!"

"I know you do, Chanel, but we need something to tell

her, don't we?"

Chanel understood. "Yes, we need something to tell her."

"I am going to the library. I need you to promise to stay put and to be here when I return, promise?" Chelsea demanded.

"I promise," Chanel agreed.

"Pinky-promise?" Chelsea countered to confirm.

"Pinky-promise," Chanel agreed again and raised her pinky for Chelsea to lock hers with. As they locked fingers Chanel smiled at her sister's support. "But hurry, I need to go to see her."

Chelsea scooped up her car keys and left for the library. She felt Chanel would be all right alone as long as she stayed put in the house. Maybe finding Cynthia Tallchief's name at a later date could resolve Ms. Ireland's state of despair.

Chanel called Jessie's house to check on her. Rebekah said she was fine and was sleeping. "Aunt Rebekah, I'm sorry for causing this trouble."

"Chanel it is fine. Everyone is safe and we are all going to be safe. Okay?" Rebekah consoled.

"Yes, ma'am. Thanks."

"You're welcome. Now, you get some rest because we have a big Thanksgiving coming up and it would be a sad sight to see you and Jessie sick." Rebekah directed.

"Okay, I will. Bye." Chanel hung up and went back to her bedroom. She was so tired and sore. Soon she was asleep.

At the university library where Chickasha's newspaper archives were stored on microfiche, Chelsea discovers complete newspapers dating back to Chickasha's founding in 1892. At one time, there were two competing newspapers as Chickasha had been booming as an agricultural and transportation center. With all the issues in archive, it took a while to narrow her search to one. The Chickasha Express was dominating in its local news coverage so Chelsea concentrated her efforts there. Slowly, she scanned each and every issue.

She had gone through 1936 and several months into 1939 before giving up on any record of a girl being found in the well. She read articles regarding Shanoan Springs Park being renovated with WPA workers and saw additional columns about the big white house that stood where the nursing home now stood. She scanned pages looking for Cynthia and Blair's family name. Nothing came up.

She even went back to the earliest paper on record and worked ahead looking for anything about the original park site or family. Two hours had lapsed and still nothing.

Chelsea knew from her history studies that the Indians relegated to Oklahoma were considered second class citizens back then and assumed that might be a reason for so little print to be about their events. But even so, a body in a well would be reported on.

She stepped outside to call Chanel at home.

"Hello," Chanel answered.

"Chanel, I am not having much luck," Chelsea reported. "Do you remember anything that Cynthia said about her family or about where she lived?"

It was quiet on the phone for long moment while Chanel thought about her visit with Cynthia in the park.

"How old was she?" Chelsea expanded her questions.

"Thirteen," Chanel replied.

"Then she must have gone to school." Chelsea resolved aloud. "Did she live in Chickasha?"

"No," Chanel started, "she and her family lived on Medicine Creek near Saddle Mountain and they camped on the Little Washita on weekends so her father could sell the furniture and leather goods that he made.

"Wait!" Chanel blurted. "She gave me a brooch that someone had given to her from the Indian school. She went to an Indian school that started with the word *river*."

"Okay, good!" Chelsea was relieved to have a more definitive starting point. "I'll go back in and try looking for articles on the school. Are you still alright there?"

She returned to the microfiche and began the tedious search for the name of the Indian school.

Chelsea found mention of a Rainy Mountain School for the Kiowa-Apache in Gotebo, Oklahoma and then later she found that an Indian School was celebrating its twentieth year in its new facilities in 1898 near Anadarko, Oklahoma. She read about its formation and the many tribes that sent their children there. The school's name was Riverside Indian School!

The newspapers mentioned little else about it so Chelsea went to over to the computer and *Googled* Riverside Indian School -- the nation's oldest federally operated American Indian boarding school.

In 1878 the Wichita-Caddo School was moved to its present location along the Washita River and was renamed Riverside Indian School. For a half-century Riverside Indian School served Wichita, Caddo, and Delaware students. Then, in 1922, Kiowa enrolled there after the Rainy Mountain Kiowa Mission School closed. Navajo students began attending in 1945. The Indian boarding school system emphasized agriculture, vocational and basic academics. College preparation wasn't added until 1990. At last census, there were approximately 600 students enrolled.

Searching further, Chelsea pulled up the official Riverside Indian School web page. She scrolled through the links and read about the school. It dawned on her that Cynthia's family might have sent her siblings there and there could possibly be a connection to follow. She read more intently looking for the name Tallchief. She found many, too many. In fact, she found that a teacher named Tallchief had worked there for over forty years. What a dead end it had become. Chelsea was about to go back to the mundane research in the archives when she noticed what had eluded her initially. It was the teacher. Her name was Cynthia Tallchief. Ms. Ireland's Cynthia!

Chelsea stared at the faded photo of the beautiful woman receiving her retirement plaque. She was strikingly beautiful. A group of people stood around her smiling. Something else caught Chelsea's eye.

A tall man with a wedge shaped face stood in the background watching Cynthia. Everyone else was facing the photographer. Chelsea knew him from somewhere. His face and his eyes were familiar. She went back through the web site. She found him in several photos. He was never smiling and Chelsea noticed that a shadow was behind him on the wall wherever he stood. It was an odd bird shaped shadow like a crow or an eagle. Nevertheless, he was watching Cynthia as she received her award and the shadow was still there though he stood far away from any wall! She pressed the print button to save a copy of the photograph. It was an odd feature but it did not take from the fact that she had found Cynthia Tallchief. Chelsea found the school's phone number on page one of the website and dialed it.

She visited with the receptionist who passed her on to the

school's librarian. The librarian was also the school historian.

"Yes, Cynthia Tallchief was a teacher here. She came to teach at the school in the late forties or early fifties. She was the English and folklore instructor," she pointed out to Chelsea.

"English folklore?" Chelsea asked.

"No, English Language and Indian Folklore." The librarian went on to expound her duties, "We had so many children from so many tribes that we integrated their native folklores to help them relate to American historical and literary figures. Ms. Tallchief's father was a Kiowa Shaman. She took teaching very seriously."

"I see." Chelsea got a clear picture of Cynthia's integrity. "Would you happen to have her phone number or would you know where she lives so I might talk with her?"

"Well, that won't be possible, miss," the librarian countered.

"Well if it has to do with privacy, just tell me what city she lives in. I will give my information to her and…"

"No, it is not that. Ms. Tallchief passed away. She has been gone for almost a month now," the librarian responded sadly.

"Oh, no!" Chelsea reacted. She had so hoped that actual contact with Cynthia would be the solution to Blair's dilemma. "Did she have family near Chickasha that I could contact?"

"No. Her two brothers and her mother died of diphtheria before Cynthia came to work here," the librarian answered. "She and her father lived on the school grounds. He passed away around 1960 or so."

"Did you know her well?" Chelsea asked, "Did she not

marry?"

"No, she never married. She and Jacob were dear friends, but they never married."

"Jacob?" Chelsea questioned. "Who was Jacob, maybe I could talk with him?"

"Jacob was the custodian here. He left the area when Cynthia was buried. We figured he couldn't stand being here without her, I don't know how you might contact him," the librarian detailed further. "Jacob was a quiet somber man. He was close to Cynthia's father as well. Rumor was Cynthia's father had passed on the Shaman rites to him. Jacob believed he was mystical."

"Mystical?" Chelsea repeated the word.

"Oh, he never said anything outlandish, but he was different. He would assist Cynthia with unruly children and he would tell stories about the old Kiowa. It was odd because he was one of the few non-Indians to work here, much less attempt to carry on traditions reserved for Indian priests."

Chelsea had a hunch. "Was he tall and thin?"

"Yes, then, you do know him?" The librarian resolved from Chelsea's description.

"No, but, I think I saw his photos on the web page."

"Oh, you probably did. He worked here many years," she conceded.

"I see. So you don't know of anyone who could talk to me about Cynthia's early years as a child?"

"No, I really don't know of anyone. Why do you ask about her childhood?" the librarian quizzed.

"My sister thinks she knows someone who was friends with her as a young girl. Ms. Tallchief's name came up and we were trying to find out for her. She would be the same age I think," Chelsea omitted the rest of the story for fear of sounding crazy.

"I really only met her a few years ago and we never discussed things that far back. I don't really know of another source for you."

"Well, I really do appreciate you taking time away to talk to me. I have one more question if you don't mind," Chelsea appealed.

"I understand that the Chickasaw owned most of the Chickasha and Grady county land originally and that the Plains tribes were located west of Grady County."

"Yes, that is true, why?" the librarian agreed.

"If Cynthia Tallchief was Kiowa why would she live in Chickasha as a child?" Chelsea asked.

"I do know the answer to that. She didn't live in Chickasha. Her father was a Shaman, a medicine man, and he traveled all around Western Oklahoma healing and advising. He was also a leather smith and furniture maker. He traveled to sell his wares. Cynthia talked about that often with her students. She said it was your destiny to share your skills. This message motivated many of her students to leave the complacent comfort of their families and to discover the world outside Oklahoma."

"Where did they live before moving onto the school property?"

"I believe they lived everywhere he took them." The librarian laughed softly. "He took them all over western and south-central Oklahoma."

Chelsea thanked the librarian and gathered her notes. She needed to talk with Chanel and then they needed to talk with Ms. Ireland.

Chapter Sixteen

Chelsea drove home assimilating, in her head, all that she now knew. She was sure that Cynthia Tallchief did survive the well. It may be a problem convincing Ms. Ireland that it was her Cynthia that taught at Riverside Indian School. With no family to confirm these facts, Ms. Ireland might not accept them in her current state of depression.

Chelsea also tried putting in perspective the events of the past week. It was too bazarre to think that a ghost was manipulating Ms. Ireland's salvation through Chanel.

She arrived at the house to find Chanel sitting on the porch. Her hair was pulled back into a ponytail and she was dressed to see Ms. Ireland.

"Chanel, c'mon, I want to tell you what I found out," Chelsea instructed through her car's open window.

Chanel stood gingerly. Her head still swam with the effects of the concussion. She found it hard to focus, but was determined to go to the hospital.

After she got in and latched her seat belt, Chelsea asked, "Are you alright?"

"I think so. My head sure hurts." Chanel set her gaze ahead through the windshield. Struggling to keep from lying back against the seat, she set her jaw and tried to be stronger.

"We can go later?"

"No. Let's go now," Chanel directed softly.

As they pulled away from the house, Chelsea could not contain herself.

"Chanel, Cynthia survived the well!"

"How do you know?"

"I talked to a lady at the Riverside Indian School and she said Cynthia Tallchief was a teacher there for forty years."

"Let's go talk to her!" Chanel exclaimed.

"We can't, Chanel. She passed away just last month." Chelsea knew how much it would mean for Chanel to talk to Cynthia one more time, even if it was as Chanel and not as Blair.

"Not last month?" Chanel implored.

"That is what they told me at the school," Chelsea continued conveying what she knew. "She never married and she and her father lived on school property. The rest of her family was gone and the closest thing to a family member, moved away after the funeral."

"Maybe we can find her to tell Ms. Ireland," Chanel offered.

"It wasn't a 'her'. It was a man named Jacob. It was sort of strange. Every photo I found of him had a shadow…"

"Did you say, Jacob?" Chanel interrupted.

"Yes. Did you meet him in the park also?" Chelsea could see the irritation in Chanel's furrowed brow.

Chanel stared distantly out the window. She could hear Zeke asking Jacob what to do with the dirty Indian girl and her white trash friend. Jacob had not participated, but he had been there and hadn't stopped the harassment. Was this the same Jacob, Chanel wondered?

"Chanel," Chelsea said again. "Chanel!"

Chanel broke from her daydream.

"What?" she asked.

"Did you meet a Jacob also?"

"There were three boys that dropped us in the well. The leader was Zeke, and there was a stupid laughing fat boy named Edward and then there was a stuttering boy named Jacob. He argued with Zeke about what Zeke wanted to do with us, but Zeke ignored him and played up to the taunting of the fat boy, Edward."

"He argued with Zeke?" Chelsea asked.

"Yes. He was stuttering and was shy sounding and I think Zeke must have made fun of him or used him as the butt of his jokes because he was so quiet."

"But he didn't touch either of you?"

"No, not that I remember," Chanel answered. Her thoughts drifted back to the incident.

Chelsea, too, was in deep thought. This Jacob could be a bigger factor than they knew.

The girls drove on to the hospital. Each traveled within her thoughts.

At the hospital Chelsea stopped Chanel as she opened the door.

"Chanel, Ms. Ireland is very sick. It is probably best if we just try to make her feel better and not to bring any of this up until she is stronger, okay?"

"Okay."

"And, Chanel?"

"Yes."

"Miss Blair is very old and this may have been too much already. She might not get any stronger."

"I know that Chelsea, that is what I've been worrying about."

They walked into the hospital and found the nurses desk.

"We are here to see Blair Ireland," Chelsea explained.

"She is in intensive care. Are you family?" The nurse questioned.

"Grand-nieces," Chanel answered before Chelsea could speak.

Chelsea's eyes rolled ever so slightly at Chanel's quick and blatantly false answer.

"Well, then, come this way," The nurse directed as she came from behind the counter. "She has not had any family to visit since she arrived. I'm sure this will brighten her mood."

Chelsea whispered to Chanel behind the nurses back, "Lying is not supposed to be so easy."

"There are dire exceptions," Chanel justified without hesitation.

"Pardon me?" the nurse turned to hear if it was her they were talking to.

"How is our aunt, it is a dire situation?" Chanel asked as they walked down the corridor.

"She is stable but weak. We are not sure how much she ingested so we can only watch her. So you guys can just have a few moments. We don't want to tire her."

"Yes ma'am." they agreed in unison.

Chelsea stopped the nurse before she left the room completely.

"Pardon me," Chelsea asked, "You don't know how much of what was digested?"

"We found high quantities of her medications in her system," the nurse divulged. "And we found polyglycol."

"What is that?" Chanel joined the conversation.

"It is automobile anti-freeze. We aren't sure how she got it but she must be really despondent," The nurse offered.

"She would not have taken poison!" Chanel defended.

The nurse arched her eyebrows and shrugged her shoulders. With that she headed back to her station.

Inside they found Ms. Ireland with her eyes closed and a look of pain on her brow. She was hooked to various monitors. Her pulse and her breathing were slow.

"Don't wake her. You can only talk to her if she wakes

up on her own. Okay?" another nurse instructed as she came in the room to check Ms. Ireland's vitals.

"Yes ma'am," they again spoke in unison.

Chelsea sat down in a chair beside the monitor. Chanel stood close to Ms. Ireland and stroked the back of her hand very softly. Soon, her brow softened and her features relaxed to one of a more resting expression. Ms. Ireland did not awaken though and the girls stood silent vigil for almost fifteen minutes.

The nurse came back in and softly asked if she had awakened any at all.

"No, but she is sleeping better, I think," Chanel answered softly.

"Then it is probably best to let her. You can come back later if you wish," the nurse directed.

"Okay," Chelsea acknowledged, "Chanel, let's let her rest."

"Alright," Chanel bent to kiss Miss Ireland on the cheek.

She had to take a chance, "Cynthia was saved," Chanel whispered slow and soft against Miss Ireland's temple. The heart monitor changed pace unnoticed by the three of them, and then went back to its rhythm. Chanel kissed her on the cheek and turned away to walk out with Chelsea.

As they exited the room, the corners of Miss Ireland's lips turned ever so slightly up. Her laugh lines deepened at her eyes and cheeks. Her pulse strengthened.

At Chelsea's car, the girls looked at each other before they got in.

"Where do we go from here?" Chanel was frustrated.

Chelsea unlocked the door.

"First we get you home. We need you strong also."

"And then?" Chanel pressed, still looking over the top of

the car.

"And then we go find Jacob," Chelsea said matter-of-factly.

As they drove off, a curtain closed from the maintenance room window of the hospital. Within seconds, a red tailed hawk was gliding over Chelsea's white Chevy Cavalier.

Chapter Seventeen

At home, Chelsea found Jaimie and Jordan sitting at the kitchen table.

"Where have you guys been?" Jordan demanded as she hugged Chanel and sat her down on the couch. "Mom called and then your dad called and we are supposed to call both of them when you two get back. I think you two are in t-r-o-u-b-l-e. How you feel, sweetheart?"

"Oops," Chelsea confessed, "I'll call them."

Jaimie sat on Chanel's other side. "How are you doing, Chanel?"

"Fine, thanks," Chanel exhaled as she leaned back against the cushions. "Just tired and hungry."

"Well how about some pizza from Napoli's?" Jaimie suggested.

"Yeah, that sounds perfect," Chanel agreed.

"I'll call it in." Jaimie got up to get the phone.

"Pepperoni?" Chanel requested.

"This time, cause you're sick," Jordan answered for Jaimie. "Next time it is the Supremes. '*Stop in the name of love. Put all the fixings on*'!"

Chelsea came in from the other room.

"Well, I got another lecture," she announced, "I probably deserved it."

"We are ordering pizza," Jaimie said. "Do you want that or lasagna?"

"Better get two pizzas. Steph and Dad are on the way home now," Chelsea alerted in an ominous tone.

"So, where were you guys?" Jordan asked.

"We went to see Ms. Ireland. She is in the hospital, in intensive care," Chanel answered.

"And guess what?" Chelsea sat against the fireplace mantel.

"What?" Jaimie inquired as she hung up the phone.

"Cynthia Tallchief survived the well!" Chelsea started. "She taught school at Riverside Indian School for over forty years!"

"So, there is a Cynthia Tallchief? How did you find this out?" Jaimie looked at Chanel resting on the couch and shook her head.

Chelsea explained how she had *Googled* the Riverside Indian School's name on the computer and had eventually found her listed in the faculty pages. She told them that she had called the school and what the school historian as told her and then brought up Jacob and what Chanel had said about him.

"I think we need to find this Jacob," Jordan agreed. Then in her best *Murder She Wrote* voice, "He could be the one to close all the loop holes."

"Not all of them," Jaimie argued. "This whole wishing well, cell phone and hawk thing is beyond explaining. I don't care if this Jacob tells us it was him that saved Cynthia from the well. It has been too weird around here."

"And besides that," she went on, "these people's names that Chanel knows supposedly without Ms. Ireland telling her. It either means Chanel went into the well or we are all sharing the same dream."

"Anyway, how we supposed to find this Jacob?" Jordan resumed her line of thought.

"Well," Chelsea started, "we know that the Cynthia's friend Jacob is into Indian mysticism as was Cynthia's father. We know that Jacob lived near the school for many years and we know that he stuttered as a child; that is, if he is indeed one of the three boys that Chanel said put the girls into the well."

"Okay, I agree, that is a lot of CSI stuff right there," Jordan offered. "Or, we could call the historian, get his last name and then look in the phone book."

They all looked at Jordan and then at each other.

"Duh!" Chelsea admonished her lack of logical reasoning "I'll call. I never even thought to ask."

She went out to her car to get her notes. As she turned to walk back into the house she saw the hawk perched on the streetlight post.

She stopped and shaded the sun from her eyes to look at it. "What is it that you know, Mr. Hawk? Are you leading us somewhere or just enjoying our plight?" She laughed at herself for talking to a bird and went inside.

She got on the phone to call the school.

"I'm going after the pizza. Jordan you going with?" Jaimie announced as she picked up her car keys.

"Sure!" Jordan jumped up to go and squeezed Chanel's knee. "Be right back, Sweetie."

Chelsea got the historian on the line.

"Hello, this is Chelsea Lane again. I talked to you about Miss Tallchief."

"Yes, I remember, Chelsea. What can I do for you?"

"We wanted to visit with Jacob. Could you tell me his last where-about or even his last name?"

"Well, honey, I wish I could but we have a privacy policy here and you are not related; so, it wouldn't be fair to Jacob for me to disclose anything else."

"I understand, but this is kind of an emergency." Chelsea pleaded.

"What is the emergency?" The historian needed

135

justification.

Chelsea knew that she could not tell this ghost story and have any credibility.

"Well, not really an emergency, but their mutual friend really would like to know about Miss Tallchief."

"I can understand but I have responsibility to our staff," the historian ruled.

"I know that, but, is there anything that you could tell us to shorten our search?" Chelsea crossed her fingers.

The historian was quiet for a moment and then added: "Jacob is into Indian folklore and medicine. There is a council that meets near the site where the Tonkawa were massacred in 1862. In fact they meet tonight for a ceremony. Maybe someone there knows Jacob."

"Did you say they meet at a site where a massacre occurred?" Chelsea asked.

"Yes. In 1857 the Tonkawa Indians of central Texas were moved to a sight on the Washita River near Anadarko in retaliation for an uprising they had on an Indian agency near Bexar, Texas."

"The Tonkawa had a reputation as marauders and were even thought of as cannibals by their tribal enemies. There existed a great hatred between them and the plains Indians scattered throughout the southwest."

"It is assumed by historians that their opportunistic habits and the fact that they had allegedly agreed to ally themselves with a group of slaveholders in the Confederacy, prompted a group of Delaware, Shawnee and Caddo warriors to attack their camp on the night of October 25, 1962. There were two agency employees killed as well as 137 men, women and children out of about 300 Tonkawa. The survivors fled and wandered for years throughout

136

Oklahoma. Ninety-two known Tonkawa were eventually resettled near Ponca City at the Oakland agency.

"A ceremony of penitence for those actions is held there annually during the full moon following the anniversary of the event."

"Why not on the anniversary of the event?" Chelsea interrupted.

"To hold the ceremony on the date of such a horrific event might serve to glorify it. It is believed that ceremonies held during a full moon washes away transgressions. The first full moon following a tragedy and mourning is the time for acknowledging penitence.

"I think Jacob and many others from various tribes who practiced the rites of the Shaman attended this event faithfully. Perhaps Jacob will be there or maybe someone who could help with the answers you seek."

Chelsea was intrigued to think how these ceremonies still are held in the twenty-first century right in our backyard.

"Well, I thank you for all that you have explained," Chelsea offered to the historian.

"Miss Lane," the historian started, "you seem quite inquisitive. Maybe in the near future you will take the opportunity to broaden your intelligence about America's *full* history. You are welcome here any chance you might have."

"Thank you, very much," Chelsea said and then added: "However, if I could tell you all we have been through in the past few days, you might question my intelligence."

The historian laughed politely as Chelsea hung up the phone.

"Road Trip!" Chelsea declared.

Chanel had fallen asleep on the couch. Jordan and Jaimie

had not returned with the pizza so Chelsea fired up the computer to find out where the Tonkawa Massacre had occurred.

A web page in Wikipedia said that in 1954 the citizens of Anadarko set aside 200 acres of land four miles south of the city to serve as an outdoor working museum, in what was once called the Tonkawa Hills. It is believed to be on or near the site of the massacre. The museum is open to the public from 9 a.m. until 5 p.m. Chelsea surmised then that other ceremonies not 'open to the public' would be suspect for them to attend. All they could do was try to get in.

"Hello house!" came Jordan's warning as she and Jaimie returned with their pizzas. "Anybody..." She saw Chanel was asleep and her voice trailed off to a whisper, "...want pizza?"

Chelsea came out of the bedroom and told the girls to get ready for a road trip to Indian City.

"I'm not going to Indian City," Jaimie allowed. "My friends will think I'm crazy if I tell him why I'm going out there. I would think I'm crazy. And, please tell, why would I be going out there?"

"The historian would not tell me Jacob's last name," Chelsea explained.

Jordan was draping an afghan over Chanel's legs. "Is he wanted for something? We *could* make her talk, you know," she mumbled sarcastically.

"Privacy issues," Chelsea started. "She said he religiously took part in a ceremony held each year at Indian City. If we went out there we might get to talk to him or worse case, someone could tell us how to find him."

"Why tonight?" Jaimie still was doubtful.

"Tonight is the ceremony mourning the Tonkawa

Massacre of 1862. It is ..." Chelsea was cut off by Jordan's palm in her face.

"Hold it there, sister. You did say massacre?" She looked over her shoulder at Jaimie. "I'm in. Jaimie you are in also." Jordan opened the top pizza box and grabbed a slice.

Chelsea looked pleadingly at Jaimie.

"Okay, I'm in, but all we are doing is looking for this Jacob, so *he* can talk to Ms. Ireland. That's our story. We are not circling a campfire and stomping up the dust under the full moon. We are in and out. Understood?" Jaimie's arched eyebrows and tight lips demanded confirmation of their intent.

"Deal," Chelsea agreed. "We also cannot tell Chanel. At least we can't tell her just yet."

"Why?" Jordan and Jaimie asked in unison.

"Cause she'll want to go," Chelsea explained. "She is not well enough to go. If she doesn't know where we are, she won't sit and worry about us going."

At that, the door opened and Chelsea's dad stepped in.

"Hello girls." He sat his lunch cooler down on the floor beside the door. "You three look as if you ate the canary."

"No canaries. But we got pizza," Jordan declared as she held up a box for him to smell.

"How is Chanel since you drug her all over Chickasha with a brain concussion?" Dad was being facetious.

"She is fine Dad," Chelsea protested. "And, I didn't drag her. We went to check on Ms. Ireland and came straight home. She wanted pizza, but fell asleep before the pizza got here."

"Okay," he accepted. "Has Steph called?"

"Yes," Jordan answered. "She should be here anytime, so we got her a Supreme with extra black olives."

139

"Great! How long has Chanel been asleep?" He hung his coat on the peg by the door.

"Maybe thirty minutes," Chelsea guessed. "I think we are going to go now that you are here to stay with her."

"What about all this pizza?" he quizzed, tilting his head to show he knew something was up. "Where are you three going?"

"Uh, I'm going home to change into my comfortable clothes," Jaimie excused herself.

"And Jordan and I have a party to go to. You know, college stuff." Chelsea avoided making eye contact with her dad. "I might take a slice with me. What about you Jordan, you want more for the road?"

"Sure." She grabbed a paper towel and dropped two pieces on it. She then threw an arm around Dad's neck and kissed him on the cheek. "After while crocodile."

"Later. Bye, Jaimie." He gave in to those two. But, he knew Chelsea better than Jordan and Jaimie.

Dad looked at Chelsea to see if he could read her face about what was really going on, but Chelsea rushed out the door to avoid having to lie to her Dad. He smelled a rat and was about to follow when Chanel awoke.

"Hi, sweetheart." He turned back and squatted on the floor beside her. "How do you feel?"

"Fine. Better," she disclosed.

"How is Ms. Ireland?"

"Dad, she's not doing so well. She's in the hospital. Did Chelsea tell you?"

"Not about that. How about you, Chelsea said you wanted pizza?"

"Where is Chelsea?" Chanel asked as she looked over the back of the couch.

"She and Jordan had a thing and Jaimie went home. Did they tell you where they had a thing at?" he interrogated.

"No." Chanel thought about the earlier conversation. Maybe Chelsea had found Jacob. She knew Dad would not approve so she changed the subject.

"Pizza smells good," Chanel changed the topic.

Steph walked in at that and the three of them sat down for pizza and *I.B.C.* root beer. Chanel was thinking about Jacob. He might have come back to the well. She had a feeling he could have been capable of doing that.

Chapter Eighteen

The road leading to Indian City from Anadarko wound through blackjack oaks and eastern red cedars. There was no traffic and the eerie shadows cast by the full moon dappled the way ahead. The road fell and climbed through the rugged hills in an attempt to shake the girls off their path. Chelsea drove too fast and her screeching tires at the curves forced Jaimie to comment.

"If we don't get there alive will they have a ceremony for *us* later?" Jaimie hinted.

Chelsea slowed. "I'm sorry," she said. "I just want to get there and talk to this Jacob."

"You know, just like Ms. Ireland, he is also eighty-something years old," Jaimie reminded Chelsea.

"Do what?" Chelsea let off a little on the gas pedal.

Jaimie took her eyes off the road to make her point. "He might not be making this ceremony anymore."

In all the discussions with Chanel, Chelsea could only envision Jacob as one of the mean boys. And even after seeing some of the old photos from the Riverside Indian School directory, she never put his true age into perspective. He might not be here tonight and even if he was, his health might preclude him from being of much help. She slowed way down.

"The lady at the school seemed to feel he might still be active," she justified. "But, if he is not here we will leave and try something else."

"Do you think they will let us in?" Jordan broke in.

"I don't know. In all the books and movies you have to have a secret handshake or something," Chelsea tried to lighten the foreboding mood that was threatening.

"We could all high-five and say 'Hey-Ya-Hey-Ya'," Jaimie joked to give herself more confidence.

"Hey-Ya?" Jordan asked. "That was a song by *OUTCAST*. I thought we were supposed to give a '*HOW*' or something."

"That is just not right, Jordan," Chelsea admonished. They glared at Jordan's political incorrectness.

As they silently admonished, the sign to the entrance came into view. The car eased to coasting. A chain stretched across the entrance, blocking their progression. Wooden animal figurines hung from the chain and symbols fashioned from twisted cedar boughs were affixed to the ten-foot high columns with red strips of cloth. Deerskins draped over the INDIAN CITY sign blocked the word CITY.

A full minute lapsed before the girls took their eyes off the spectacle.

"Well, that's it. It's closed," Jaimie offered.

"Wait a minute," Jordan protested. "It's just closed to tourists. I think."

"We ARE tourists," Jaimie corrected her.

Again the car was quiet.

"I think it's okay if we go in. The historian at the school would not have told me to come here if it was not alright," Chelsea said.

"Yeah? Where are all the cars? How did the ceremony people get here?" Jaimie argued.

"Maybe the *ceremony people* unlocked the chain let them in and then put it back," Jordan explained matter-of-factly. "It's not a big deal. Let's go."

She got out of the car and left the door open for Jaimie to get out from the back seat. She went to inspect some of the figurines.

144

"These are so cool. This is a bear and here's a coyote and a lizard." Jordan walked along the chain. "And look! The chain is not locked it's just hooked to this ring."

Chelsea turned off the headlights and the engine and joined Jordan. She, too, marveled at the intricate carvings as well as the manipulations of the cedar stems. Two fluorescent lights were mounted to the entrance sign, but they were not lit. The full moon, however, bathed the area in a surreal glow.

The door shut quietly behind her as Jaimie joined Chelsea and Jordan.

"You do have a flashlight?" she requested from Chelsea.

"Yes, in my trunk. I'll get it."

"And a gun or pepper spray or baseball bat? You know, just in case," Jaimie added.

"How about a wooden stake and a mallet?" Jordan teased.

"How about your garlic breath from eating that pizza. That should be enough," Jaimie replied to Jordan's teasing.

"Girls!" Chelsea stopped the escalation.

Chelsea retrieved the flashlight and the three of them stepped over the chain. Walking close together and with senses alert they stayed on the road that led to the museum and gift shop. All was dark and still, except for the crickets and the occasional lightning bug.

"I think the scariest part is all the things that are racing through my mind," Jordan offered.

"Yeah, well that part is called common sense," Jaimie said. "You are supposed to be scared of the situations that you know are potentially dangerous."

"I know that, Jaimie, I'm talking about all the monster stuff from the movies; not the Jeffrey Dahmer or the Zodiac killers. You know, not the stuff that really happened," Jordan clarified.

"Oh my god, you did not have to bring up specific real monsters, Jordan," Jaimie stopped in her tracks.

"Guys, I really think this is okay. The historian brought it up and offered it as a chance for me to find Jacob or one of his friends. I don't think this ceremony would be an evil event," Chelsea reassured.

"Did the historian say she had come to this before?" Jaimie hoped aloud as she caught up with Jordan and Chelsea.

"No. She didn't. But she also didn't say she had not been here," Chelsea answered.

"She could be like Igor was to Baron Frankenstein or like Norman was to the old murderous lady in Psycho," Jordan said.

Chelsea and Jaimie stopped in their tracks.

"Norman *was* the murderous old lady in Psycho," Chelsea corrected Jordan.

"I know, I just couldn't think of any the other assistant's names right off the bat," Jordan acknowledged as she walked on without them. "But you get my drift."

They continued on and soon were standing on the porch of the gift shop. Together they peered inside the dimly lit building. In the stillness they heard voices coming from behind one of the native villages that had been set up to display each of the seven tribes represented at the park.

The village was a series of houses built in tribal fashions. The Navajo Hogan was constructed of pine logs laid in a circle and covered with adobe to seal out the wind and weather. A small oven of adobe was in front by the entrance. The Apache Wikiup was crudely built of boughs covered in

146

grasses and skins. It was obviously a throw-together type structure as the Apache were very nomadic. The Caddo built a more permanent "wattle and daub" structure using post and twigs mixed with mud also to seal out the elements. A willow bough roof laced the top. The Pawnee Earth lodge was made of posts circled around a tall center column of pine. It resembled a dirt mound from the outside. The Pueblo Indians built a cubicle rock and adobe structure with pine post over-hangs at the entrance.

The Kiowa "tipi" was the most familiar of the seven. It was light colored deerskins draped conical over lodge-pole pines. A fence of willow bough branches and grasses served as windbreak around the structure. It was from the dense trees behind this house that voices could be heard.

The girls' apprehension slowed their pace through the fenced section of the Kiowa house to the trees. A glow within a large circle emanated from an open area in the trees. A man spoke to the members seated in the circle turning slowly to allow each participant his attention. An opening in the circle was to the east of the gathering. Leaves and petals covered the ground of the opening like a carpet. They seemed to represent a bridge between two worlds.

The girls walked slowly towards the circle but stayed in the sanctity of the woods. They squatted down behind plum thickets to watch.

There was a wooden bowl being passed from person to person and a small herbal button was taken from the bowl. As the bowl reached the final person the man speaking walked over and took the bowl. He went back to the center of the circle and raised the bowl to the sky and asked the Great Spirit to bless the participants and the purpose of the gatherings:

"Greatest Spirit, the maker of all things blessed. Walk with us at this gathering of the faithful and guide our thoughts to purity and purpose. Unite us in our dream and our intention this night. Resurrect the honor and strength that was those who came before us. Bless this key, we partake of, to open our hearts and minds. Reward us with vision. Cast from our thoughts that which would distract us from our penitence."

At that he lowered the bowl and took for himself one of the herbal buttons. Touching the button once to his heart and then to his head, he then placed it in his mouth. All in the circle did as such.

Three men sitting outside the circle in the fringe of the glow began a slow rhythm on drums of animal skin. The drummers were blindfolded. A fourth man, also blindfolded, chanted softly accenting key syllables with a turtle shell rattle. All in the circle lifted their faces and open arms to the sky.

"What are they taking?" Jordan whispered.

"I think it is a mushroom." Jaimie whispered back.

"No. I think it is peyote. I read where it is legal if you are a member of the Native American Church," Chelsea continued the whispering.

"What does it do?" Jordan focused on the ceremony ahead.

"It is a hallucinogen like LSD or mescaline or ecstasy," Chelsea elaborated.

"I've heard of LSD and ecstasy. What is mescaline?" Jordan asked.

"I will bet that you can probably ask Chelsea's dad or Uncle Steve about all of them," Jaimie interjected, "They lived during the time when they were all legal."

"*And* during the times they all were *illegal*," Chelsea added.

"So, getting back to my original question, why do they take it?" Jordan's sarcasm dripped to the ground.

"They believe it opens their minds to see things that would otherwise be polluted by everyday thoughts. In fact in my psychology class a doctor named Timothy Leary tried to get it legalized as therapy for manic depression and psychosis," Chelsea pointed out.

"How long does it take to …" Jaimie's finger tips halted Jordan's questioning.

"What?" Jordan protested.

"Look!" Jaimie pointed to a light in the woods beyond the drummers.

A light was dancing snakelike through the trees; first only one and then several. They moved fluidly through the trunks and then some appeared in the branches.

Many voices from the circle joined the chanting. Harmonizing in a bass and baritone chant, they soon drowned out the drums. The lights increased their glow and were scattered throughout the woods now.

Out of instinct, the girls huddled closer.

As the chanting rose to a crescendo, one by one the participants rose and slapped small leather tassels across their shoulders. Each flagged first the left shoulder and then the right.

The man in the center was releasing white doves from the bowl as each participant sat down from his flagellation. The palm size bowl that had once only held the buttons miraculously held enough doves for the circle of over twenty men.

The girls watched as the doves circled over the fire. As

the last dove flew they gathered as a white cloud over the fire. Dancing and flitting about without touching, they scurried in a mass of white feathers. The drumming reached a loud crescendo and stopped. The birds flew straight into the moonlight and disappeared.

The girls' captivation ended. They looked back down to the circle to see what was to be next and found it empty of all participants. Looking to the perimeter for signs of their departure they saw only the three drummers and the chanter. All four were looking up through the protective cover of brush that held the girls segregated from the event. Their blindfolds were down around their necks and they were looking directly at the girls.

All around them were sounds of the forest undergrowth being rustled. There were wings fluttering in the darkness above their heads and hurried footprints in the dry grasses and leaves behind. To both sides of them, small trotting footsteps were heard.

Between the panting and soft grunts rustlings and flutters could be heard all around them. Small trotting footsteps broke twigs and rustled leaves. A cry-like whistle echoed in the treetops. The girls were surrounded by the noises, but never threatened directly by an intrusion of their own circle.

Then it stopped.

The drummers again started the rhythm and the fire blazed to that of a huge bonfire. The blindfolds were again over their eyes. A cloud eclipsed the moon and the wind elevated the treetops to a loud roar. The girls watched as the cloud passed and the moon flooded the area with light again. The drumming stopped abruptly.

They looked again to the circle and all the participants were standing in their original places. And, they were looking at the girls.

A small branch broke behind them. The man that had been leading the ceremony was now standing to Jordan's right side. He was smiling softly and his eyes danced in the moonlight.

"Why don't you join us in the circle?" he invited.

They looked at each other and rose to walk with him. He led them to the opening on the east of the circle and stopped them there.

"Are there any among us who entreat these guest not to enter into the gathering of priests?" he posed to the circle.

No one spoke.

"Forest of our ancestors," he began, "embrace those who would join us and celebrate in our gifts."

As one voice, all in the circle chanted: "Peace fall upon us, forgiveness reside in our hearts and honor be in our souls!"

The girls were led across the petals and leaves of the east entrance to a spot that now had a blanket draped over a small log. They sat and faced the fire that held center of the gathering.

"And to what pleasure to we owe your visit, Maidens of the Plums?" their leader solicited.

The participants all smiled. The girls' faces reddened with heat.

"We came looking for Jacob. We were told he was a member of your group and we wish to speak with him about Cynthia Tallchief," Chelsea answered for the group.

"Jacob is not with us now." the man said to Chelsea. "Is there someone else who could help? We all knew the teacher, Cynthia Tallchief."

"I am not sure. We were told Jacob was a lifelong friend

of Ms. Tallchief and her father. We had questions for him about Ms. Tallchief when she was young," Chelsea explained.

As Chelsea spoke, Jordan looked around at the circle. All the participants were seated on a blanket different to the next. Figurines of wood carved in the likeness of animals were placed in front of where they sat. One blanket was empty between two men. A figurine of a hawk sat upright in the sand before it.

"She will always be young as she was a teacher and was the daughter of a Shaman. Most of us came to know her after she was grown to be a woman. Jacob may know more, but he is not here." the man explained.

"Can you tell me how we can ..." Chelsea started.

Jordan interrupted Chelsea. "Who was sitting there?" She got up and walked to the empty blanket and hawk figurine. She picked up the figurine and brought it to the leader.

"That is the seat of Jacob. And as you can see, he is not here," the man reiterated as he gingerly took the figurine that Jordan handed to him.

From beyond the circle, high in the trees a limb rustled and then something flew over the gathering and off into the night. The leader looked skyward and smiled.

"Could you tell us how to contact Jacob or even what his last name is?" Chelsea continued uninterrupted.

"Jacob is independent of phones and such contraptions. If one of us happens to see him, we will tell him that you wish to speak with him. Would that suffice?" the leader asked.

"And his name?" Chelsea asked one more time.

The leader turned slowly and walked back to the empty blanket seat. He placed the figurine back in its original position.

152

"Jacob was once Jacob Ingals Huffman. He was the adopted son of a freight hauler named Luther Huffman. After an incident of his childhood involving Luther's eldest son Ezekiel and a cousin called Edward Gary, Jacob renounced the name as well as the family and took another," the leader said as he walked back from Jacob's blanket.

"And his new name is?" Chelsea probed further.

"Tallchief," the leader announced as he now stood toe to toe with Chelsea. "He took the name and the responsibility afforded a brother to Cynthia Tallchief."

Chelsea's mouth fell open and Jordan pointed to her own to let Chelsea know.

Chelsea closed her mouth and Jaimie muffled her laughter with her hand. 'I'm sorry." she apologized to Chelsea.

The leader smiled at Jaimie and then turned back to Chelsea.

"You are correct in that Jacob will know more about Cynthia Tallchief. He would know what a brother would know. As far as any of us, that which we would know is for our knowledge only. It is not correct to speak of someone that is away and unable to correct or defend."

Chelsea looked at his face. "And I respect that. It is only for a family friend that I come here seeking Jacob," she justified. "If I left a name and phone number for Jacob would someone see that he gets it?" She pulled one of her Dad's cards from her hip pocket but the leader waved it away.

"Your card is not necessary, Chelsea Lane, sister to Chanel and friend to Blair Ireland. Jacob will know that you seek him and he will know how to contact you."

"But…" Chelsea started.

"If you will excuse our haste, Miss Lane, we have penitence to reflect for past transgressions. We appreciate your interest and also your quiet observation in observance of the ceremony. You are still welcome to stay if you like, but I must reserve the circle for those who are priests."

He escorted Chelsea and the girls from the circle and back to the plum thicket. "Was this a good vantage point? You are welcome to sit here." he offered.

"No, we need to be going. It is getting late," Jaimie excused as she rolled her eyes to Chelsea. "Thank you for the invitation, though."

"I see," he replied. "Perhaps, next year, then?"

"Maybe," Jordan answered over her shoulder as she had turned to move towards the main building of the area.

Chelsea stepped to follow Jordan and Jaimie.

The speaker stopped Chelsea with a hand to her elbow.

"Young Chelsea, you are admired for assisting your sister and Ms. Ireland, but be aware that when you revive history, you revive all of history. As well as righting a dark wrong you can force the dark ones to defend themselves. It is wise to proceed with caution."

"What do you mean?" Chelsea's brow furrowed. "Who are the dark ones?"

"That will be for Jacob to explain in his way," the shaman rationalized. "However, as you are Kiowa you know to open your heart to what you know and with the guidance of those who love you, the rest will be revealed." He turned and walked back to the circle.

"But, I am not Kiowa!" Chelsea protested.

The speaker turned slowly and smiled. "Are you not?"

"No," Chelsea explained, "my father's grandmother was part Chickasaw, or so I have been told. And my mother's family was Irish."

Smiling with the assurance of one who knows a secret the speaker turned again to join the ceremony. He stopped at his original position. "Miss Lane, the rich Kiowa blood flows through your veins. Trust me on that."

"Chelsea, come on!" Jordan directed behind her. "We'll find Jacob for Ms. Ireland."

Chelsea caught up and joined the girls. They walked without speaking back through the Kiowa camp and then through the gift shop parking lot. When they reached their car and were safely inside with the doors closed Jordan exclaimed, "Holy Mother of Pearl Bailey! That was the freakiest thing I have ever seen. I need a drink. Chelsea, stop by the *Sonic* when we get to Anadarko."

"Did you see how many doves he pulled from that little bowl and the way they hovered over him while they beat themselves with those dusters?" Jaimie sounded out.

"Those weren't dusters they were riding crops," corrected Chelsea.

"I don't care if they were truck crops. How did he get all those doves from that one bowl?" Jaimie laughingly demanded.

"Just like the magician that pulls the rabbit from the hat," Chelsea retorted.

"Speaking of rabbits," Jordan started, "how about all those little animals running through the forest around us. There had to be hundreds!"

" I think there were twenty-eight," Chelsea said.

"Twenty-eight? Not thirty-three or seventeen? Twenty-eight?" Jaimie grilled.

"There were twenty-eight in the circle counting the high priest or whatever he was," Chelsea resolved matter-of-factly.

"You counted them?" Jaimie asked.

"Yes."

"Then you miss-counted cause I counted twenty-seven," Jordan corrected Chelsea.

"No. I counted them twice while they were passing the bowl around and were all still," Chelsea corrected.

"Well, I counted them while we were in the circle listening to the televangelist talk to his gods," Jordan defended.

"Wait a minute." Jaimie started, "Jordan did you count just the people or did you include the empty seat for Jacob also?"

"That's right!" Chelsea acknowledged. "When I counted they didn't know we were at the thickets watching.

"So, someone left when we got busted?" Jordan agreed.

"Jacob!" they all proclaimed together.

Chapter Nineteen

Jacob Ingals Huffman had been born Jacob Ingals Pendergrass to Theodore and Gladys Catherine Pendergrass near Pittsburgh Landing in southwestern Tennessee. Theodore Pendergrass was now a cotton buyer living on a farm beside Walnut Creek in Purcell, Oklahoma.

After saving for ten years to start a cotton purchasing business, Theodore had hired Luther Huffman Transportation to haul the large loads of cotton that he had purchased from two McClain County farmers. The contract was an agreement to deliver the cotton directly to the Chickasha Cotton Oil Mill owned by R.K. Wootten of Chickasha, Oklahoma. This would cut out the middle-men buyers in Purcell the county seat. Theodore's future business and the livelihood of his young family hung in the balance of this first business endeavor.

Jacob, at thirteen, had two sisters. Elwanda Lynn was ten years old, and Ethyl Francis was seven. They were used to working for their father and mother, as hard work had brought them to Oklahoma in search of a better life. Their farm in Tennessee had been taken by right of eminent domain to be set aside as part of a national park honoring the Battle of Shiloh fought in 1863 during the Civil War. The national park system incorporated their farm into the Shiloh National Cemetery Memorial. With the money given to him by the War Department, Theodore moved his family to Oklahoma. Cotton was what he knew and in 1932 the old Choctaw lands in Oklahoma were booming in cotton along the banks of the Washita River. It had been a good year for cotton. Chickasha, Oklahoma was the center of cotton production and the Wootten cotton oil mill was paying top dollar.

On November 1, 1932, Luther Huffman and his drivers had reached the banks of the Washita River just east of the Chickasha. He was commanding four trucks loaded to overfill of cotton for Theodore Pendergrass. It had been raining for days prior and the now swollen river was out of its banks leaving only the bridge rails visible.

Caskets and skeletal remains from an old Indian burial ground had washed out from a river bank site north of Chickasha where Otter Creek joined the Washita River and were entangled in the debris piling around the bridge supports. Crowds of spectators on both sides of the river watched the ghoulish spectacle.

Grady County Sheriff, Horace Crisp, had set up a roadblock to stop traffic about a quarter mile from the bridge as tides of river water and skeletons were flowing around both ends. The community of Tabler, to the east of Chickasha, was inundated with two feet of water.

Contrary to the advice of Sheriff Crisp, Huffman took it upon himself to attempt crossing the bridge to off-load Theodore Pendergrass's cotton at the mill, two miles to the west of the bridge in Chickasha. Following in his fourth truck, he sent his trucks around the roadblock. His four trucks inched along through the water and had just reached the bridge edge when the lead truck was swept south toward the main body of the Washita River. The other three trucks tipped precariously towards that same edge and lost the bulk of their loads into the swollen river. Two of the drivers as well as Luther Huffman were able to back out before a wall of water four feet high swept the lead truck into the churning muddy red water. The driver and the truck were lost to the violent mixture of trees, Indian cadavers and water.

Cursing God, Huffman backed his remaining three trucks to higher ground. He returned to the farm on Walnut Creek and confronted Theodore demanding reimbursement for his truck and payment for his shipment. Theodore protested that Huffman had made the decision to bypass the county sheriff's roadblock and that, as such, Huffman should have to pay him for the lost cotton.

The two squared off with a warning from Huffman that the McClain County Sheriff will decide the outcome and with a terse reminder that the sheriff's wife was Huffman's sister. Theodore and his wife Gladys were newcomers to McClain County. They had no support to glean from the townspeople.

Within weeks a kangaroo court had convened and the verdict was in Huffman's favor. Theodore now owed Huffman for the truck and compensation to be paid to the driver's widow. As he had paid cash to the farmers for the lost cotton anticipating a return from the cotton oil mill, he was broke except for the small 150-acre farm and house that he owned on Walnut Creek.

Huffman demanded the title to the farm and house as payment. Theodore protested and pushed Huffman aside as he marched from the courthouse.

Three days later, Theodore Pendergrass' body was found in the Canadian River east of Purcell. Official cause of death was accidental drowning.

After a somber funeral attended by Gladys Catherine, her three children and some members of the Church, Huffman approached the then widowed Pendergrass with a deal. She would sign over the farm as collateral and her son would work for Huffman for five years to pay off the debt. After which, the farm would revert back to the Pendergrass family. She explained the desperate circumstances to her oldest son Jacob. Jacob agreed to the terms. He was a good son and he loved his mother dearly.

Catherine took a job in town cooking meals for the Rock Island Railroad workers as they expanded the track service south of Purcell. Jacob labored for Huffman. Huffman had one of his boys drive Jacob home on Sunday mornings so he could attend church with his mother and sisters as previously agreed. On Sunday evenings he was expected back before nightfall. He got three small meals a day, which he ate alone in the bed of one of the trucks. During the week, Jacob slept in a shed outside the Huffman truck yard. He was subservient to Huffman and his employees as well as to Huffman's three children, Gerald, Ezekiel, and Tabitha. Constant tormenting by the older Huffman boys left Jacob a shy, stuttering introvert. Even the toddler Huffman girl knew Jacob's true place in the family. Soon, he was one with the shadows that followed him.

One late night the following February, Luther Huffman arrived at the Pendergrass home. He was drunk and tried violently to force himself on Gladys Catherine. He even offered to reduce the debt if she would reciprocate. With a now swollen eye and Theodore's shotgun, Gladys forced him off her property. Huffman stopped his truck at the roadside and opened another bottle of moonshine. He took one long drink and set the bottle aside. He had another use for the pure grain alcohol that remained in the bottle.

Morning came to the smoldering ruins of a farmhouse.

Officially, Gladys Catherine Pendergrass and her daughters Elwanda and Ethyl had been the tragic victims of a woodstove igniting a fire in the attic.

Jacob had been in Fort Worth, Texas off-loading

Huffman trucks when his mother and two sisters were killed. Two weeks after their funeral, he was informed of their deaths. He believed sadly what the sheriff told him to be the truth. After all, the sheriff was a representative of the McClain County court.

As an honorable son, he was committed to pay his father's debt. As a young boy alone, he worked that one day his family's farm on Walnut Creek would be his.

Jacob knew little of the events that had previously transpired between his father and Huffman. He was considered a child and was never present during any of the legal proceedings.

Jacob was a minor and as no one was alive to look after his best interest, Luther Huffman went to court and ceremoniously had Jacob legally adopted. Many in the town saw it as a magnanimous gesture. Those who knew Luther Huffman, knew it for what it was.

From that point, Jacob was indentured to Luther Huffman. Jacob Ingals Pendergrass was pressured to become Jacob Ingalls Huffman. Jacob was old enough to understand that he would never see the family farm again.

It was this relationship that had brought him to be with Zeke and Edward that fateful day in 1936. They had off loaded some rocks at a WPA work site near Shannoan Springs in Chickasha. Zeke had stolen a bottle of liquor from his dad and was passing it to his cousin Edward when he saw the Indian girl by the well.

Even under the influence of alcohol, Jacob knew dropping them into the well was wrong. His guilt was sobering but Zeke was overbearing and Jacob left his courage at the well with the two girls, but only temporarily.

Cynthia sat in the cold water nursing her throbbing left arm. Shivering uncontrollably, she stood to get her body out of the water so she could warm up. The pain in her arm returned. Stooping to soak it in the cool well water, her thoughts wandered to Blair's efforts to save her. Would she return with help, or had the boys found her?

Looking at the shadowed walls, Cynthia felt around with her right hand for the handholds that the darkness threatened to cover. Maybe if she took her time, she could climb out. Finally finding the lowest indentation, which was as high on the wall as her thigh, Cynthia formulated her plan. It would take all her strength and coordination to get a foothold in there and still jump up to the next handhold.

Summoning up her inner strength and wedging her toe into the first handhold, she jumped skyward. With a surge of energy and the grace of God, the next handhold was found. Cynthia clung precariously to the face of the wall. Her right hand held the wall just above shoulder level. Resting briefly she took deep breaths before attempting to go further.

Her left arm throbbed intensely. It rested tense at her side. Her body was sore and cold. The shivering had stopped with her physical efforts, however, and she found solace in that.

Under her breath she began the chant of courage that her father had taught her. She looked up to see if she could make out the next handhold. It was too dark now. Her left arm was useless and she couldn't let go with her right hand lest she fall.

With her left foot she explored the wall between her right foot and her right hand. She found another indentation in the wall.

She placed her left foot firmly into the crevice and shifted her weight to it and relaxed her right foot some. In her mind's eye, she thought she could see a pattern in the handholds. The way things were so far, the next hold would be to the left of and a little above where her right hand held her body to the wall face. Maybe shifting her weight to her left foot and standing her leg straight, she could reach the next hold with her right hand before falling backwards.

Still chanting softly she rocked a little to give herself a cadence to try move up. On the third rocking motion she lunged.

Perfect!

She rested again. Sweat ran into her eyes despite the cool air of the well. She envisioned her family for strength.

She had no way of knowing how far she had to go. The fall had been so quick and the interruption by the bucket of water had distracted any sense of distance she might have had. Her determination to escape was strong, her physical strength, not so.

In retrospect she estimated that Blair had taken only ten or fifteen movements to get out. Maybe the top of the well was very close.

Her weight rested on her left leg and her right hand and her right leg dangled. Cramps in her calves knotted when her toes pointed down. She brought her right foot up to find the next hold. It was easy to find. She now had a pattern if only her right hand could hold out that long.

She shifted her weight to the right leg. Again, trusting in her mind's eye, a visualization of the next handhold pushed her to make ready. This time it would be to the right of the one that she now clung to.

She chanted and rocked. Lunging with all her energy, she found the handhold but almost lost it when her finger jammed into an outcropping of the indentation. Throwing her head and shoulders forward she found it and snatched onto it. She was now breathing laboriously and her right forearm was weak with exertion.

She rested again.

Suddenly she heard voices from beyond the rim of the well. They were getting closer.

Fear overwhelmed her when she recognized the gruff hateful tone of the boy called Zeke. She pressed herself closer to the wall as she heard him right above her.

A lantern cast eerie shadows and glows on the rocks around her.

"Well, Edward, look at what we have here!" Zeke exclaimed. "Our little red princess is a spider! She's a dirt brown insect!"

"I don't see her, Zeke," the fat boy known as Edward protested.

"There, right below my lantern," Zeke directed.

"I see her!" Edward laughed. "She does look like a spider. But where is her friend?"

"Surely she is down below in the water, Edward. Hello the water! Are you down there?" Zeke called to the depths below.

"Let me get a limb to swat this spider we have found, Edward."

Zeke pulled away from the rim of the well. With that motion he took away the only light that Cynthia had enjoyed. Now, again, she was in the dark.

Cynthia had lost her concentration. She couldn't remember now whether the next handhold was to the left or right of her current one. She prayed for guidance.

Then as if sight had been given her she remembered. She

164

extended toward the sky with all her weight on her left leg and reached simultaneously to the left of her current handhold.

She found it!

Dangling her left leg to relax it a bit and knowing she couldn't rest too much longer; she needed out before Zeke returned.

Finding the left hold quickly with her foot she shifted weight and sprung upward again. Searching frantically with her right hand for the ledge that was sure to be on the right her movements accelerated.

Again, success!

Resting for only a second, she heard Zeke's obnoxious voice getting closer to the well.

"This should reach that brown recluse. Spiders really are the scourges of our being. Don't you agree, Edward?" Zeke asked rhetorically as they reached the rim again.

"Here, Edward, you hold the light and I will swat this bug off the wall."

He reached in with a long limb and swung viciously at Cynthia's head. She ducked as far as she could without losing her grip and he swung again with a backhanded thrust. This time the limb struck her on the shoulder and neck.

She felt the impact and the splinters dig into the soft skin behind her ear. She felt the tearing of her flesh as the weight of the limb pulled in its momentum.

She held on.

"Maybe it is the web that she holds to!" Zeke cried out as he changed his tactics.

He swung the limb towards her right hand. Once, twice, three times it landed across her wrist and knuckles. Cynthia held with all her might.

Suddenly she felt a joint in her index finger pop. She chanted softly for strength.

The next blow dislodged her hand. Instantly she fell. The water came quickly and the rock floor below came up even more so. Her ankle wrenched.

Before she could look up to curse Zeke she heard Edward exclaim, "Zeke, she *is* by herself. The other girl is gone!"

"So, what!" Zeke dismissed Edwards's alarm.

"That means she got out and has gone for help. We've got to get out of here before someone comes!" Edward explained to Zeke.

Zeke stood upright and looked around.

"Perhaps," he agreed. "Perhaps you are right Edward, but who would give a moment's loss at this Indian girl except that she is fouling the water with her presence."

He threw the stick away and took the lantern from Edward.

"C'mon I'll race you to the trucks!" Zeke called out as he bolted from the well.

It was dark again.

Silence engulfed Cynthia and the well. Her head hung in despair. A soft whimper escaped with a tear.

She caught herself and stopped her moaning. She was the daughter of a Kiowa Shaman. Her grandmother had been a Kiowa priestess. She would live and, if necessary, die with dignity. She began the warrior's chant that she had heard at the ceremonies she had attended with her father. Her voice strengthened with each verse.

She had sung but a few moments when light bathed the well walls above her once again.

Was it her brothers who must surely be searching for her?

166

Or maybe her father had returned from his business and had found her. Of course, Blair had sent help!

"A…a...are y..you al…all r..r..right down there?"

It was the Jacob boy. Was he here to torment her now?

"H..hello. C..can you …hear m..me," came his voice as he lowered a lantern a bit further down the well.

"Yes, I hear you." Cynthia stood and held her right hand to shield her eyes from the lantern. "Did you come also to throw sticks at the Indian girl?"

Jacob pulled the lantern from the well and darkness came again to Cynthia.

Suddenly a hank of rope hit Cynthia square in the chest.

The light came back to the well.

"G…grab this and p…p..pull yourself out," Jacob instructed.

Cynthia picked up the rope and called out to Jacob.

"I can't. I think my arm is broken," she explained.

The light disappeared again.

She could hear movement above. Her mind raced. Maybe Zeke had come back and confronted Jacob. She heard no voices. Maybe Jacob had a change of heart.

'Hello! Are you still up there," she called out.

Then the light was back. Jacob tied it to the spindle that held the pulley above the well. His legs came over the rim and he started climbing down with the rope in his hand.

When he reached the water he found Cynthia bruised and battered and wet.

"I'm sorry," Jacob apologized without stuttering. "I'm sorry."

Cynthia said nothing.

"C…can ..y…you hold on m…m…my b…b…back if I c…c..carry you out?"

167

"I think. I am heavy though and the wall is straight up." Cynthia doubted his ability to carry such dead weight up the face of the well. "Can you make it with me not helping?"

"I will make it," he answered adamantly, with no stutter.

Cynthia got on his back and threw her right arm over his shoulder and neck. She then wrapped her legs around his skinny waist. This boy was far too skinny and fragile to carry her out of the well.

Jacob could feel the burden that he would bear up the wall. It was great.

He added it to the burden he had been carrying since he hadn't stopped Zeke earlier.

One handhold and foothold at a time brought them to the well rim. They were free of the dark, cold well. Jacob had just pulled the rope up and untied the lantern when Cynthia heard the far off voices of her brothers and father calling her name.

"Over here," she cried out, her voice quivering with emotional release. Tears pooled in her eyes. "Over here!"

Her family eyed Jacob with contempt when they arrived. Cynthia sat on the ground in a heap with her arm cradled in her right hand.

"He saved me, Father," Cynthia defended, recognizing the look on her father's face. Looking up at the shy boy, she ended it there.

"Thank you, son." Cynthia's father held out his hand to Jacob.

Jacob soaked up the word "son". He had not heard it in forever. He shook Cynthia's father's hand.

Her brothers helped her to her feet but she was too weak to walk. Her father scooped her up and started off into the night.

168

Cynthia's brothers fell in line with him.

The last brother stopped and motioned for Jacob to follow.

"Come, you must be hungry and thirsty. Mother will feed you," he told Jacob.

Jacob stepped in behind the family carrying their injured sister. He followed and never looked back.

Chapter Twenty

Tabitha Huffman-Cross walked from the hospital to her idling Cadillac parked near the entrance to the emergency room. Her driver met her at the rear door. After assisting her into the Deville, he took his place behind the wheel.

"Where to, ma'am?" the words flowed like molasses.

"To the nursing home." She lit a stubby unfiltered cigarette. Smoke framed her masculine face with only a blood-red glow of charged embers breaking the sinister shape. "Park the car and make sure that woman's room is clean of your handiwork. Except for the empty vial in her purse, I want no traces of the capsules left in this building. And I want that juice cup destroyed. Don't leave any traces of the anti-freeze."

"Yes, ma'am." The driver's response was rote. He opened her car door.

"And I want Jacob found!" she demanded as she stalked to the building. "If you can't do it, I'll get someone who can. You said you could get that decrepit step-brother of mine to sign the deed papers and you've failed." She turned on him to make her point. "You have one more chance! Do *you* hear me? I want him found now!"

"Yes, ma'am, I will find him again and I will convince him to sign."

"You said that before we used the old woman he looks after as bait and that has been weeks now! How much more time do you need?" she ranted as she slithered into the rear entrance of the nursing home.

"Yes, ma'am," he replied under his breath as he reached for the door handle. The door shut in his face. Rolling his eyes, he grasped the door handle with white knuckled fist and jerked it open. He stepped in and spoke to an empty hallway. "He'll come around soon enough."

Ms. Huffman-Cross's office door slammed ahead of him.

"Yes, he will come around, because I want that property!" she turned and screamed to her closed door.

"Yes, ma'am," her driver answered under his breath. Turning down the hallway to his left, he headed to Ms. Blair's room.

He knew all too well that Tabitha Huffman-Cross would stop at nothing to get all the property that her father had stolen from Jacob's family. In his ignorance, Luther Huffman had failed to get the mineral rights under the farm signed over to him when he adopted Jacob. Now there was oil being discovered all around the property and Tabitha Huffman-Cross could not get her hands on the royalties being paid to other landowners.

"I'll get the old man to sign," the driver mumbled to himself, "and I'll also get my portion of that oil money. I haven't risked going to jail for you Tabitha Huffman-Cross just because you are my aunt. I have a share coming. My father Edward Huffman served both Luther and Zeke far too many years for me to not benefit."

He entered Blair's room and searched for any evidence that he had spiked her food with anti-freeze. Crawling around on his hands and knees he found several of the capsules that he had doctored. Satisfied with the evidence being gone, he left the room.

Chapter Twenty One

Chanel awoke to the smell of wet leaves and damp wood. Staring at the ceiling, trying to let her eyes focus in the darkness; she sensed the presence of someone with her. Holding her covers near her eyes she inched up against her headboard. Summoning strength, she looked beyond the comforter holding sentry at the foot of her bed. Grasping the covers tighter as a shield should she need one; she leaned forward to see more. With saucer eyes, she stared at the apparition.

As a life-sized holograph, an old Indian chanted quietly on the ground near her bed. His chiseled features honored his age. Chanel could make out the patterns on his shirt as similar to those on Cynthia's blouse at the park. His silent chant was obvious only by his open mouth and moving lips.

He drew smoke to his face from softly glowing embers at his feet. Sifting a substance into the embers, the old man fed the glow to flames. Chanel straightened up in bed at the sight of the growing blaze. Was her room going to catch on fire?

Examining at the floor around her bed, Chanel could make out that was forest floor and movement in the twigs indicated life existed within its debris. She looked deeper at the floor trying to distinguish insect from animal in all the broken limbs and rocks. Slowly raising her eyes, she found a clear sky and stars where once her ceiling had been. A breeze shifted her hair from her forehead.

Lowering her eyes from the vision above, Chanel found the old Indian hovering in front of her. He was shaking a turtle rattle in his left hand and clutching a necklace in his right. Chanel recognized Cynthia's necklace that her

Grandmother had given her. It was her tai-me.

"Who are you?" Chanel softly questioned the apparition.

He gave no effort to respond.

"Why do you have Cynthia's necklace?" her voice grow stronger.

The Indian apparition stared into Chanel's eyes.

"Tell me what you want me to do! Am I to help Cynthia or Miss Ireland?" Chanel's voice rose in its demand.

The wind picked up in its intensity from the breeze on the floor.

"Where is Jacob? Tell him to come to me," Chanel said to the still figure above her bed. She was sitting against her headboard with her hands at her side. Trying to raise them but finding them pinned by an invisible force, Chanel could feel panic rising within.

The wind blew harder. Leaves swirled behind the Indian.

"Say something!" Chanel screamed.

The Indian returned to chanting his silent chant. His eyes rolled back into his head and he raised his chin to the stars.

When he brought his face back to look at Chanel it was different. It was longer. His nose was dark and his ears were pulled back towards the crest of his head.

"You don't scare me," Chanel challenged. "You need me for something and so you won't hurt me!"

The Indian raised his head again to the ceiling. His chest and neck quivered and his hands dropped to his side. When he brought his chin down again his was the face of a wolf. His gray and black hair covered his jaw line and the bridge of his nose. His head shook left to right and a low guttural sound emanated from his throat.

"You don't scare me, I said! Tell me how to save Cynthia and Blair. Tell me now!" Chanel screamed over the wind

173

noise that now engulfed her room. "Tell me what to do!"

Suddenly, there was a rattle at her door knob.

"Chanel! Chanel what is wrong? Open the door."

It was her dad.

"Daddy, I can't open the door. I can't move!" Chanel yelled back.

The wind intensified.

"Daddy, he is in here again and I can't move!" Chanel cried louder.

The debris that was on the floor now engulfed the air around Chanel's bed. The noise was deafening.

Suddenly, the door burst open. Wood splinters from the door-jamb joined the debris whirling around Chanel's bed. Her dad stumbled in as his shoulder busted the door free from its latch.

Moving quickly to the window, he slammed it shut. The wind stopped and the noise with it. Flicking on the light, he swept Chanel up in his arms.

The Indian was gone as was all the forest debris.

"Sweetheart, what is it? Who is in here?" he asked as he brushed her hair in place.

Chanel knew that nothing was in the room, now. It wasn't when Steph burst in before and now it wasn't when Dad did the same.

"Daddy, I don't know!" she sobbed.

Stephanie came in tying her housecoat around her. "What is it honey?"

"I think it was another dream, Steph," Chanel's dad reassured her.

"Was it, Chanel?" Steph was skeptical. She knew the answer already.

Chanel looked lovingly at Steph.

"No, it wasn't a dream, mom." Chanel stopped crying and leaned into her dad.

"I am to do something for Blair or for Cynthia. I don't know who, but I have to be the one to do it," Chanel resigned as she left her dad's arms and got out of bed.

She walked around to the right side of her bed and stood looking at the floor.

"Chanel, I thought we had decided that the dreams were from your accident. You are not seeing real people," dad tried to reason with her.

"No," Chanel started, "then what is this?"

Dad and Steph walked around to where Chanel stood looking at the floor.

Three human footsteps a bright red tail feaher and then three paw prints were marked in the carpet with moist soil from the woods. They stopped six feet from the window sill. One paw print, leaving the window sill sprinkled in wet soil, had scratched the wood with four light scratches.

Cynthia's tai-me lay on the floor ncar thc ashcs of a burned effigy of a small dog.

"Dad, I have to go now," Chanel made clear her resolve.

"You have to go to where, Chanel?" her dad asked as he stood beside the bed.

"Dad, I don't know where for sure, but I have to go to the well to find out." She turned to face him. "Will you take me there?"

Dad looked at Steph and she stood motionless. Her eyebrows arched in disapproval.

"I'll go with you and I'll go with you into the well." Dad answered.

Chanel took his hand I hers. "No, Dad, I have to go in by myself. Things were not as clear when I had Jessie with me.

175

So, I know they would not happen as they are supposed to if you go. Just take me to the well and wait. It will just be a wrinkle in time till I'm back."

"You are not going to let her go into that well, are you?" Steph interrupted. "And even more; you are not even thinking about letting her go by herself, are you?"

Chanel and her dad stood face to face. They were reading each other's eyes. There was always an understanding of character between the two of them. Chanel, as her dad, believed in following your heart. To not do so would be to leave a hole unfilled in your life. She could not rest until this played out.

Chanel's dad had previously been convinced that she had been dreaming these events in her imagination. Now, with these footsteps and paw prints, his concerns were of a different nature. But now he was thinking that going into the well with her father standing at her side might bring the closure Chanel needed to move on from this obsession.

Chanel believed that until now her dad didn't quite believe her. But the marks on the carpet and the tai-me were the evidence that something was indeed happening and they now shared the challenge to see this to its end. She knew he was going to say yes.

His laugh lines deepened around his eyes. A smile raised the corners of his mouth ever so slightly. Chanel smiled softly back at him.

Steph raised her hands in disapproval. "Are you kidding me?"

Chanel's dad took his eyes from Chanel's and eased over to Steph's side. He put his arm around her shoulders and led her out into the hallway.

176

Chapter Twenty Two

November's morning veil shielded the rest of the world from Chanel and her dad as they walked to the woods from the house. Stephanie stood alone on the porch behind them. She knew that the past week's events were more than mere dreams and after last night, she now feared for Chanel's safety. She also had an understanding of Chanel's intentions by going back into the well and that she thought she needed to do it alone, but, that understanding was not enough to ease her fears.

They talked softly as they headed to the well.

"Sweetheart, I know what you are thinking. You are thinking that you alone can resolve this issue. But, we have always been able to team up on our problems." Chanel's dad tried not to be overwhelming.

"Why not let me help?"

"Dad, I know who and what I'm looking for when I go to the well. Some things will seem to be putting me in danger but they won't be because I have a reason to be there and that reason will work itself out. I know if you are there you will step in and maybe change the course." Chanel continued, "You will step in because you are a daddy. That is your job, as *you* would see it." She smiled.

"Exactly, and that is why I wrestle with letting you go alone into the well. A *good* daddy wouldn't let you put yourself in harm's way," he reasoned, still not wanting to pull rank.

"A good daddy prepared his children to stand alone. I am not an adult, but I have a better understanding of the well because it called to me and it has directed my every step." Chanel slowed her pace and took her Dad's hand in hers.

"Daddy, I am not afraid anymore. I know whatever I am to do will be laid out for me and it *is* something that I *can* do.

"Do you remember when we talked about things in the divorce being my fault or your fault or Mom's fault and you said some things are bigger than us as individuals?" Chanel led the discussion to the answer she wanted.

"Yes, but…" he started.

"This is bigger than us as individuals. I have been called to do this, dad. I don't know why, but I have been called because someone knew I could do this and I know I can do this. I would only let myself down to run away from it." Chanel reached over and took his other hand in hers. "Is that what you would want me to do?"

They arrived at the edge of the woods and Chanel stopped to look for the well.

Her dad took the opportunity to try once more. He bent down to one knee and hugged her tight. He put her at arms reach and looked into her eyes.

"Honey, *you* might not be scared, but, *I* am very scared." His voice quivered with emotion. "This world we know and live in offers many opportunities to get hurt. I haven't a clue about this world beyond the well."

"So, you believe me that it is a place and not a dream, don't you?" Chanel confirmed as she pulled away from him.

Still on his knee, her dad smiled, "Chanel, do you remember the old Indian woman at the arts festival that told your mother and I that we would have a child that carried a gift?"

"When Mom was pregnant with me? I remember the story."

"Yes," he went on, "all this time I thought the gift was the artist's eye that you saw with. You were drawing at three years old and were seeing things from a perspective we could never enjoy. Maybe . . . the real gift is what you have just discovered. Maybe this gift is what you bring to the well today."

"Then, I can go alone? Because, I just knew you were going to stop me. I could hear it in your voice."

He smiled as he rose to his feet.

"Yes, I figured if I couldn't talk you out of it before we got there, I would have to just say no," he confessed.

"Dad, that makes me stronger that you can let me go," Chanel confided.

"Well, it makes my knees week that you are going." He laughed to hold back tears.

He dusted the grass from his knee and inhaled deeply. He began to pace the clearing around them. "Here are the rules," he turned to Chanel, "you have one hour to come back and to report to me what you are doing. You have to talk to me as long as you can hear my voice as you travel into the tunnel and you have to remember that it is still okay to change your mind. Do you have your watch?" he asked matter-of-factly.

"Yes," she responded fighting back the tears welling in her eyes.

"Is your voice strong?"

"Yes." Her shoulders and back straightened with resolve.

"Do you want to change your mind and go back for pancakes with me and mom?"

"No, daddy, but I would love some when I get back." She was smiling at him when she heard the rustle of feathered flight behind her.

A piercing scream echoed through the silent woods. A blur of motion passed through the mist and alighted on the bare branches over the well.

"Is that your guide?" He motioned at the majestic red-tailed hawk perched above them.

"Yes, I believe he is."

She walked the last few yards with her dad's hand in hers. At the well, she stopped.

"Dad, sit right here on the well. I will be but a moment, you'll see."

Chanel's dad sat down on the edge of the well. Chanel stepped over and started down the hand holds. At the bottom she yelled up to her dad.

"Can you hear me now?"

"Yes!" he replied with a smile.

"Good!" she answered back over her shoulder as she started down the tunnel toward her greatest adventure. This time, Chanel did not have Steph's sweater or the brooch from Ms. Ireland. Chanel wore around her neck, the *tai-me* necklace that the chanting Indian shaman had given her. It would prove to be her passport to an event like none she could have imagined.

Chapter Twenty Three

Chanel came out of the tunnel into what she knew to be the park. The park was very different. It was wilder and with no man- made structures, but the landscape was similar. It was basically a small depression with a creek flowing through it from the west.

Chanel could still tell that she was still near the Shannoan Springs, even though there were more trees and the small lake was gone.

She walked towards the creek and slowed at a large hole in the ground. Water trickled from sandstone outcroppings.

"So, this is the famous springs!" she acknowledged aloud. "This is so cool."

She bent and drank of the cool water. It was almost sweet.

The only noise was the wind in the post oaks and here and there a crow would caw in echo from the trees beyond Chanel's view. She turned and walked up the hill to the west where the well had been in her original visit with Cynthia.

She walked far before realizing she had been climbing out of the small valley that made up the park. The woods were deeper now and she had determined to return to what had been the park. In a clearing, she stopped to go back. As she turned, she heard horses. From out of the woods to her right came ten or more Indians in buckskin leggings and cotton shirts. Rifles were draped across their legs and two young boys drug travois behind their horses loaded with bundles of hides and meat. They stopped about ten yards from where she stood. All eyes were on her. Even the ponies focused on Chanel. Except to flick away nagging flies with their tails, they too were motionless.

Chanel's skin prickled and her heart raced as the tallest Indian walked his sand colored pony towards her.

"Hacho wasichu?" he demanded.

She stared blank at the fierce face of the warrior.

"Quien es senorita?" he interrogated next in Spanish, "De donde eres?" He moved his pony to within twenty feet of her.

Chanel recognized he now spoke in Spanish but other than being able to count to ten, she was unfamiliar with the language. Not knowing what to say, she remained motionless and quiet.

"Who are you, girl?" the Indian at last asked in English. "Where are you from?"

Chanel could sense a less threatened situation.

"I am walking to find Cynthia Tallchief. Do you know where she would be?" Chanel offered as explanation.

"Why do you look for Cynthia Tallchief?" The Indian asked as he shifted his weight to get more comfortable on his horse.

"Are you Kiowa?" Chanel asked.

"I am Kiowa." his answer was short.

"Then you may know Cynthia's family. They are Kiowa also." Chanel tried to convey friendliness.

"The Kiowa are not as many as before but they are many. I do not know Cynthia Tallchief. That is an English name. It is not a Kiowa name." The tone of his voice grew more challenging. "Why are you alone on this land of the Comanche?"

"I search for Cynthia. I thought this was Kiowa land," Chanel replied.

The Indian grunted under his breath. He leaned forward and looked long at Chanel's necklace.

"If you can help me, I would like to find Cynthia. If you cannot, I would return to my search." Chanel tried to sound confident.

"You will go with us." The Indian motioned for assistance from the party behind him.

Two young men leapt from their horses and ran to secure Chanel. She was placed on the bundle of hides. She knew not to resist. One of the men pulled a strip of braided horse hair from his waist and started to tie her hands. Chanel looked at the Indian that she had been talking to. Their eyes met.

He said something to the younger Indian and he put away the strip of rope. Chanel was not tied but she knew she would be staying on the travois. Her fear made her stomach weak but her curiosity empowered her to be strong.

For hours, they rode west. Chanel recognized geographic formations that she had seen from the highway when her Dad had driven her back to Elk City. She knew that she was near the present town of Verden, ten miles to the west of Chickasha but there were no roads, houses or buildings; only the huge red dirt cliff that overlooked the town from the south.

They turned north and after another long while they came to a red rolling river. Chanel knew that this must be the Washita River as we know it. It might very well be named something else to the Indians. Across the river, to the north, she saw gray wooden buildings congregated like a school or college. Her party avoided it and kept moving west.

They followed the river for miles and stopped in a bend to water the horses. Chanel walked over to the leader as he tended to his horse.

"Where are you taking me?" she asked after he

acknowledged that she was standing close to him.

"My people would know what to do with you. You will go to my camp," he answered.

"Why do you have to know what to do with me? Could you not just help me find Cynthia Tallchief?" Chanel felt demeaned.

"You walked the Comanche lands alone with a Kiowa tai-me across your heart. I would have left you without it," he explained. "It is not for me to make a choice now. It is the tai-me of Santanta. Santanta's family will choose what is to become of you."

Chanel touched the necklace that Cynthia had given her.

"This is not the tai-me of Santanta. It was left to me by Cynthia Tallchief. It is the tai-me of Tallchief. I don't know Santanta. Who is he?"

"We know him as Set-tainte. Set-tainte means White Bear Person. Santanta is an English name just as Cynthia Tallchief is an English name." He motioned to the travois. "Return to the travois we have more land to cross."

Chanel did as he directed, but her discomfort was overwhelming. How was she to find Cynthia so far from Chickasha? If the family of Santanta was angry over the tai-me, then everything could change. Everything changing could preclude Chanel's mission or worse still, it could keep her from ever seeing her family again. She felt for her watch on her wrist to find comfort. She remembered that time stood still at the well and envisioned her dad standing sentinel.

Soon the group of Indians with their intruding guest topped a ridge and there below was an encampment practically surrounded by the river. A small pathway from the north allowed them to walk their horses through oaks and cottonwoods into the Indian camp.

The camp reminded Chanel of the dioramas at the Omniplex History Center in Oklahoma City. She remembered the tipis and campfires with dear and buffalo skins draped on stretching racks. Only this time they were full size not two inch replicas. There were also wagons and a few galvanized metal wash tubs. These looked out of place but their presence meant Chanel might not have gone too far back into time.

Chanel did know this place was decades before Cynthia. Panic raced her heart and the smell of the hides she rode on almost made her swoon in her anxiety.

Once in the village, she was surrounded by children and women. Her fears overwhelmed her. Chanel fainted and fell from the stack of hides.

Chapter Twenty Four

She awoke in a tipi surrounded by women. Some wore blouses and long skirts while the older women wore buckskin. All wore moccasins decorated with colored beads. Wisps of smoke in a birds nest holding embers from a fire were being passed over her by callused hands. A man chanting behind her head raised his volume when her eyes opened. She could see from the opening that it was dark outside. How long had she been unconscious?

Chanel tried to sit up but her hands and arms were weak. She lay back down. A young woman rose and ran out of the tipi. Soon she returned with another woman.

The woman was taller than most of the others in the tipi. She was dressed in blue gingham blouse with a long black skirt. Silver jewelry adorned her wrists. Her hair was in braids along her neck. She had a kind face and she smiled when Chanel made eye contact with her.

"You sleep hard and talk to those unseen," she said softly.

Chanel rose to her elbows.

"My dad says I talk in my sleep when I'm tired. I hope I didn't say something stupid," Chanel offered.

"I don't know what is *stupid* but you mentioned Cynthia in your dream talking and you mentioned 'misireland'. What is 'misireland'?"

"Ms. Ireland is a friend. She is also a friend to Cynthia Tallchief from before I met her. Do you know the name Tallchief?"

"I don't know Cynthia Tallchief. It is not a name from our village."

"She said she was Kiowa. Is your village Kiowa?"

186

Chanel was nervous.

"Yes, we are Kiowa. When did you talk to this Cynthia that she would tell you she is Kiowa?" the woman asked.

Chanel knew that she could not relate the meeting with Cynthia in any reasonable explanation. She could only attempt not to lose this new ally.

"I met Cynthia days ago, back at the woods where your people found me while hunting. The hunting leader said that it was Comanche land where he found me," Chanel started. "If that was Comanche land and this necklace that belonged to Cynthia is Kiowa, then I am way confused."

"Who are the 'wayconfused' and where do the 'wayconfused' come from?" the woman asked as she sat down next to Chanel.

Chanel laughed aloud.

The woman rose suddenly and glared at Chanel.

"Am I to be laughed at? I came here to help you and you laugh at me!"

The woman started towards the entrance to the tipi.

Chanel jumped unsteady to her feet. "No, wait!"

The woman stopped and turned. Her eyes once soft were hardened with anger.

Chanel walked to her.

"I am sorry. I was not laughing at you. I was laughing at the way I butcher the English language. Please don't leave." Chanel's eyes were pleading.

After a brief moment, the woman's face relaxed. She and Chanel sat back on the pile of soft deerskin that Chanel had awakened on.

"I met Cynthia a few days ago. She told me of her family and that they were camped a few miles south of where your hunters found me. She said she was Kiowa and gave me this

187

necklace as a gift. It had been her grandmother's," Chanel explained.

"She gave it to you? And what did you give her in return?" the woman asked.

Chanel was embarrassed about the exchange or lack thereof. Cynthia had wanted her Harry Potter watch and actually the chanting Indian had left Cynthia's necklace in Chanel's room. It was just convenient to believe Cynthia wanted Chanel to have it.

"I didn't give her anything. We were talking and some freighter boys interrupted us." Chanel was leery about telling the entire story because she could not find the well at the park nor did she even recognize the park. It was obvious that she went farther back in time than before. To tell of her and Cynthia's time in the well would be very confusing to the woman.

"These freighter boys were Kiowa also?" the woman asked trying to fill in the blanks.

"No they were like me, except mean." Chanel tried to leave it at that.

The woman leaned back and eyed Chanel curiously.

"What is your name?" Chanel asked the woman.

"I am called Guapahka. It means *Little Dog or Fox of the Woods,*" the woman elaborated knowing Chanel would ask.

"Guapahka, who is Santanta and why does your hunter leader tell me I have his tai-me?"

"Santanta was a great chief to the Kiowa. He was the son of Red Tepee, keeper of the tai-me for all the Kiowa people. He was known as White Bear Person before he went to walk with his fathers and grandfathers before him."

'He's dead?" Chanel confirmed the walking with fathers and grandfathers explanation.

188

"Yes. He is, as you say, dead. He has been gone five seasons. He was a great leader and a great voice for the Kiowa. He led the Kiowa at the great Medicine Lodge Council of Kansas in the year 1867. It is why we came here to the Oklahoma reservation. It is also why the Comanche, Arapahoe, Apache and the Kiowa walk each other's land.

"After we came to Oklahoma, Santanta and my father Guipago, whom the soldiers called Lone Wolf, fought with words about the Kiowa future. Santanta led a raid against freight wagons to bring food back to the reservation and was sent to a soldier prison in Texas. It is said that he jumped from a tall building to die rather than to be caged. He was the brother to my father. I don't believe that he jumped to kill himself when so many here were suffering. Something else happened to Santanta.

"The men in the Washington City, the wasichu, put us all together as a herd. Tell me, is it a wise person that herds the wolf and deer and bear and the rabbit all together because they are all animals? Would you herd the Kiowa, Arapaho, Comanche and Apache all together because they are all Indians?" She paused. "Did you see the buildings at the river when our hunters brought you to our camp?" Guapahka asked Chanel.

"Yes," Chanel replied and then asked, "who lives in those buildings?"

"Those buildings house the sons and daughters of the Wichita and the Caddo children that were forced to leave their homes to live and learn the ways of the white man. It is called the Riverside Indian School." Guapahka went on, "It is not an Indian school. It is a white man school for Indians."

"Forced?" Chanel questioned the use of the word.

"Forced." Guapahka reaffirmed louder for full effect.

189

"There is also a school for the Kiowa, Comanche and the Apache. It is called Rainy Mountain Boarding School. Our children must live there and stay until they can speak and write the English language. They will learn to work in houses and on farms for money. This *money* will allow them to barter for the white man belongings. Skills and crafts will no longer be necessary to learn. Only working for money will bring to you the things that you need. Our Kiowa children are being taught to be *servants* to money," Guapahka almost hissed the word servant.

Chanel listened intently. She also found little favor in being made to go to school but she knew the probable outcome if she were to quit. Guapahka was very distressed over the exchange of skills for learning menial labor practices.

"If our children want more American education they must go to Carlisle Indian Industrial School in another place called Pennsylvania. It is very far from here. We fear we would never have our children with us if we let them leave. Some are afraid they would be ghosts from our world as the tatonka have been."

"Some?" Chanel started. "Guapahka, the school is not to be feared. My father taught me that my school education is a tool for me to use along with the tools that he and my family will teach me. I will never lose those family tools just because I added the tools from my education."

"There are some that also say this within our camp. Some believe as you say. I am fearful." Guapahka took a deep breath, looked up at to move her neck muscles and relaxed her shoulders. She was accepting some of what Chanel said about education because she knew the power of knowledge. But, the loss of tradition would be a tremendous loss.

"I have these fears because we have seen the results of this education from Washington City. We have seen the results of *American* educated men."

"What do you mean?" Chanel dug deeper.

"The Council and Treaty of Medicine Lodge gave us land to live on in Oklahoma. It gave us the unseen boundaries that were to be ours. But the treaty placed us side by side with people that we have never seen as brothers and sisters. We were Kiowa. We are not Kiowa-Apache or Kiowa-Comanche.

"Then, for money, hunters from the cities east of Oklahoma came and killed all the tatonka for their skins only. They left hundreds of skinned tatonka to rot in the heat. We were a hungry and beaten people. Did the educated wasichu from Washington City not see how this would beat down the Kiowa? Did they not see that beating down the Kiowa would only make the Kiowa a burden to the wasichu?" she demanded, although not expecting Chanel to answer.

Chanel knew some state history, but her school version had left all the details fuzzy. She knew that Oklahoma had been little more than a prison colony for Indians prior to statehood. She never knew how it had come about.

But Chanel could not be sidetracked from her mission. She still needed to find Cynthia . . . or did she?

Did Cynthia give her the tai-me to come to this place? What does the tai-me offer to Chanel?

"Guapahka, what is this tai-me that Cynthia gave me? What does it mean to me?" Chanel held the necklace out for the woman to see clearly.

"Child, I don't need a better look at your tai-me," she

smiled.

She pulled on a thin strip of leather from around her neck. She pulled an identical tai-me from under her blouse.

"The question is, what does it mean to me that you have mine?" Guapahka put her hand under Chanel's chin. "What do *we* have together with this Cynthia Tallchief?"

Chanel looked incredulous. The necklaces were identical. These were not mass produced costume jewelry. These were handmade, twisted from slivers of pine and willow twigs and adorned with small feathers. They were distinct effigies of a hawk but they were identical!

"Come with me, child." Guapahka instructed as she took Chanel by the hand. Walking through the crowd of women, Chanel cast her eyes towards the old Indian who had been chanting behind her. Her heart skipped a beat. It was the Indian shaman from her bedroom.

His eyes opened to meet hers, but the chanting never stopped. Saliva dripped from his lower lip to a puddle on his wrinkled belly.

"I have seen him, Guapahka!" Chanel exclaimed. "I have seen him in my room!"

Guapahka touched her finger to her lips. "Shh, child," she admonished as she tightened her grip on Chanel's hand. "Come with me."

Chapter Twenty Five

Guapahka took Chanel to the creek north of the main village. It flowed over rocks and submerged branches to the main river she saw from the hill overlooking the village. Cottonwoods were releasing their seeds in the breeze and the gurgling creek was soothing to hear. They sat down on a red sandstone rock that hung over the cool water. Guapahka took her moccasins off and eased her feet into the ripples.

Chanel took her shoes off and did the same. Instantly a memory of her dad and her doing the same in the creek that flowed through the woods came to her. Sadness tried to envelope her. The creek in Chickasha seemed like a lifetime ago. Chanel felt older but, with the release of a slow breath, a bit wiser also. She knew she was on a mission and she knew that she was alone in this adventure. Still, many 'friends' had been found along the way and there was a reason for these people to be in her journey. She wasn't sure if she was getting nearer the end or simply ending the beginning.

"Chanel, what do you know about the Kiowa people, especially the Kiowa shaman?" Guapahka quizzed while twirling a floating twig with her foot.

"Nothing, really, until I met Cynthia I only knew of Indians. I didn't know much about the different tribes or legends," Chanel responded.

Guapahka hesitated but then got to the point.

"Chanel, the spiritual world of the Kiowa is usually the man's domain. Very few women are part of it. Did Cynthia tell you this?" Guapahka wanted to know the extent of Cynthia's conversation with Chanel.

"No. We never talked about those things."

"Did she tell you of the secret lodges of the priest or what we call shaman?" Guapahka tried to jog Chanel's memory further.

"No." Chanel repeated.

"Did she ever say anything about shape-shifting or skin-walking? I think that is what the Indian Bureau man called it," Guapahka elaborated her question.

"No ma'am, she didn't." Chanel went on, "what is shape-shifting and skin-walking?"

"The Kiowa don't call it shape-shifting, but that is the best word I know that you'll understand." Guapahka started, "Each Kiowa has a guardian that directs our actions. That is, if we allow it to happen. If we don't, we wander without purpose. This guardian is found when we are very young."

"Who is your guardian?" Chanel interrupted.

"I was a young girl when my grandmother took me to the woods far from our village. It was not a normal thing for a girl to do. Religious issues were for the men of the village, but my grandmother told me I bore a gift."

"Why did she take you to the woods?" Chanel posed. "Were you leaving your village?"

"No, I was not leaving my village, but I was leaving the life that I knew. I was going on a vision quest," Guapahka confided softly as she remembered the details.

"A vision quest?" Chanel scooted closer to Guapahka.

"Yes, I was looking for my purpose. I didn't eat for two days but I had the water from a gourd that my grandmother had brought. I prayed with her for these two days and then she left me sometime in the night. I awoke to find that a mist had covered the hill where we camped. Dew wet my face and nose so that smells were nourishing above the usual. I could smell and taste the world around me. I could sense the locations of the different animals and of the plants that we gathered for medicines. I felt more of a part of my world so I prayed harder."

"What were you praying for Guapahka?" Chanel was very in tune with this desire to find answers.

"I prayed for my family and for direction. I prayed to know what my future was to be also," Guapahka explained. "I prayed for a hand to show me who and what I was to be."

"And you found what?" Chanel needed to know what could be found in prayer. She too had prayed to know who she was to be. Her parents' divorce had left her with a void. She knew they loved her and they told her there was no fault of hers in the separation. Chanel couldn't help but wonder if she could have said or done something to have kept their family together. Even as a small child she wondered why things had happened different for her than for her brother and sister.

"I found myself becoming one with my surroundings." Guapahka continued, "I could smell, taste and hear things as never before. Then, as I sat there I felt a deep sleep overwhelming me. And I closed my eyes."

"I awoke to darkness but with a clear moonlight. The mist was gone and I was alone on the small hill that we had spread our deerskin. I could hear footprints and wings all around me. I stood to look through the trees, but fell in my weakness from hunger. But soon that left me and I was strong in spirit and my alertness."

"I had just closed my eyes to pray again when a noise directly in front of me made me open them to investigate." Guapahka started but Chanel interrupted her.

"What was it?" Chanel asked then answered. "It was a fox wasn't it? It was your tai-me come to be your guardian, wasn't it."

Guapahka smiled, "Yes, it was, child."

"Do I have a tai-me?" Chanel asked.

"You have mine." Guapahka motioned to her necklace.

"But it is yours, Guapahka. Do I have one?" Chanel stood.

"Yes, you do and I think I know that it is the same, but only you will know," Guapahka replied and stooped to pick up her moccasins.

"How important is it for you to know?" Guapahka asked while tying her moccasin.

Chanel knew where this was going. She stood up.

She walked to the creek and listened to the noises. She could feel nature embracing her and it was comforting. This must be the reason she was here.

"Guapahka, will I be here for a long time?" Chanel inquired over her shoulder.

"Maybe you will be here a long time and maybe not so long. Is that too great a sacrifice?" She raised the question as she placed her hands on Chanel's shoulders.

"No." Chanel admitted as her confidence lengthened her stature.

"Then so be it." Guapahka turned to walk away.

"Guapahka," Chanel started, "I understand tai-me, now, but you asked me about shape-shifting. Will my time here answer that also?"

"Chanel, I believe you have a gift. I believe that is why we are together. I don't know what that gift is, but it could be that you are to be included as you are Kiowa. I don't know what you will be granted, but I know you will soon find out. For that is why you are here."

"But Guapahka, I am not Kiowa." Chanel had a puzzled

196

look on her face.

"Yes, child, you are." Guapahka left Chanel alone on the embankment. Chanel sat on a bleached oak log and closed her eyes. She prayed to God for guidance. A mist crept over the glade where she sat. Darkness cloaked Chanel's being. She prayed harder.

Morning came and Chanel was still sitting with her eyes closed. She had fallen asleep in her search. The heat of the dawn awoke her to her hunger and thirst. She crept down to the creek and looked into the water.

All her life she had looked at the creek as a flowing of dirty water. Sediment, leaves and debris floated by. Now, and not just because she was thirsty, she saw the creek as life. She could smell the sweetness of it and the floating pieces were merely sharing the sweetness. She drank from her hand and felt the coolness wash over her. She returned to the spot where she had awakened.

It was at this time that she noticed the circle of objects around her.

A small cairn of rocks was piled with twigs representing limbs wedged at various places. A wooden bowl with dried vegetables and small bones sat to the left of the rocks. Fur and feathers were wrapped in grapevines as the circle continued. All around her were small effigies that had been placed while she had slept. Two lines of ground cornmeal formed a path out of the circle. Chanel could feel a sense of comfort to be in the midst of them so she closed her eyes and prayed more fervently.

In her weakened state, sleep came again. Or was it sleep? Could she be moving into a world parallel to the world she knew?

Chapter Twenty Six

Chanel's dad was sitting on the edge of the well after Chanel climbed out of sight. A large red-tailed hawk flew to the branch above his head. Their eyes met. The hawk settled on the branch as if to wait alongside her dad.

"She'll be right back," her dad spoke aloud to the hawk and he pulled his sleeve down to his hand to wipe his face.

The hawk brought his wing across his beak and settled it back in place to his side.

"This is way weird, Mr. Hawk," Chanel's dad proclaimed as he turned to peer into the darkness of the well. "It is way weird."

The hawk settled himself on the branch.

Chapter Twenty Seven

Chanel dreamed vividly about the shaman from her bedroom. He was the same shaman from the tipi. A burning bird nest was at his feet. Charms and effigies were positioned in a circle around him also. One effigy of a large dog or perhaps a wolf was located on the back of a tortoise shell near the smoldering nest. She could hear his chant but could not understand it. With eyes wide, he stared at the moon. He did not acknowledge her presence.

She approached him but his chanting never stopped. She moved in closer and let the wisps of smoke come to her face. She could hear the chant more plainly. She could understand the words:

Spirit within me hear my call
Take from me this burden
Spirit within me hear my call
Take from me this burden
Bring life to my tai-me
Through my eyes
Bring life to my tai-me
Spirit within me...

Chanel backed away from the smoke and the chant became foreign again. She sat across from the shaman and pulled the wisps to her face with open palms. Her understanding to the words returned.

Spirit, take this veil from my life that I may run with your world
Open my heart to who I am
Spirit, take this veil and cast it from me
Let me run in your world

The old man raised his hands to the air and the smoke

from the nest of twigs and feathers emanated from his palms. Chanel raised her hands and repeated the chant she had heard.

Spirit, take this veil from my life that I may run with your world
Open my heart to who I am
Spirit, take this veil and cast it from me
Let me run in your world

For what seemed like eternity she chanted. Soon she was lost to the chant. Time was gone. She stared at the moon. It appeared to move closer to her. When it had engulfed her sight she closed her eyes to protect them from the brightness. She chanted fervently as the old shaman sitting across from her did also.

She opened her eyes and looked down to the ground in front of her feet. A red fox with black stocking feet stood before her. He bowed his chin to the ground and then raised it sharply to the air. He dug with his front paws in the dirt while keeping his eyes on Chanel. He kicked dust from behind his back paws. Three times he repeated this and then turned to run away from her. He stopped to see her follow.

Chanel resumed her chant.

The old Shaman slowly stood as he chanted, palms still raised in the air. He turned his palms down and Chanel saw the glow of embers between his fingers.

He clapped his hands together and smoke and ash clouded her vision of him. When it cleared he was gone.

A gray wolf stood before her.

Chanel raised her eyes to the moon and continued to chant.

Spirit, take this veil from my life that I may run with your world

Open my heart to who I am
Spirit, take this veil and cast it from me
Let me run in your world
Spirit, take this veil from my life that I may run with your
world
Open my heart to who I am
Spirit, take this veil and cast it from me
Let me run in your world

The wolf lowered his chin to the ground and then raised it sharply to the sky as the fox had done before. He did this three times and turned to run.

Chanel bent as she chanted and took the nest into her hands. She raised it to the sky and then sat it down. She stood with her palms held upright.

Smoke rose from her hands. She felt no pain from the embers between her fingers.

A mist fell across her eyes and she could smell cool grass and earth.

She clapped her hands and the dust and ashes whirled around her head. She could feel the grass on her chin and under her feet and hands. Her arms were like springs and she bolted from this position. She found herself running through the woods and eventually into the open field.

Soon she was entering the moonlit Indian camp. It was empty of people outside their homes. She ran through the passages between each tipi. She was eye-level with the cooking pots and tipi openings. She turned between two tipis and saw the legs of Guapahka. She pulled abruptly and slid to a stop in the loose dirt. Her eyes met Guapahka's.

"Run, Little-Dog-of-the-Woods, run," Guapahka said softly and turned her back.

Chanel turned and ran back to the creek as hard as she

could. She was breathless, but her energy was immense.

The old shaman was there. His hands were upturned and a smile adorned his face as he rocked back and forth on his seat.

The wolf was gone and the moon was going down and Chanel lay down beside the old shaman. Twigs snapped and she awoke from the dream. She was alone again on the creek bank. She looked in the darkness for the shaman, but he was gone. The circle of effigies was gone. She looked for signs of the burning nest but found nothing. Dew had covered the grass except for the spot from where she had she had awoken. She sat back down and soon fell back into a deep sleep.

When she awoke to the dawn's heat again, Chanel stood and looked around her. All was as she had left when she went to sleep. Dew still covered the grasses around her and the world smelled of sweet honeysuckles.

She went down to drink from the creek. As she leaned to scoop water into her palm she noticed the ashes, dirt and debris on her hands. She looked at her feet and found them also covered in ashes, dirt and debris. Her reflection in the water revealed dirt under her chin.

Chanel smiled.

Chapter Twenty Eight

Tabitha Huffman-Cross read over the deed in her hands as she had a hundred times before. The Huffmans had kept the taxes up on the abandoned farm in McClain County all these years. Her father's short sightedness now kept her from owning the one portion of that farm that now looked to be a gold mine, a *black-gold* mine. Oil was being extracted from every section of land around the abandoned farm and Tabitha Huffman-Cross wanted her share.

Her father told the family that the farm with the burnt foundation was theirs. It had been given to him as collateral in a debt and it was family property. For reasons unknown to the family, he evaded ever discussing the debt.

Now, it seems that all these years after his death, the worthless farm had sat on top of a pool of Oklahoma oil and though the surface rights were Huffman's, the mineral rights belonged to that stuttering old fool that swept floors at the nursing home. She would get that stuttering old fool to sign the mineral rights over to her before any other heirs to the Pendergrass family were discovered. One way or the other, Jacob Pendergrass would do as she demanded or his precious Blair Ireland would suffer for his inaction.

The powder ground from Blair Irelands heart medicine capsules had been slipped excessively into her food. It brought her to the brink of death. Showing the empty capsules to Jacob and demanding that he sign the mineral deed only stiffened his jaw.

"Surely, you don't believe anybody would listen to a demented old janitor in a nursing home claiming the old woman that he had all but stalked for seventy years was being poisoned. And, I have the only copy of the mineral deed and you wouldn't know your way around a courthouse to find another. She has no family and you have no family, why not sign the paper and be done with it? If she dies, who would believe your story? And, if she dies, her blood will be on your hands for being a greedy old bastard!" she had threatened him the night Blair Ireland was rushed to the hospital.

Chapter Twenty Nine

Footsteps seemed to be right behind Chanel. She slowly turned, but saw no one. She heard the footsteps and smelled the familiar scent of a body. She turned more to her right and soaked in the essences that her senses revealed. Within moments she could see Guapahka emerging from the woods. Guapahka was almost fifty yards away. Within the familiar scents she knew to be Guapahka, Chanel could smell food also.

And sure enough, Guapahka had food wrapped in a cloth when she arrived. The smell was overwhelming as Chanel hadn't eaten for days. How many days? The question arose in her mind.

"Guapahka, how many days have I been here?" Chanel asked as she stood to greet the beautiful woman.

"As many as you needed." She smiled as she held out the venison and bread.

Chanel sat down and began devouring the food.

"Slow down little one," Guapahka warned as she sat next to Chanel. "You will have to chew some before you swallow."

Chanel was embarrassed. "I'm sorry." She was famished. "My stomach is so empty."

Guapahka handed her a canteen.

"Drink this between bites and it will slow down your feasting." Guapahka recognized the survival instinct taking over Chanel's need for manners. A smile formed that softened her face and endeared her to Chanel.

Guapahka watched as Chanel ate the food. When it was gone, Chanel wiped her mouth on the cloth.

"Guapahka, I had the most amazing dreams!" she started.

"I dreamed of the Shaman and of running into you at your camp. I dreamed of a wolf and of running very fast."

"Did you now?" Guapahka shifted her weight to be comfortable.

Chanel began telling the whole story and as she came closer to the end, it dawned on her that Guapahka was not amazed. It then dawned on her that Guapahka was nodding her head as if each portion of the tale was as planned.

"Guapahka, something changed with me, didn't it?" Chanel asked.

"Yes child. It did," Guapahka replied softly.

"Forever?" Chanel wondered aloud.

"If you want it to be forever," Guapahka confirmed.

"I don't understand." Chanel leaned forward and took Guapahka's hand in hers.

"You were given a key to your gift. The gift has always been yours. You just never knew how to open it," Guapahka explained.

"And now that it is opened, what am I to do with it?" Chanel pressed further.

"Whatever brought you to this place brought you here to fulfill a task. I don't know what that task is, Chanel." Guapahka continued, "Cynthia Tallchief is the river that runs between you and me. I don't know who Cynthia is. I only have a guess that she is part of me also."

Chanel sat back and thought silently for a moment. Cynthia and Guapahka looked similar. The shape of their faces were the same. Guapahka was beautiful and so was Cynthia. Both had dancing eyes. Both were bright and accommodating to Chanel.
Both had the same…

It was then that Chanel knew.

"Guapahka, what year is it?" Chanel probed as she rose to her feet.

"Why child?" Guapahka looked up at her standing there.

"What year?" Chanel repeated.

"It is 1887, child, did you not know this? After all it is a white man's date," Guapahka replied.

"Are you married?" Chanel was confirming a hunch.

"Yes," Guapahka was suddenly aware where this was going.

"Do you have children?" Chanel went on.

"No, but..." Guapahka hesitated.

"No, but what?" Chanel stepped closer.

Guapahka rose to her feet. She moved slowly and softly towards the river.

"What?" Chanel pleaded.

Guapahka's hands cupped her lower abdomen as if to cradle it.

"I soon will." She turned smiling. "I soon will have a child and you have just told me that she will bear a granddaughter!" Tears rolled down her cheeks.

Chanel rushed to hug Guapahka. She pressed her face to Guapahka and then looked up at her, still wrapping her arms around her waist.

"Cynthia told me that she couldn't give me the tai-me because it was something special that her grandmother had given her." Chanel elaborated on their first meeting.

Guapahka's face changed expression.

"Then what are you doing with it?" she challenged as she pulled Chanel's arms from around her waist.

Chanel was startled at the abruptness.

"The old Shaman left it in my room the night he sang on my floor." Chanel tried to explain. "I am sorry I lied to you about her giving it to me, but I didn't want you to think that I had stolen it."

"Then you did lie?" Guapahka demanded.

"Yes, but…" Chanel started.

"Chanel, you cannot lie! You cannot hold the gift and be true to its promise if you are one who lies!" Guapahka insisted while wiping the tears from her face with her sleeves.

"Guapahka, listen, I came from another time! How can I explain that without you thinking that I am crazy?" Chanel defended. "I am lost as to why I am here. Last night or the night before or even the night before, I dream that I am running through an Indian camp. Then you tell me that it is 1887. Cynthia tells me that it is 1936. Guapahka, I was born in 1992!

"I don't know what to tell you or your hunting party or Cynthia that any of you will understand, because I don't yet understand all of it!" Chanel screamed as tears flowed down her face.

"If I am crazy and I came from this same year as we live in now, how else would I have your tai-me?" Chanel demanded from Guapahka.

The two of them stood as if waiting for an answer. Neither knew what to say.

After what seemed like an eternity, Guapahka walked over to Chanel and encircled her within her arms. She guided her over to a fallen log and sat the two of them down.

"Tell me everything, Chanel. It will be then the two of us working on your mission instead of you having to find your way alone," Guapahka directed.

For hours the two of them talked as Chanel detailed all the events with the well.

As the events were revealed to Guapahka, a directive unfolded.

"Chanel, I understand some of why you are here," Guapahka began. "But, I don't understand who you are to save, if you say that Cynthia grew to be a teacher in the Indian school after falling in the well."

"I first thought it was Ms. Ireland. She was very depressed and was almost giving up on her life. I thought that knowing what really had happened to Cynthia would ease the guilt that she had been bearing," Chanel's tone of voice was full of doubt.

"But now?" Guapahka pursued her doubt.

"Now, after all that has happened here and during this time, I am not sure.

"In fact," Chanel added, "before the old Shaman that left the tai-me came to me, there was another ghost or spirit that came while my head was hurt."

"Another?" Guapahka probed.

"Yes and this one was scary and cold." Chanel described the visit. "The spirit told me to leave *her* to them. I don't think it was the Shaman. I think it was a woman's voice. It was almost … evil! It was threatening me and I was really scared to have been visited by it."

"And what did it want from you?" Guapahka quizzed.

"I think it wanted me to stop looking to help. I think it wanted me to leave whoever I was to save for them. And I don't think they would have helped her," Chanel finished.

"Chanel, as there is good in the spirit world there is also evil. Whatever forces are guiding you could also be fighting with the evil that men do," Guapahka explained.

"Evil could sense that you are now involved and your being part of the event could change the outcome of whatever happened or was about to happen," Guapahka elaborated.

"It could be that…" Guapahka started, but Chanel interrupted her.

"Do you hear that?" Chanel asked as she rose to her feet.

"Hear what?" Guapahka rose also.

"I hear women screaming. I hear cries from the camp," Chanel said.

She turned on her heels and headed towards Guapahka's camp. Guapahka soon over took her and ran deftly through the dense woods ahead.

Chapter Thirty

Chanel followed close on Guapahka's heels as she ran. Soon Guapahka heard the wailing and commotion also.

A crowd of people were gathered near the tipi that Chanel had been brought to. In the center of the crowd, three wagons loaded with children of various ages sat as if on display.

"What is going on?" Guapahka demanded as she made her way through the crowd of women and old men.

"They are taking the young ones," a woman wailed. "They are taking them to the white school. They are taking them away from us."

Guapahka made her way to the group of white men that surrounded one of the families. They were armed.

"What are you men doing with those children?" she demanded.

A man in a rumpled suit turned sharply. He was holding papers with names listed down two columns.

In a gesture of frustration, he threw his hands down to his sides and rolled his eyes to the men that came with him. "I'll say it one more time!" he announced, obviously repeating himself. "Though many of us disagree, Interior Secretary Harlan feels that this nation cannot adopt a policy of exterminating the native people who have been subjugated after years of warfare. He has therefore directed, with the approval of these signed leaders of the Kiowa tribe, that all children under the present age of fourteen years old and over the present age of eight years old, would get a six year education. Theses ages are as of January One of each current year of our Lord. The only school for your tribe is the Rainy Mountain Boarding School. It was, and is, the desire that these children are not going to remain savages in Oklahoma only to become wards of the Territory."

Guapahka looked at the papers he held.

"Are these treaties?" she asked.

"These are the same as," he began. "These are the names of the families and of the children in your band of Kiowa. And I might add if there are children not on this list but present in this camp and you don't turn them over to us it is a federal offense punishable by prison! Do you understand what I am saying? Now, quit making such a commotion. You all know where the school is and in December, you will be able to visit your children. If you have someone who can read and write or desire to have someone with the BIA do it for you, you may write letters to your children. But, mark my words, if there are any disparaging words in those letters encouraging your children to run away or to disrupt the indoctrination process, it would be paramount to treason, as this is a federal program. Treason is punishable by imprisonment, also. Do you understand what I am saying?"

The women looked around at each other. The men were away hunting and no one stood as being able to confront these government bullies.

Guapahka stepped in closer to take that position.

"These children will stay here until their fathers return. Their fathers and mothers will bring them to the school if that is their wish. You will not shackle them to a wagon and steal them away from us. Do you understand what I am saying?" Her fist doubled instinctively. More of the women moved in to support her.

Suddenly two men rushed in to take Guapahka by her arms.

"Squaw, if I have to shackle you to a tree to let me do my

job I will." The suited-man stepped closer to Guaphaka to make his point. He rolled the papers into a tight cylinder. "These children are not shackled to these wagons. Their parents have agreed, albeit reluctantly, to let their Kiowa leaders to represent the will of the Kiowa nation. The Kiowa leaders' decision and the will of government of the United States prevails. They are going off to be educated. They will be allowed to rejoin their people after that fact." He jabbed the rolled up papers to her face as if they were a saber.

Guapahka raised her right foot kicked him square in the chest as the two men inadvertently support her weight.

"Why you…" The man doubled up his fist to strike Guapahka.

Chanel jumped in between them pushing the man off balance. He leaned forward to strike her.

"Let me see those papers!" she shouted. "I can read them!"

The man stopped his advance.

"Who are you?" he demanded.

"I am Chanel…" she hesitated but a moment. "I am Chanel Tallchief and I can read the words on those papers."

Guapahka stopped struggling to watch Chanel.

"You can either give me that chance or you can fight this whole camp of mothers! Which would you rather do?" Chanel offered.

The men looked around at the large group of women encircling them. There were six of them and they were armed but the men had no intentions of firing their weapons at these mothers.

"Very well," the suited-man said. He straightened his tie and vest where a dusty footprint marked Guapahka's rage. "You have five minutes!"

He glared at Guapahka as he backed away.

Chanel read the order slowly. The entire camp watched her closely. Only Guapahka knew her.

Then after what seemed like an eternity, Chanel approached Guapahka and the two men that held her arms.

"Tell your goons to let go of her!" Chanel ordered to the suited man. "I will try to explain this order since you don't have the courtesy or decency to tell how this affects these children and their parents."

"I am obligated to the United States Indian Commission, not to the ragged protectorates thereof." He bowed up.

"C'mon Bill, I don't want to fight this whole camp!" one of the goons holding Guapahka urged as he let go of Guapahka's arm. "We got children too, William. Let the girl help."

The other man let go as well and Chanel took Guapahka by the hand and led her out of the crowd.

"Guapahka, this letter says that the Treaty of Medicine Lodge signed on October 28, 1867 by several Indian Peace Commission members and including several marks and signatures with printed Indian names beside them, agreed to compulsory education of the Kiowa children for six years per child or until their fourteenth birthday. I see Santanta's mark and name here, Guapahka.

"It has allocated two thousand dollars per year to provide for them. It also says that they can be schooled in Oklahoma if a school is available but if not, they would be authorized to take them to Carlisle, Pennsylvania to be schooled. Guapahka, that would be a hundreds of miles from here!"

Guapahka's, shoulders sagged.

"Guapahka, remember me telling you that Cynthia grew up to teach at the Indian School?" Chanel appealed.

215

"At this school?" Guapahka wanted to know.

"I am not sure, Guapahka. My sister said it was at Riverside Indian School. But, it means that Cynthia saw a need to teach the children. She also saw a need for another Indian to teach these children and she was able to accomplish that. She must have attended school to know this."

Guapahka's eyes reddened, but she would not let the men see her at a weak moment.

"It is if they are taking them to prison just as they did Santanta," Guapahka explained. "Santanta died at the white prison."

Chanel put her arm around Guapahka's waist.

"Guapahka, you have been a great teacher to me these last few days. It is something that will make me stronger. And, I will admit there are times when I don't like going to the school. But my dad says that knowledge is the only tool you have that no one can take from you. It is important for me to have it. If your people are to survive and live with any successes in the white man's world, it is important for your children to have it also.

"I can read this list of names. You know them so we can say them aloud to their parents to make sure the right children by age are going," Chanel offered. "I know I am asking you to trust the one who lied to you about how I came to have Cynthia's tai-me. I understand why I can never lie again. I understand my responsibility to have your trust. Mostly, though, I understand my responsibility to define my gift."

Guapahka looked deep into Chanel's eye. She sought reassurance.

"Chanel, you lied about your last name to these men,"

216

Guapahka said softly. "Would you lie to me, even if it was good for me?"

"Guapahka, I wouldn't lie to you, again, for any reason in the world, I pinkie promise." Chanel held up her pinkie finger to confirm.

Guapahka tried to smile, but it wouldn't surface. She looked at the mothers waiting for her direction.

She nodded to Chanel and curtly to the suited man. She and Chanel moved in closer to the wagon and spoke to the camp. The bureau men grumbled at the delay.

Reluctantly, the mothers and grandmothers agreed to let Chanel read the names aloud. Several of the children were younger than the list described and they got to stay with their mothers. Several boys stepped up to announce they weren't on the list, but would go to keep their tribe whole and to watch over the younger children.

Belongings were loaded on the wagons next to the children and goodbyes were said. Keeping brave faces for their children the mothers stood in stoic honor.

As the loaded wagons prepared to depart, the suited man and another large man approached Guapahka.

"You are under arrest, squaw!" the suited man sneered.

"For what!" Chanel protested.

"For striking an agent of the United States government!" He declared. "And you, you half-breed, if you don't want to go to prison with her, you'll sit quiet!"

The big man grabbed Guapahka's arm and Chanel rushed to intervene.

"Stop!" Guapahka ordered Chanel. "I will go. I struck him."

"But Guapahka, you…"

"I don't want our children to bear the wrath of this man,

drunk with his treaty-power, because of me," Guapahka declared.

"There you go," the suited man sneered. "Now you are seeing things as they are."

"Robert, shackle her and put her on the front wagon," he ordered, "and, if she causes you any trouble, shackle her to the axle!"

"You can't do this!" Chanel protested.

"It is done, half-breed." He said as he turned to mount his horse. "Now go back to your people and prepare them for when I return for the rest of their progeny."

Chanel watched them pull out and followed them to the edge of the camp.

"And half-breed," the suited man called out to Chanel. "If you follow, I will arrest you also. And if I see the hunters following, I will shoot your friend first!"

Chanel stood alone in front of the women. Darkness came slowly. Chanel knew many in the camp felt she might have betrayed Guapahka. Their silence weighed heavy on her.

She returned to Guapahka's tent. She found the Shaman inside. He watched her walk across the blankets on the ground. She settled on a buffalo robe directly across from him.

They sat in silence facing each other. His leathered skin hung dull against his silhouette. His emotionless face challenged her to seek life within his dark eyes. For almost an hour they sat in silence.

Suddenly a coyote howled in the distance. Chanel cocked her head and listened. A smile surfaced on her lips. She understood her gift.

Chanel rose to her feet and started gathering familiar

218

things in the tipi. She placed them in a circle around her and laid her tai-me in front of her. She knelt in the center of the circle facing the old shaman.

"Okay, old-man-of-my-dreams, how do I do this again?" Chanel asked matter-of-factly.

Chapter Thirty One

Chanel could smell the horses in the grass and dust. It was as if a florescent trail lay before her. She ran at a measured clip trying not to overrun the scents that directed her. The prairie grasses brushed against her chest and stomach.

Occasional piles of dung nearly made her swoon with their strong odors. Off to either side of her she could smell and even see animals parallel with her. They were spectators to her dilemma. Neither support nor obstruction came from them, but she knew they were along for the ride.

Running long into the night, Chanel was oblivious to what direction north, east, south or west she travelled; but then, the direction was meaningless to her. She knew the destination and her senses unfolded the path to follow.

Topping a mesa, a breeze cooled her face. Water must be close. Chanel found the wagon odors mixed with those of people and burning wood. She could distinguish Guapahka's scent from the rest, long before she saw the camp.

The campfire light on the horizon signaled the end of the journey. Chanel slowed to a walk.

Darting from rock to bush, she soon came over the edge of dry wash and saw the school wagon camp. Searching the group of men and children she was unable to find Guapahka.

The water smell was stronger and Guapahka's scent also. Chanel headed for it.

As she rounded the contour of the creek she saw Guapahka. The suited man stood guard over her as she washed the plates and cooking pans used for their meal.

She could smell alcohol on his breath as he chided Guapahka doing her work. Chanel could smell his sweat and even his fear. He was thirty yards away!

This man feared Guapahka, but there was something else. There was something more sinister. Chanel could sense his hatred.

Chanel did not want to give him time to act on it. She knew as soon as Guapahka had finished her work, this little, evil man had plans for revenge.

Chanel watched, hoping for a plan.

Suddenly, Chanel was aware of another smell!

At the moment she discerned what it was. It appeared.

A gray wolf bounded over the creek bank. It ran snarling for the suited man. He rose and tried to bring his rifle up to fire, but the wolf was too fast. It struck a jagged bite to the man's wrist and ran past. It stopped abruptly and attacked his ankle sending the man tumbling into the water. The man fired his rifle with one hand sending the barrel backwards into the bridge of his nose. Blood flowed down his wet shirt.

The large man that had shackled Guapahka had seen the wolf and heard the gun fire at the creek. He had been listening to his boss snipe at Guapahka. He had no intentions letting his boss take advantage of the situation with the Indian woman.

"You men take care of these children!" he ordered as he ran from the campfire to the creek.

The men and the older boys started putting the children on the wagons.

"Wolf!" the suited-man shouted through gasps of creek water. "Shoot that son-of-a-bitch!"

The gray and black wolf ran across the ridge away from the melee.

The large man fired a shot from his Winchester carbine. Sand kicked up hard in front of the wolf's hind feet causing it to stumble and tumble down the hill. The man fired his carbine again and quickly cocked his weapon. The wolf ran back towards the suited man and slowed to a stop. Again, the large man fired as the wolf jumped forward. He did this another time and as before, the man barely missed hitting the wolf.

At ten yards the wolf slowed as if to repeat the procedure. This time the shooter knew what to do.

As the wolf stopped, the man fired again and as quickly, cocked his rifle. Anticipating the wolf jumping forward again, the man rotated his hips to lead his next shot. He fired!

The wolf did jump as anticipated! He jumped directly at the suited man!

The 40 caliber bullet hit the suited man squarely in the ribs. He fell forward into the water. The wolf's front paws pushed off the man's shoulders and he bounded away to a point overlooking the floating body and stopped.

Chanel's eyes met the eyes of the wolf. Were they the eyes of the old Shaman? They were one and the same. Chanel took her cue.

Guapahka had pressed herself against a bluff at creek-side during all the shooting. Her feet were under her and tucked out of the line of stray bullets. Chanel bolted down the river bank and stopped beside her. Her presence startled Guapahka. Chanel cocked her head slightly and turned to trot off. She stopped on the ridge.

Guapahka looked at the little red fox and smiled. She looked over at the wagons. The oldest boy motioned for her to run. She waved back as a tear clouded her vision. She picked up one of the canteens that she had previously filled for the wagons and ran up to the ridge along Chanel's path.

At the highest point she stopped and looked back at the wagons.

"I will join you at the school!" She called out to the boy in their native language. He waved and nodded in approval.

The large man had dropped his rifle and was struggling in the creek pulling the suited man from the water. He laid him on the bank. With a gasp and several coughs, the suited man tried to sit up.

"Sit still, boss," the large man directed. "I've got to get you to a doctor."

"What about the wolf?" The injured man's voice faded with distance as Chanel and Guapahka ran into the darkness.

Chanel slowed to allow Guapahka to keep up on her trail. As she was, she knew she could never get close enough for Guapahka to touch her though she wanted to wrap her arms around the woman.

Chanel had feared the worse for Guapahka. Sensing the anger in the school man and the way he was treating her at the creek, Chanel knew she had gotten there in the nick of time.

It would be a long night, but Chanel knew where she was going.

In her mind, she answered the age old question: Do animals smile?

Chapter Thirty Two

Into the night they ran. Chanel was routinely altering her pace for Guapahka. But, throughout the night, the temptation to run after adventurous sounds and smells nearly sidetracked her mission. She needed to get Guapahka back to the camp.

Chanel was emboldened with new energy. There was a spring in every step and her endurance was boundless. The wind tickled her face as she ran. The sounds of the night had been described in books and movies, but to actually hear them in this resonance was incredible.

As she ran, she could actually hear movement under ground. She could hear the flutter of wings above her even without seeing what made the noise. And the smells!

Chanel felt as if she were travelling through an incense fog of multiple odors. Some such as the cedars and dirt, she could easily recognize. Others were unfamiliar, but she seemed to be able to differentiate between types of animals.

She could somehow tell the difference between carnivores and herbivores. She could smell their breath! Worse still, she could smell their scat and could tell the difference between digested grasses and digested animal matter.

She could also see for long distances even though the moon was gone. She was aware that Guapahka was depending on her for that very reason.

What she didn't know was how this was going to change her life. Was she going home through the tunnel as she knew home to be? Was she going to look at her family and friends as species? She certainly didn't want to smell anybody's scat!

Suddenly, she heard Guapahka gasp.

"Stop, Little One! I have to rest!"

Chanel had been so preoccupied in her thoughts that she had lost the pace that she was keeping for Guapahka.

Guapahka fell to her knees and panted. After a moment she drank a little from the canteen.

Chanel walked closer, but stopped short of being beside Guapahka.

"You have come a long way, Little One," Guapahka commended after she had caught her breath. "And you have farther to go."

Chanel cocked her head to listen.

"I thank you for my life, but I am not sure about thanking you for the lives of our children," Guapahka started. "I am trusting you to show me how Cynthia Tallchief came to be. I am trusting that she became a teacher for the good of her people."

Chanel felt lost as far as responding to Guapahka. She wanted to be voicing her thoughts to Guapahka but she needed to be able to find the Kiowa camp in her present state.

The fact of the matter was, Chanel needed to find the Shaman to know exactly how to return to who she was. Or to return to who she is!

Guapahka stood and readied herself to continue. "Okay, Little-Dog-of the-Wood, take us to our home."

As dawn broke, Chanel could smell the camp. Stopping to look back, she could see Guapahka straining her neck to see the camp as she must have recognized the area.

Stopping one more time to let Guapahka rest and drink, Chanel tried to convey the nearness of the camp to Guapahka through just her thoughts. Somehow, Guapahka knew.

"Go, Little One," she said, "you have things to discover."

Chanel hopped to her feet and turned a short circle and stopped, facing Guapahka.

Guapahka laughed aloud at her dance.

Then Chanel took off to sneak into the camp. She knew she was taking a risk coming into the camp in broad daylight, but she had to find the Shaman and she had to find him fast!

Guapahka calling the camp 'our home' stuck in Chanel's mind. Chanel already had a home. In fact, she had two of them.

Maybe as the card she had given her dad for his birthday had said '*Home is where there is love*." Maybe there is love for Chanel at the camp also. The Kiowa loved family. And, because of Cynthia, Chanel had been able to see that. Her previous shortsighted view of the Native Americans has been lengthened and enlightened. She could easily love the Kiowa.

As she neared the camp she saw many women busy tending to the day to day tasks of feeding and caring for their families. She heard crying coming from many tipis. Too many voices were lamenting the loss of their children.

She skirted the main camp area and darted between some buffalo grass and a cedar dead-fall. Pausing to check if the coast was clear she scurried to Guapahka's tipi. The old man was there chanting.

Chanel ran to where she had knelt the night before. She looked at the old man as he chanted. Blood was caked on his ribs and on the top of his leg. She rushed over to him. She sniffed him and smelled the blood and the sweat and the creek mud that was mingled in his wounds. It didn't look like a puncture wound from a bullet. The skin was peppered and filled with sand and tiny rocks.

The Shaman ignored her and continued chanting.

She returned to the buffalo robe that she had sat on. She waited for the Shaman to acknowledge her. He kept chanting.

A veil of darkness fell upon her. Her heart raced. Panic consumed her. Chanel was losing consciousness.

What if she could not change back?

Chapter Thirty Three

Chanel awoke to someone running their hands through the hair on her temples. The warmth of someone's lap comforted her head. She opened her eyes and saw Guapahka leaning against one of the tipi poles and humming to herself. Her eyes were closed.

When Chanel stirred Guapahka looked down at her.

"My, how you sleep hard Little One," Guapahka smiled.

"How long have we been here?" Chanel asked as she sat up.

"It is time for the mid day meal. Are you hungry?" Guapahka asked.

"I'm starving-marvin," Chanel acknowledged.

"You are what?" Guapahka had a puzzled look on her face.

Chanel smiled, making sure she didn't laugh aloud.

"It is just a saying meaning I am very hungry," she explained to Guapahka.

"Are the men back from their hunting?" Chanel was afraid they would come back and go after the children.

"No," Guapahka said, "I will tell the men what has happened and I will go with them to the school," Guapahka stated decisively.

"Please, don't go by yourself! I fear the suited man will have you arrested," Chanel pleaded.

"Perhaps he will. But, I have to go because I am the one that you taught the meaning of the words on the papers."

"I understand. Just don't go by yourself," Chanel reiterated.

Guapahka stood and stretched. It had been a long night for her also.

"Let me get us some food. You have things to tell me and I am sure you have things to ask," Guapahka said and then turned to leave the tipi.

She returned with some flat bread and venison. Chanel remembered her dad making venison on the grill and even making jerky, but none ever tasted as good as this. There was honey on the bread and some pumpkin that had been cut into strips and roasted.

Guapahka sat down and they ate in silence for a moment.

"Guapahka," Chanel began as she set the cloth holding her food down on her legs, "have I become something?"

"You mean more than a girl with a gift?" Guapahka asked.

"No, I mean a freak of some sort," Chanel looked deep into Guapahka's eyes.

"What is a 'freak'?" Guapahka's eyebrows furrowed in confusion.

"Have I become something against nature?" Chanel tried better to define her question.

"Little One, it was nature that gave you this gift. If you use it for good as nature intended, then you cannot be against nature." Guapahka sat her food down also. She turned to face Chanel.

"If you are worried that you have lost who you were, then the answer is a little yes and a little no. You will always be Chanel. You will always have the gift. You will always be burdened with deciding when you should use your gift as it is not for you to abuse. It is a privilege to have. But when you are not asking to use the gift, you are still Chanel and you should live Chanel's life also."

"Will I have more control over it?" Chanel relaxed at Guapahka's assurance.

229

"What do you ask?" Guapahka again was perplexed at Chanel's question.

"Like now, I have shifted from me to the fox and back again in a time of need. And only the Shaman has been there to witness. I feel as if the gift has control of me instead of me controlling the shifting back and forth. Will it always be like that?" Chanel asked.

"Little one, I don't have the gift," Guapahka started. "My father had it and I learned and watched what I dared. But, I never watched the change. When it happened, he was away from his family. I do know that he said it is not to be witnessed by those who don't share the beliefs of our people."

Guapahka continued. "This gift is a power of good over the darkness that drives people to do bad things. And, it is not for the betterment of the person who holds it.

"It is my understanding that you cannot change without a purpose and that is why you ask your tai-me for guidance as you did in the woods during your vision quest," Guapahka explained.

"That is something else." Chanel was not satisfied. "If your tai-me was the hawk, as was Cynthia's and you and I shared a vision quest about the fox, why isn't your tai-me a fox?" Chanel asked.

"Your tai-me is your protector. Your protector and your spirit can't be the same. They are two." Guapahka answered.

"Why was I given the gift and not you?" Chanel asked.

"That is a question for 'He that watches over us'. Perhaps we all have the gift. Maybe I didn't know to chase it or how to hold it. I don't know all that is. You will need to seek out those who know more than you do if is your desire to use your gift when you return."

230

At that, Chanel heard dogs barking in the distance and horses walking.

"Do you hear that, Guapahka?" Chanel quizzed.

"Yes, Little One, why?"

"I am afraid I will hear, taste and smell things more than I did before. I worry that I will be confused all the time about who I am," Chanel confessed.

"Maybe you will hear, taste and smell things before others, but if you know and have the strength about who you are, those senses can just be more of the tools that your father told you to find. Don't make them a burden to bend your back."

A woman burst into the tipi. She said something to Guapahka. Guapahka nodded. The woman looked at Chanel and smiled.

"She said the men have returned. It may be best if you accompany me to explain the paper and words," Guapahka directed as she rose to exit.

She and Chanel left the tipi and walked out to meet the riders.

The men did not dismount. Someone had met them outside the camp and told them of the children.

The same Indian who had directed them to bring Chanel spoke directly to Chanel after he and Guapahka had spoken.

"Guapahka says that I should not go to bring my children back to their families. She says you read the words on the paper that tell us that Kiowa chiefs have decided this school was for our children. Do you tell me that I know less about what will make my sons and daughters strong than the white man's government?" His tone was indignant.

"No, sir. I can only tell you what I know will happen to the Indian in my lifetime and in the lifetime before me.

"I have read that the Indians will struggle to keep their identity. They will fight becoming white. There will be many famous Indians in the history of the United States. Many will be famous for fighting and many will be famous for what they do for their people. I don't remember in my history lessons that the two were ever one and the same."

"Why do you say in your lifetime, you are near as old as I." He challenged her credibility.

Chanel looked at Guapahka.

"I will have to tell you of this Little One and why she is here," Guapahka said. "It is my wish to let our husbands eat and rest. It is then my wish for you to take me to the school. It is not my wish to go there to bring our children home unless the school is not what the words on the paper said it is to be. I will tell you more while you eat if that is what you see to be a wise action."

The hunter looked at Chanel.

"And do we take this one with us?" he asked.

Guapahka moved to stand beside Chanel.

"She has been on a quest. Now she has a mission. It is my desire, if it is your desire, that we as a people explore this school and the treaty words for ourselves. This Little One needs to return to her path."

The man looked intently at Chanel. He motioned to one of his riders and said something to him in Kiowa. He then dismounted and went to the tipi that Chanel had been taken to. The rest of the riders unloaded their bounty and disappeared into the camp with their families.

"Little One, walk with me." Guapahka put her arm around Chanel's shoulders.

"My husband will send a rider with you to return to the passage to your world. I think you have received what you came to receive and it will take you to Cynthia Tallchief.

"Are there Kiowa people living where you live?" Guapahka inquired.

"I will find them," Chanel stated.

"The Kiowa will understand if you explain. It will be hard to get to the person you seek because you are not a man and these gifts are usually given to the men. It is important if you want to use this gift that you seek more guidance. If it is too much for you, let it go to the winds and do not think of it. Hohn-day-ohn-day." Guapahka held her palm open towards Chanel.

"What does that mean?" Chanel wondered if she should already know it.

"It means 'everything is good', Guapahka explained, 'if you keep your heart open, everything will be good."

Chanel wrapped her arms around Guapahka's waist. Guapahka looked to the sky above her and then pressed her cheek to Chanel's head.

"I will always think of you Guapahka," Chanel said as tears filled her eyes.

"And I will think of you Little One." Guapahka hugged her tight.

"I ask one favor, Little One," Guapahka said as she pulled away.

"Anything," Chanel confirmed.

"I sensed in you strength when you came into our camp, but I also sensed in you a feeling of being alone. In our talks you have mentioned your family. It is there that you will maintain that strength. Always keep them close. Remember that it is all of the rocks that make up the mountain."

"Yes ma'am," Chanel acknowledged.

The young hunter mounted his pony again and led one

233

over to Chanel.

She had never ridden bareback. She looked wide eyed at Guapahka.

"Hold with your knees," Guapahka said softly.

"Yes ma'am," Chanel smiled meekly.

Guapahka helped Chanel on to the horse.

Chanel reached into her shirt and pulled the tai-me out to be seen.

Guapahka held hers up to Chanel.

"When I see Cynthia again, I will tell her how crazy her grandmother was," Chanel announced with a big smile on her face.

"Crazy was good for her grandmother?" Guapahka asked with furrowed brow.

"Crazy is good for Guapahka and will be good for Cynthia Tallchief." The hunter pulled her lead rope around to head out of camp.

Chanel grabbed two handfuls of mane as she started to tumble backwards off the pony. She looked over her shoulder at Guapahka as she regained her balance. Guapahka waved. Her eyes now filled with tears. She caressed her tai-me softly in her fingers.

Chapter Thirty Four

Chanel and the young hunter rode at a trot for almost an hour without speaking. Sensing his anger at having to escort this girl, Chanel kept to herself and made good time of acquainting herself with the landmarks back to Chickasha. She recognized many of the features surrounding the river from her trip to the camp. Finally, she could see the buildings on the north shore of the Washita River. She knew them to be an Indian school.

She kicked her pony softly to come along side the hunter.

"Do you speak English?" she asked him.

"I speak English," he huffed back at her. "I speak Kiowa and I speak much Mexican. How many languages do you speak?" He never looked at her.

Chanel was sure he was not happy to have been delegated to take her home. He wouldn't make eye contact when he spoke.

"Only one but I will take Spanish in school," Chanel explained.

"School!" He scoffed.

Chanel edged her horse closer to him.

"Yes, can we slow just a little bit? I want to ask you about those buildings over there."

The young Indian looked over at her and reined his pony to a walk. He looked over at the buildings on the other side of the river.

"It is a school for white people that we are taken to by force. It is a school that washes the ways of the Kiowa from his head and fills it with white lies. It is to make the Kiowa a little man and the white man bigger. That is all that it is!" He looked at Chanel as if to challenge her to deny it.

"Why do the Kiowa not go to this school instead of the Rainy Mountain School? It is closer?" Chanel asked.

The boy snarled at the fact that she did not know as much as he did.

"This is Riverside Indian School. It is for the Wichita, Delaware and Caddo. It is not for the Kiowa and the Kiowa are pleased to not go there," he explained.

As he talked, Chanel could see that he was not much older than she if older at all.

"How old are you?" she inquired.

"Old enough!" he stated emphatically.

"Are you old enough to not to have to go to the school?" Chanel dug deeper.

He pulled his reins to his chest and looked at her. She could sense anger in his eyes.

"What is your name?" Chanel asked as she stopped along-side him.

He was looking at Chanel, but his mind was racing to another place and time.

Finally he offered his name.

"My name is Walks-With-Fire, but the white eyes call me Goombi," he said.

Chanel understood that a Kiowa's name was reflective of a Kiowa's personality or an event in that person's life.

"And why are you called Walks-With-Fire?" she pressed further.

His cheeks flushed and he smiled as he reminisced.

"It was at my quest that I saw an owl land on a rock in front of me. He had yellow and red cloth in his claw and I thought it was fire. It was as if he was bringing me a power."

"Well, Walks-With-Fire, I am Chanel. I think you would be a wiser man to go to the Indian School but I can understand why you would be afraid to go," she offered.

"Afraid!" he bowed out his chest and whirled his pony around. "I am not afraid!"

"That was not what I meant!" Chanel interrupted hurriedly. "I meant that I would not want to be forced to be taken from my family and the things I loved."

He glared at her.

"Move! We have a long journey to your world," he snarled again and kicked his horse to a gallop.

"Wait!" Chanel hollered in vain as she tried to catch up to the angry hunter.

And again, for what seemed like eternity, they rode in silence.

At a creek he pulled up to let the horses drink.

Chanel dismounted and led her horse to the water next to his.

"All I've been trying to say is…" she started.

"All you are saying is too much!" he cut her off.

"But, I want to …" she began again but this time he put his hand over her mouth to silence her.

He raised his fingers to his lips and slowly looked around the creek bed to his right. He was listening.

Before he could turn to look over his left shoulder they were upon them.

Two Indians bolted from the brush behind them.

"Whoa ha! What falls to the hands of the Comanche?" shouted the bigger of the two on a snorting Appaloosa .

"It is a lowly Kiowa and a white girl from the city!" shouted the other ambusher, as he edged his pony in to force Chanel and Walks-With-Fire into the deeper water.

From the cottonwoods along the shore, three more young hunters guided their ponies in to circle their quarry.

237

Chanel was petrified. They were all about the same age as Walks-With-Fire but they were intimidating nonetheless. It was unsettling seeing real Native Americans in a scene straight from a Hollywood movie. She was certain it was no movie, but the entire event was surreal.

The big hunter roared, "This is Comanche land and you must pay to cross through it!"

"The Kiowa walk this land *with* the Comanche. It is the white man's law!" Walk-With-Fire shouted with the same fury as the Comanche hunter.

"The law is the law of the strong! The strong make the law and the Comanche are stronger than all the Kiowa. The Kiowa are all women and women-boys!" He laughed hard and the rest of his band laughed with him.

Walks-With-Fire braced his legs, for he knew what was coming.

The Comanche rode hard at him in turns and tried to kick him as they passed. His own pony bolted from the creek and ran to the edge of the cottonwoods to avoid the melee.

He fell into the waist-deep water, but righted himself before the next onslaught. The Comanche were skilled riders and could turn their horses on their heels to make quick runs at Walks-With-Fire. Soon, fatigue got the best of him and he fell again.

As quick as cats they were all over him. They held him under for what seemed like an eternity and raised him once to get his breath. Before he could gather himself, they held him under again.

Chanel knew there was nothing she could do but she darted in to try anyway.

"What is this?" cried one of the Comanche. "This white girl needs to see fish also?"

He grabbed at her neck to get control. Chanel turned and bit him hard on his hand. Her dad had taught her some self-defense that was in a bully-awareness program at school. She brought her palm up under his chin and his teeth rattled as they closed involuntarily. He fell to his knees in pain. The other Comanche were laughing at their struggling brother.

"She is a white girl!" the leader admonished. "She is no stronger than a Kiowa!"

The Comanche were watching her escape and it was giving Walks-With-Fire time to catch his breath.

But Chanel was more than just a white girl. Her adrenaline was racing and her defense was up. Knowing what Guapahka had taught her, she could sense a presence within her.

Chanel bolted for the trees on the upper bank. She was quick and agile. Two of the Comanche let go of Walks-With-Fire to pursue her. The one she had hit was still nursing his mouth.

The other two held onto Walks-With-Fire but were watching the chase. Chanel disappeared into the cottonwoods.

The respite gave Walks-With-Fire time to get both his breath and then his wits. He brought his heel down onto the inner leg of the hunter on his left. When the hunter loosened his grip to catch his balance Walks-With-Fire brought his left forearm to the throat of the Comanche on his right. As the Comanche's head snapped back Walks-With-Fire hooked his arm under the reeling hunter's leg and tumbled him over into the shallow water. The Comanche must have hit his head on a submerged rock for he stood up dazed and stumbling. He then brought the heel of his foot up to the stomach of the other and it took that one's breath away.

Grasping his ribs the wounded Comanche boy fell to the shore coughing.

Walks-With-Fire gathered his pony's reins and the reins of Chanel's pony and followed the chase after the quick white girl. As he topped the bluff that Chanel had disappeared over, he stopped. There was Chanel standing behind a huge Cottonwood waiting for him.

He smiled at her and held the reins out to her. She easily jumped onto the pony's back. Chanel started to gallop away but Walks-With-Fire had other plans. She stopped to watch him.

He jumped his pony into the creek and across the bank. Leaping with the grace of a dancer; he jumped to the ground and gathered the reins of the Comanche ponies. Climbing back onto his horse, he crossed the creek once more to join Chanel.

They ran until the tree-lined creek was out of sight. On a red dirt mesa, that Chanel recalled to be the present day town of Verden, they stopped to look back.

"High five!" Chanel breathlessly offered her palm to Walks-With-Fire.

She laughed aloud when she saw his puzzled expression.

"Never mind!" that was so awesome, Walks-With-fire," she panted.

He smiled at her enthusiasm.

"Chanel is a fighter of men?" he asked.

"No." She explained, "my dad was more worried about the mean *girls* at school."

"At school?" he was astonished.

Chanel looked at him and smiled.

"Yes, I go to school also." She had her breath back. "Walks-With-Fire, I think you should try the school. You can always leave," Chanel said and then added sarcastically: "Besides, I've seen you run."

Walks-With-Fire smiled and turned to continue the journey.

Over his shoulder he said to Chanel.

"Fourteen. I am fourteen of my years."

They rode in silence for an hour or so. Chanel could see the Washita River where it flows north above Chickasha. She motioned for Walks-With-Fire to follow her now. After a long while she could recognize what was to become Shanoan Springs Park. She knew where the tunnel was and she knew better than to show Walks-With-Fire.

"Stop here," she directed.

She dismounted and handed the reins to Walks-With-Fire. Until now she never realized how cute he was. She wished she could tell him that she lived in the twenty-first century and all about Cynthia and Blair, but she would only confuse him as much as it all confused her.

He got off his pony and walked over to her.

"Where are your people?" he looked around at the emptiness of the area.

"They will be here soon." She looked around confirming this to be the right place.

"I will wait," he offered.

"No, you go back to your camp. You have been gone long enough."

He looked at her frowning. After a few seconds he turned to remount his pony.

"You are ashamed to be seen with a Kiowa so I will let you go to your people alone." The disappointment in his voice was obvious.

Chanel stepped quickly over to him and put her hand on

his knee.

"Walks-With-Fire, I have never been as proud of the Kiowa as I am now. I fear that you will struggle in the years to come, but I will tell you this: the Kiowa will survive all your trials and the Kiowa will always be a proud nation. Please trust me on that." Chanel backed away from his horse. "It is time for you to be with your people. You still have the Comanche at the creek to deal with."

He looked at Chanel and smiled. He pulled a leather bag from his waistband and tossed it to her.

"Think of me when you are in your school, for, soon, I will be in my school thinking of this day when Chanel defeated the Comanche," he said. "And if I don't like this school, I will leave it."

Turning to the west, he kicked his pony to a gallop. His right hand came up as he rode. His palm was to the sun.

"High five!" he hollered to the wind. "High five, Chanel!"

His voice echoed from the west as he rode away.

Chanel watched him ride away, wondering if ever she would see him or Guapahka again. She would cherish this adventure. It was a gift in itself.

Chapter Thirty Five

Chanel entered the tunnel. She was exhausted and dirty.

Her dad was sitting on the edge of the well when she started climbing out.

Chanel's dad heard her below him climbing up from the bottom.

"Change your mind!" He leaned down into the well.

"No, Dad, I went there, "she defended as she reached the top. She threw her leg over the rock perimeter and teetered with exhaustion. "Here, Walks-With-Fire gave you some jerky." She threw him the leather pouch.

"Honey you have only been gone…my gosh, what happened to you!" He exclaimed when he saw the scratches and torn clothing from her ordeal. He helped her get her feet on the ground.

"Sit down, Dad, we have to talk." Chanel sighed as she rested on the well.

As he studied the bag and sampled the jerky, Chanel spent the next hour describing what had happened to her. It was too fantastic for belief, but he could not argue with the details of the story.

Chanel had described the rural area between Chickasha and Anadarko in detail. This was rural area that in his youth her dad had hauled hay for farmers and as a young man, he had rough-necked in the oil fields. Chanel would only know the topography details of their highway trips back to Elk City. The red bluffs at Verden were still visible from the highway but not the views of the river bends and the clapboard buildings that had been Riverside Indian School in the Eighteen-Hundreds. The current Riverside Indian School north of the Washita River in Anadarko was now made up of modern buildings of red and tan concrete and mortar. Chanel would not know these things. He had no choice but to believe her.

"Well, Sweetheart, I think we need to go home and tell Mom what happened to you on *this* trip," he proposed. "I think she will be as perplexed as I am."

"Dad," Chanel started, "you believe me don't you?"

He stopped and knelt down in front of her.

"Sweetheart, I didn't want to believe what you are telling me. I didn't want to admit that there is more to our world than I could ever explain to you. Plus, these past few days are too fantastic to comprehend." He looked at the ground soaking up all that she had said. Finally, "but, I think maybe you are not just special to me because I'm your dad." he relinquished. "I think you are special with a purpose."

She threw her arms around his lanky neck and they held each other for the longest time.

"C'mon," he said as he stood up, "we got a lot of talking to do and I'd rather do it at the kitchen table instead of out in these woods. They are starting to give me the willies."

"Okay, Dad."

They had walked a few steps when Chanel put her hand out to stop him. "Did you know we are part Kiowa?"

"Yes, I knew that. Did I never tell you?"

"You said my great grandmother was Chickasaw," Chanel answered.

"No, I told you she was raised by the Chickasaws. She was Kiowa. Rumor was, she was the daughter of one of the Kiowa leaders who went to prison for a wagon train attack during the Indian relocation in western Oklahoma. A mission worker coming from Santa Fe to Fort Smith brought her to Ada and left her with the Chickasaws when she was just a toddler."

Chanel thought about Guapahka relating Santanta's death at the prison. This is the connection eluding everyone. Chanel had the gift because Santanta passed it to her. Cynthia's great grandfather Lone Wolf was Santanta brother. Cynthia and Chanel were blood relatives!

They continued home but had no more than taken a few steps when Dad's cell phone rang.

"Hello," he said into his phone.

"Dad?" questioned a girl's voice.

"Yes."

"Is Chanel with you?" It was Chelsea.

"Right here with me," he answered and then asked, "Chelsea I can barely hear you, what's up?"

"Dad, Miss Ireland has disappeared. The staff won't talk to me except for the aid we talked to the other day. She said Miss Ireland might have walked away from the nursing home. And Dad," Chelsea started to cry, "they said a new bottle of her medicine has been emptied and thrown on the floor. They think she might have tried to take her own life."

'Chelsea, calm down, where are you? " Her dad couldn't understand her now that she was crying.

"I'm at the nursing home parking lot."

"Okay, I heard you better then. Stay there," he directed. "Chanel and I will get to my truck and meet you there in ten minutes."

He hung up the phone and put his hand in Chanel's.

"There is something wrong at the nursing home, Chanel, do you think you can run with me all the way to the house to get my pickup?" he was shaken at Chelsea's allegations.

"Yes, I can." she was wishing she could explain just how far and fast she could run now.

"Okay, we are going to …" he began.

"Meet Chelsea at the nursing home, I know," Chanel cut him off. "Dad, I don't believe Miss Ireland would take those pills to hurt her self."

"How did you know about the pills?" he asked as he turned to run.

"*I* could hear Chelsea fine, Dad."

He raised one eyebrow and grinned. "Okay, then, she's waiting for us at the nursing home. Or would you rather twitch your nose and let *me* two-leg it to my truck?"

"Dad!" Chanel smiled.

Actually, she had considered it.

Chapter Thirty Six

Tabitha Huffman-Cross was pacing the cold cement floor to the basement storage area. A dirt-dauber clod clung to the single light bulb glowing dim against the gray ceiling. Her cigarette hung loose in exquisitely manicured fingers. Her nephew and henchman stood over Jacob pinning him down to a chair by his shoulders. A pen and several documents were under his nose at an old typewriter desk in front of him. Furnace noises blanketed most of what Huffman was saying but Jacob knew what she wanted.

"You could sign the papers and get on with your miserable life, Jacob. I don't know what an old orphan planned to do with the land anyway!" she ranted.

"Say something, you old fool!" her driver demanded.

Jacob stared at the documents before him. The farm on Walnut Creek was a distant memory. Until Miss Huffman-Cross, the owner of the nursing home and a sister by adoption, had brought up the mineral rights, he had not known they existed.

Now when he thinks of the farm and of losing his sister and parents to accidents, he wishes he had returned to McClain County to investigate their lives and his roots. But had he done so, he would never have been able to watch over Miss Tallchief after her father had died. And now he secretly watched over Miss Blair Ireland.

He knew who she was from that day at the well so long ago. He could never tell her who he was. It was a shame he'd suffer through alone.

He remembered back to the day that had followed Cynthia and her brothers to their camp on the Little Washita. Cynthia's arm was broken and her mother was disapproving

247

of Jacob being at their home.

"Jacob, you have to defend the rights of the weak at the *very moment* your heart sees the wrong. Even if you stand alone against those you walk with daily," she had admonished, "It is a greater testament to character than merely hoping for a chance to redeem an injustice."

But Cynthia's brother had come to his rescue.

"Mother, Jacob carried Cynthia from the well on his back. Is it not also true that a man is valued by the burden he is willing to bear for the weak?" he had defended.

And so it had been for years to come. Cynthia's brothers and her father taught Jacob the way of the Kiowa and her Mother taught Jacob the way of the good man. Jacob found them to be one and the same. Character traits the Huffmans never enjoyed.

When Jacob was eighteen and had proven himself to be a good man, Cynthia's Father noticed a gift Jacob had been given. This gift would be enhanced by the way of the Kiowa Shaman.

And, subsequently, many years later, Miss Huffman-Cross had stumbled across Blair Ireland's connection with Cynthia, Jacob and the well. Jacob's tie to Ms. Ireland was the leverage she needed.

Now as then, Jacob was faced with adversity. He would sign all the documents to gain Miss Ireland's release if he truly believed that she would be released. He knew Huffman-Cross's heart. He knew that the woman had taken a bold step in kidnapping Ms. Ireland. He could smell fear and anger in Tabitha Huffman-Cross. To Jacob, that exposed her deceit. Jacob needed to gain his release to search for Ms. Ireland.

Tabitha Huffman-Cross intended to let her die if she

wasn't already dead.

"You are but a few years younger than me, Tabitha." Jacob finally spoke. "What plans does an old fool of a woman have for the property?"

Tabitha Huffman-Cross sprang across the room and struck Jacob backhanded across his ear knocking him from the chair to the floor.

He recognized the blow. It had been administered by her father and mother many times before he had left to live with the Tallchief family.

"Pick him up!" she ordered her nephew.

The driver grabbed handfuls of Jacob's lapels and raised his frail body off the ground. With his right foot he slid the wooden chair back under Jacob's knees and pushed him down onto it. Blood etched a trail from Jacob's ear to his jaw-line.

Tabitha Huffman-Cross bent down to bring her nose to within inches of Jacob's. She pinched his ear with arthritic fingers and pulled it to her lips.

"You will sign right now or your precious Ms. Ireland dies in the cellar." Her hissing voice was soft and menacing. "I will live without the mineral rights to watch you suffer for her death if that is what I am left with. It is your choice, old man."

Through the ringing in his head, Jacob tried to think. He had to get out in order to save Blair Ireland. As a red-tailed hawk he could move effectively. He knew he had to give in to be able to get out of this underground cage.

"If I sign, will you take me to her?" he moved to get the ball rolling.

"Immediately," Tabitha Huffman-Cross answered still holding his ear in her talon-like fingers.

Jacob pulled his chair closer to the table to sign the papers. He was dizzy from the blow to the head and had to steady himself with both arms on the table top.

The nephew backed up to the wall and reached behind him to get a grip on a short two by four. He leaned against it.

Jacob signed the documents as Tabitha Huffman-Cross pulled each signed paper from under his pen.

Jacob signed the last and tossed the pen to the table in front of him. Both his arms were laid across the table to steady him.

"Now take me to Ms. Ireland," he demanded.

Tabitha Huffman- Cross looked at her nephew and smiled wickedly.

"Sure, Jacob," she agreed and nodded.

At that instant, the driver swung the two by four down across Jacob's arms breaking both just above the wrist. Jacob fell to the concrete floor hitting his head. In his mind's eye he was soaring. In reality, he was losing consciousness.

"Put him in the cellar with the old woman! Everyone will assume they fell in together as two old people stumbling in the darkness. It would be obviously in her dementia, that Ms. Ireland convinced this old custodian to assist her in running away and escaping from her nursing home. We do have nursing records that Miss Ireland had abused her medication as recently as last week," Huffman-Cross thought aloud to her nephew as she inspected the signed documents.

"I have to get these post-dated and filed. Do you think that you can handle that or do I have to come back and do THAT myself also?" The nephew knew the question was rhetorical.

Her step was purposeful as she exited the room.

He scooped Jacob from the floor and draped him across his shoulders. Jacob's arms hung twisted over the driver's back. He carried Jacob out of the room and up the concrete steps into the back offices of the nursing home. No one would see him load the body in the back of the Cadillac.

In the middle of the now vacant concrete basement, a single feather rested against a drop of blood where Jacob's body had lain.

Chapter Thirty Seven

Chanel and her Dad arrived at the nursing home to find Chelsea sitting in the family waiting area. A police officer was talking to the head nurse at the nurse's station.

"Dad, they are saying that Miss Ireland's room was empty when they checked on her at three a.m. Her clothes were gone and all her photos from the dresser. Betty says that an empty pill bottle was found under the edge of the bed." Chelsea was talking ninety miles an hour. "They also say that the custodian's keys were found near her closet and his belongings are missing from his room in the basement."

"Slow down, Sweetheart," her dad calmed. "Where is Ms. Huffman-Cross, the nursing home manager?"

As if on cue, Ms. Huffman-Cross appeared walking towards them from the hallway. Chanel's senses were instantly heightened.

"Dad, that woman is evil!" Chanel whispered through gritted teeth.

"Did you need me?" she asked as she approached them.

"Yes," Chanel's dad replied. "What can you tell us about Ms. Ireland?"

She had an obvious mask of concern on her face.

"Nothing, I'm afraid." she started, "as you are not family or the authorities, I have to respect Ms. Ireland's privacy until this is resolved."

She turned to walk away. Over her shoulder she added, "I'm sure the local reporters will get out a by line out as soon as the police release it. You can then read the details in the newspaper."

Chanel's dad caught up with her at the nurse's station and put his fingers on her shoulder to get her to face him.

"Ms. Huffman-Cross," he said, "you know me from the reading sessions. You know how close Ms. Ireland and my daughter are."

She turned quickly.

"Sir, if you put your hand on me again, I will have this officer arrest you," she snapped with an icy glare.

"Officer," she announced with her voice rising. "These people are not family members. They don't have family members here and have harassed my staff and residents on two separate occasions now. Could you ask them to leave so they don't hinder our search for Ms. Ireland?"

Her eyes never left Chanel's dad's eyes.

"No, we'll leave," He moved his hand. "We will leave you to find Ms. Ireland.

"Come on girls." he directed as he backed away from the wretched woman.

"But, Dad!" Chelsea protested.

He motioned her to silence by bringing his hand up.

Tabitha Huffman-Cross walked back down the hallway to her office. Chanel's dad watched her unlock her office door. Before entering she stole a glance at him. He knew she was hiding something. Chanel was right about evil forces in Ms. Ireland's life.

"Dad, Chanel's gone!" Chelsea broke his concentration.

"What?" he turned to scan the rest of the nursing home.

"Where did she go?" he asked Chelsea.

"I don't know. When you said let's go, I turned and she was gone."

At that moment Betty motioned for Chelsea.

She was behind the police officer who was busy again taking a statement from the head nurse.

She motioned that Chanel had left the building through

the front door and with raised palms and shrugged shoulders, she indicated she didn't know where Chanel had gone after that.

Chelsea grabbed her dad by the sleeve of his coat and pulled softly.

"C'mon, Dad, now we have to find Chanel," Chelsea alerted fearfully.

Chanel's dad took Chelsea by the hand to slow her haste. He looked out the door of the nursing home and across the Shannoan Springs Park that it stood sentinel over. Scanning the park quickly, he relaxed his tension.

"No, Sweetheart," he decided. "I think we need to stay out of her way."

Chapter Thirty Eight

Chanel could feel the dry November grass on her legs and belly as she ran around the nursing home building. Darting between air conditioner units and garbage bins, she could smell and hear so many odors and sounds, it was overwhelming. She needed to differentiate the common signs from the signs she was searching.

She slowed her pace and raised her face to the sky. Walking slowly in the dimming light of dusk, Chanel concentrated on the odors and sounds around her.

She had found no traces of Ms. Ireland leaving the nursing home on foot. That meant that she had not waked away with the custodian even if they had just walked to a parked car.

Ms. Ireland had to have left some other way.

Chanel stopped in her tracks as the whir of a garage door opening from behind the building caught her attention.

Turning the south corner of the building, Chanel caught the distinct odor of a familiar person. She couldn't place it because it was mixed with a scent of nature. She recognized the sent, but not from where.

Suddenly, she knew. It was the man who had been at the well in the rainstorm. She recognized the scent and remembered the talon-like hands that had helped her to her feet the night she found Jessie propped against the tree. She had smelled it on the coat that had been draped over Jessie.

A Cadillac backed out of the driveway and stopped. The driver saw Chanel standing by the driveway. He was puzzled at the sight. He had never seen a red fox and now one was watching his every move.

He put the car into drive and watched Chanel watch him

as he turned to exit the drive. Driving fifty feet or so, the nephew of Huffman-Cross looked in his rear view mirror. The fox was following him away from the nursing home.

He stopped the car and got out. Looking all around he tried to find his pursuer. The fox was gone. Shrugging his shoulders and laughing at his paranoia he returned to the car.

Turning left and driving south along the edge of the park, the driver followed an overgrown road long ago closed to through traffic. Post oaks with thick barriers of English Ivy and plum thickets blocked the road from view of the nursing home. The old covered path to the old Mandeville Estate property that bordered Shannoan Springs Park on the southwest was the perfect seclusion for a mission of evil.

It was that way with the woods and glades. They harbored worlds separate from the world around them. It wasn't that they were evil. They were just perfect environments for hidden agendas.

The agenda could be beautiful as 'stopping by the woods on a snowy evening' or sinister as 'the wolf racing ahead of the little girl to beat her to her destination'. The beauty or darkness of a wooded area hinged on motive.

Chanel and her dad had used the woods to shelter their visits from distraction. They had walked them and talked in them to make sense of a divorce and the consequences of a divorce on an eight year old girl. They had served as a familiar comfort during some very rough times.

Tabitha Huffman-Cross now used them to cover up deeds of envy and greed. The old Mandeville Estate mansion was kept up by the grandchildren of John Jernigan. John had been an oil property buyer from the boom-time nineteen thirties. But the mansion was only to be opened on the anniversaries of Chickasha's founding. No one lived in it.

The two acres of woods that bordered the park on the west and south were un-kept and wild. The six foot security fence kept a solid barrier from casual hikers. Few people knew about the gate from the park as it too had been over-grown with ivy. That is until Tabitha Huffman-Cross had directed her nephew to 'handle things'.

And now, as he stopped to open that gate, the thoughtless accomplice was counting his yet-to-be-received rewards as he 'handled things'.

It was his plan to leave the gate ajar and to drape a few of Ms. Ireland's belongings on the thickets around the entrance. He would drop more along the path after he left the last two obstacle to his fortune in the cellar of the old estate house.

Unaware of the red fox hidden in the thickets behind him, he eased down the last hundred yards to the abandoned cellar.

Chanel followed the car carrying the scent of the man who had saved Jessie's life. She knew something important was down this path. She had never seen this place, but the familiarity was intense.

When the car stopped, Chanel took cover under some vines. The car backed up to a concrete slab. A metal framework with rusted cables attached to two corners of a wooden door was the only structure on the slab. Neglected flower beds framed the slab on three sides. An old slat porch-swing with natural oak supports was piled in a heap to the west of the flower beds.

Roses, left from some long ago garden, had overtaken the pile and had strewn vines in all directions. Many vines were crisscrossing the slab to impede maneuvering through the door.

The driver got out and moved over to open the heavy

wooden door. Pulling latex gloves from his coat pocket, he reached for the rusty handle of the cellar door.

"You still in there old woman?" He mocked as he pulled against the heavy weight.

The scent of Ms. Ireland wafted in the breeze to Chanel's nose. She could feel anger welling up inside her. If she had the capabilities she would charge the bullying henchman of Miss Huffman-Cross and teach him a lesson in justice. Not knowing her capabilities she stayed under the bush to observe.

The nephew then went back to the trunk of the car and opened it with his key-fob remote.

"Still with me, old man?" He again mocked his victim. "Yes. It looks like you are still in here. Out cold, but still in here."

He grabbed Jacob by the belt and roughly pulled him to the edge of the trunk opening where he could get an arm around his waist.

He scooted Jacob over the rear bumper and let him fall to the ground. Jacob's arms lay deformed at his sides. Chanel reeled at the sight of this poor gentle man's condition. A low growl surfaced from her throat.

The driver grabbed Jacob by his shoulders and dragged him down the stairwell of the cellar. Placing him next to the shivering and unconscious Ms. Ireland, he laughed. A large knot was on her temple and her lip was also bloodied.

"Here's your boyfriend, Blair," he proclaimed. "Now, do I need to chaperone the two of you or can I trust you to a proper courtship?"

He took his finger and wiped some of the blood still oozing from Jacob's lip and walked over to the stairwell. He smeared some on one of the steps.

He took another finger and got some blood from Ms. Ireland's lip and wiped it on the wall of the stairwell.

With both hands he scooped dirt off the floor and started up the stairs. Inching up the stairs backwards, he sifted the dirt from his hands to cover both the drag marks from Jacob's heels and his own tracks.

Feeling confident in his cover up, he went back to the trunk of his car and grabbed a pry bar and the bag that he had gathered from Jacob's room to look like he too had run away.

At the door he tossed Jacob's few belongs into the cellar. Then he pried the cable eyebolts from their moorings so as to appear that the door broke free of the framework to close on it's own behind the two victims. He was hoping an investigation would conclude Jacob and Ms. Ireland had hit the door on their fall into the cellar breaking it and allowing it to close behind them.

The temperature was expected to get down into the low thirties tonight and that exposure plus the 'accidental' blows to the head should be enough to tie up these loose ends.

He would exit the property through the front gate thereby avoiding any undue traffic from the hidden path to the nursing home.

"Perhaps Ms. Tabitha Huffman-Cross will recognize just how smart I am. I'm not just her nephew to be bossed around like white trash." He spoke aloud as he got into the car to leave.

Chanel watched him drive off from the slab. When he had turned around the old mansion she crept out of her hiding place to investigate.

At the door she could hear labored breathing. It was erratic and feeble. She knew that neither would last the night in these temperatures.

She was sniffing around the edges of the door when the déjà vu came upon her. She had been here before. She could almost feel her own presence at this spot from a previous time. Chanel, in her mind's eye could see Cynthia's face and could hear her saying "this is my favorite…"

"Gotcha, you little vixen!" Chanel heard before the tree limb came crashing down across her back and shoulders. Blackness crept over her as the nephew grabbed her by the nape of her neck. Stunned and confused she hung limp from his grip. He carried her over to a large rock plant potter beside the concrete slab. He put her down to free up his hands. He bent to the potter and wrapped both arms around a wooden planter to remove it from the rock planter that held it. The planter broke up in his hands and fell to the ground scattering old soil and broken slats of wood.

"Oops," he laughed. "That thing was as old as our friends down there."

Chanel could only lie dazed from the blow. She tried to rise, but he was on her immediately.

"Hold on there red fella," he chided. "I'm about to do you a big favor." Looking at the fox that he held in his hands and then down at the hole he had just exposed by moving the round-rock planter, he explained, "You see, down this hole is a meal fit for a king. In fact you might say it has been aged just for your enjoyment." He laughed at his morbid humor.

He held Chanel over the hole and shook her to bring her to full consciousness. When she was fully alert she bared her teeth at him.

"That's it. Wake up," he prodded. "There is enough meal down there for a den of foxes."

He let go of Chanel and with an unforeseen grace she twisted in mid-air to land on her feet. She stumbled and rolled when she hit. She was now at the feet of Jacob and Ms. Ireland on the floor of the cellar. Ms. Ireland blinked and opened her eye to see what had just happened. The light from the removed planter allowed a soft haze into the cellar. She gasped softly when she saw the dusty red fox standing at her feet.

Chanel was bruised and battered but she was conscious to the fact that she was not seen as a friend in this circumstance. Ms. Ireland was trying to back up from the fox.

"Sir," she said to the man lying next to her. "Sir, wake up."

Jacob stirred but the pain had overwhelmed him. His arms throbbed and his head was spinning from the rough treatment he had received. He moaned softly.

"Sir, you have to get up!" Blair exhorted.

"SIR, YOU HAVE TO GET UP!" The nephew yelled down the opening, "A FOX IS GOING TO EAT YOU!"

His laughter was fading as he placed a few broken boards over the opening to the round-rock planter.

Chanel walked to the opening and looked up. She could see his taunting grin as he placed the broken pieces of the wooden planter over the hole.

As she looked up she was again experiencing déjà vu. She had never seen this man before now. She had never seen this house or this garden. And except for the round-rock planter she didn't recognize…

The planter! The round-rock planter!

Chanel let her eyes follow the opening of the planter down.

A chill shook her body!

There were the footholds from Cynthia's well!

The cellar was carved from the original well!

As he placed the last board across the opening, most but not all of the moonlight faded. The cellar would be totally dark after the moon passed across the November sky!

Chanel had to do something quick. She could not reveal who she was to Ms. Ireland. The gift was not to be witnessed by non-believers!

Ms. Ireland was rising to her feet behind Chanel. She was focused on the fox in front of her.

Chanel turned to look at her. She knew that Miss Ireland could not raise the heavy wooden door from the stairwell. Maybe she would be strong enough to climb out of the well one more time.

Chanel eased around Jacob's weakened body to herd Ms. Ireland towards the well shaft.

"Shoo, fox, shoo!" She waved her hands at the animal as it crept around the wall of the cellar towards her.

"Shoo!" she said as she backed away along the perimeter.

Chanel did not want to create too much fear as Miss Ireland was old and possibly more ill than Chanel was aware. She stopped to let Ms. Ireland rest.

A soft moan escaped from Jacob. Ms. Ireland heard it and stooped to comfort him.

"Go away, fox!" she warned. "I won't let you harm this man!"

Chanel could not stand it any longer. She had to let Ms. Ireland know she was on her side.

She backed away so Ms. Ireland could tend to Jacob. She sat beside him and cradled his head in her lap avoiding

262

moving his arms. With her skirt she wiped the now drying blood from his cheek.

"Who are you that you and I are thrown together in this pit?" she murmured softly. "And where is this pit, that I sense recognition?"

Jacob stirred ever so slightly.

"And you, Little Fox, are you here to make certain of our demise?" she demanded with authority. "Well, let me tell you now that you are mistaken if you think you can scare this old woman to panic. I have been in tighter situations than this!"

Chanel wished she could laugh aloud. She sat down and smiled at Ms. Ireland. She had never been as proud of someone as now.

Chanel looked around the room as the shadows grew darker. She saw Jacob's bag and had an idea.

Running over to it she grabbed it by the handle. Dragging the bag to Ms. Ireland she released it and went back to where she had sat before and watched Ms. Ireland's reaction.

Ms. Ireland pulled the bag close to her and then looked back at the dusty red fox that sat monitoring her and the injured man.

"You are a strange little fox, you are," Ms. Ireland decided. "Are you trying to tell me something? Is there food and medicine in this bag?"

Ms. Ireland opened the bag and looked through the contents. There was no food nor was there medicine. There were only a few personal belongings and some letters.

Ms. Ireland looked at the letters before the light had gone completely. They were addressed to Jacob Tallchief.

"Jacob Tallchief?" she asked the man that she was comforting. "Are you Cynthia's brother?" Her frustration at

263

his lack of response was getting the best of her.

"Oh, please wake up and talk to me," she begged. "I need to know if you are Cynthia's brother."

She stared ahead of her for a moment and opened one of the letters.

The writing was old and in pencil. It was difficult to read in the pale moonlight.

She opened more and more until she could find one that was clear in this poor light.

Finally she found a letter written to Jacob when he was in New Mexico. She read it aloud: *"Dearest Jacob, I hope you are well and are learning much from your trip to the Sacred Mountains. Father says you are strong in the spirit and are learning much"*

She read on: *Mother says you have grown to be a man as the Kiowa are men. She is proud of you and the anger she had struggled with for so long is buried deep in her memories. She is not well and I fear she will not live here with us for much longer. The tuberculosis is taking a toll on her. When you saved me from the well and from your brother's wrath, I was not shocked but was…"*

"What?" Miss Ireland could not believe what she was reading. "So you are Cynthia's brother!" Ms. Ireland exclaimed. "But what was this about your brother's wrath? Is your brother not her brother?

"You saved Cynthia from the well? That is, that is so wonderful to know. I have struggled with that fear for all these years!"

Chanel sat quietly. She could not believe what she was hearing. This man had saved Cynthia. This man must be Cynthia's brother. But why was her mother so angry at him?

Ms. Ireland read on: *"Jacob, I can't wait to see you again*

264

and to hear what you have learned about your gift. I know it is foolish and Father would admonish my envy, but I am jealous! To be able to fly over the lands that our father's walked. And as a hawk at that!"

Ms. Ireland had a puzzled look on her face.

Chanel was on her feet now. This man, a hawk. Is this Chanel's hawk? Is this the man responsible for her gift?

Chanel was looking him over. Yes, he could be the man that saved Jessie in the storm but was he also the hawk that guided Chanel to the well?

Enthralled with the wonderful news, Ms. Ireland read on: *"Jacob, I know you fear being like your brothers but do not. They were not your true brothers. Zeke was a bad person and you will never revert to being like him or his father. In fact, since you got out from under his abusive ways, I haven't heard you stutter once! We feel you are the good man that you desire to be and their influence has not corrupted, and never will corrupt, who you truly are. I can't wait to see you. Your sister, Cynthia."*

Ms. Ireland looked up from the letter and looked down at Jacob.

Chanel looked at Jacob also.

Their mouths fell open!

Jacob began to stir. He was weak and badly injured. Chanel and Ms. Ireland could only stare at him.

Here lay one of the boys that had dropped them into the well. Here was one of the heartless creatures that had impacted their lives with great remorse for having abandoned Cynthia to the well.

"Jacob, can you hear me?" Ms. Ireland asked softly.

Jacob stirred again and his eyes opened as mere slits.

"Yes, Ms. Blair Ireland, I can hear your wonderful voice

265

and it gives me great pleasure again," he responded softly.

"Again?" she asked.

"Yes. Again. Can you help to me sit up?"

Blair got her hands under his shoulders and helped pull him to an upright position against the wall.

As he gained composure the feeling came back to his arms and he grimaced. Sweat formed on his forehead. He was very pale.

"Just rest, Jacob," she instructed. "You are hurt badly and need to sit still until I can find a way out of here."

"I need to tell you before time runs out and I won't be able to explain," he defended.

Chanel moved to stand close to Jacob.

"And you, Little Dog of the Woods, I know who you are also," Jacob smiled at Chanel.

Chanel could feel tears welling in her eyes. Can foxes cry?

"Ms. Ireland, after Zeke and Edward drank to unconsciousness, I came back to carry Cynthia from the well. We went to her family home from the springs and didn't return for many weeks. Your father had moved on from the WPA work and we could never find where the two of you went. That summer, I lived with Cynthia's family. Cynthia and I went to the boarding school in the fall after harvest. I had missed my education working for the Huffmans. By the way, they adopted me after my real parents were killed in accidents. I was never really a Huffman.

"Cynthia's father sent me to school to catch up on what I had missed. Riverside Indian School only allowed me to go for a year as I was not Kiowa. I went to the white school in Carnegie after that."

266

He grimaced again as the pain was almost unbearable.

"Please rest, Jacob," Blair pleaded again. "You don't owe me explanation."

"No, I need you to know. You need to know also because I could see you worrying about Cynthia. For many years we searched for you. After Cynthia passed away I decided to go to see my real parent's farm in McClain County. I knew Luther Huffman's daughter Tabitha owned the nursing home here so I came to see what she would tell me. I wasn't sure anymore how to find the old farm."

He caught his breath for a moment.

"While here, I heard your name mentioned by a girl during the reading sessions. I investigated and found you. I was afraid to tell you who I was so I just took a position as custodian to look after you."

Tears rolled down Blair's face.

"Jacob, did you think I was incapable of forgiving you?" she asked.

"No, quite the contrary. I quickly found out that I could tell you but at the same time Tabitha was threatening me to get me to sign the mineral rights under the property over to her. I was afraid to show how important you were to me that she would harm you to get to what she wanted from me," Jacob explained.

"Well, obviously that worked." Blair smiled.

"No, it was too apparent that I was looking out for you," he said. "That is why I recruited our little friend here."

He looked at Chanel.

Blair frowned. "I don't understand what you are saying."

Jacob smiled at Chanel. "Ms. Blair, I will have to explain *that* to you some other time.

"Right now we need to get help before the November

cold gets the three of us," Jacob said. He tried to stand but his strength was gone.

"Jacob, sit still!" Blair admonished. "Tell me what to do and I will do it!"

He closed his eyes in pain. After a moment, he opened them and looked to the wooden door.

"See if you can push that door open. I think it is too much, but we need to try before we discount it altogether."

Blair walked slowly through the shadows, feeling her way until she reached the staircase. She ascended the steps in near darkness. At the landing, she pushed on the door with all her strength. She too was weakened from illness and the abuse she had just been handed. The door wouldn't budge.

"Jacob, it is too heavy for this old woman." She sat on the last step and rested.

Chanel ran to her and turned around in a circle. Ms. Ireland was hesitant to have the little fox that close to her.

Chanel then ran across the cellar to the well shaft and turned once again. She ran back to Ms. Ireland and repeated the motion twice more.

"I think she wants you to follow her." Jacob said.

"To where? And, how would you know that?" Ms. Ireland questioned as she stood up.

"To that depression in the wall, I am guessing," Jacob replied.

Ms. Ireland followed Chanel to the shaft. It was too dark now to see anything significant.

"It is just a wall, little fox. I don't know what you want." Ms. Ireland's frustration grew.

Chanel put her front paws on the wall.

"Do you want me to push it? Is it a false wall little fox?"

268

Miss Ireland asked.

She put her hands on it and pushed. Nothing happened.

She pushed on another spot and nothing happened there either.

Suddenly, a chill shook her body. She had felt this wall before!

Blair Ireland felt along the shaft until she found what she now knew to be there. Handholds!

Would she be strong enough? She had done it seventy years ago, could she again?

"Jacob, we are in the well!" she exclaimed to the now total darkness.

"Are you sure?" He was incredulous.

"Yes, Jacob and I am going up," she stated adamantly.

"Blair, it is an old well and you, if you'll pardon me, are an old woman. I do not think it to be a wise choice," he voiced his strong opposition.

"No, but it is my choice," Ms. Ireland started. "For all these years I have second guessed my decision to leave Cynthia. I have been granted a pardon. I won't allow either of us to freeze to death in this dungeon without trying."

She didn't wait for Jacob to reply. Her hands were feeling for the handholds and her feet were finding places to step into. She started to stumble, but felt two strong hands pushing up on her hips. She was able to continue upward.

"Thank you, Jacob," she said over her shoulder.

"You are welcome, Blair." He replied from behind her.

Climbing ever so slowly as age had overtaken her youth, it seemed forever to the top. Seconds turned to minutes and minutes almost to eternity.

 Finally, feeling smooth stones above her face, she pushed hard upward and knocked boards from the opening.

She was there.

Blair called down to Jacob as she stepped over the rock well and onto the ground.

"I am out Jacob! I am going for help and I promise with all my heart that I will be right back. Can you hear me?"

"Yes, Blair, I hear you!" He called out from the well.

Suddenly, Ms. Ireland stopped in her tracks. Jacob's voice had been so distant behind her when she thanked him. She put both hands on the cheeks of her rear-end. Who had pushed her from behind?

It mattered not. She had to get help for Jacob!

In the distance through the oaks and ivy she could see flashlights and people were calling her name. They were calling for Chanel also.

Blair headed towards the lights.

Chapter Thirty Nine

When the heavy wooden door was raised Chanel's dad, Steph, Chelsea, Jordan, and Jaimie pushed their way down the stairwell. Her brother Cody stood holding the door open.

There on the floor with her arms wrapped around Jacob sat Chanel. She was dressed in an old flannel shirt and khaki slacks taken from Jacob's bag.

Chanel wrapped her arms around her dad and a group hug ensued.

"Cody, when did you get here?" she asked through flowing tears.

"About an hour ago. Chelsea called me. She said you were in trouble," he answered. "Kenzie and the kids are here also."

"Steph, you guys get Chanel to the car," her dad directed. "Someone guide the ambulance to this spot for Mr. Tallchief. Cody and I will keep him company."

As they guided Chanel up the staircase Jordan asked Chanel about the fox. "Ms. Ireland told the ambulance driver there was a fox in the cellar!" Jordan explained.

"A fox?" Chanel asked. "Somebody saw a fox? I love foxes!"

Chapter Forty

Chanel, Cody, and Chelsea drove quietly to the tourist attraction known as Indian City near Anadarko. Chelsea had described her experience with the circle of elders many nights before.

A fear of the unknown kept Chanel quiet, but a confidence in her new found abilities kept her resolute to see this through.

She had been given a note on parchment that a group of "like souls" would be meeting at midnight tonight. She and Chelsea had snuck out knowing Dad and Steph would never approve. Cody had stayed in Chickasha after Chelsea and Chanel had filled him in on the events that had preceded the arrest of Huffman and her assistant two weeks before. He needed to know that Chanel was lucid and not delirious from the blow to her head. The whole tale was a bit fantastic for him. He would always wonder about Chelsea as her imagination had many times led her down wondering paths. But, all in all, he knew there was more to the time portal and shape-shifting events than just the story of a girl falling in a well and hitting her head.

As they turned up the road to the gift shop he turned to speak with Chanel who was sitting quietly in the backseat. He reached back to take her hand.

"We don't have to come here if you don't want to," he offered.

She took his hand and smiled.

"Yeah, I can bust a u-turn and we can go home to our beds," Chelsea agreed.

Chanel leaned forward. "I know we can."

She paused and continued, "I will have to do this

272

sometime or I am afraid I would just wonder the rest of my life what was supposed to come of this power that was shared with me. I am glad you agreed to bring me here. It would be real hard without you two."

"Okay, we are with you to find out. But if you want to leave just let us know and there will be no questions," Cody added as he squeezed her hand.

Chelsea pulled up to the parking area of the gift shop. This visit reminded her of the adventure she, Jordy, and Jaimie had a few crazy nights before except this time, the gate had been purposely left open for Chanel's arrival.

Exiting the car, the three of them heard chanting and drums wafting through the cold night. It was a week before Christmas. The crispness of the air and the smell of cedar smoke was intoxicating.

"It is just beyond the Kiowa Village area," Chelsea offered.

The three of them locked hands and walked through the tourist attractions towards Chanel's appointment with the elders.

At the Kiowa Village, the elder that had talked with Chanel, Jordan and Jaimie during their rendezvous met Cody, Chelsea and Chanel. He held his palm out to Chanel, "Hohn-day-onh-day".

"Yes, everything is good," Chanel touched her palm to his.

Chapter Forty One

Chanel dozed in the gentle rocking of the back seat of the pickup. The highway to her brother's house was straight and treeless. Crossing the Texas panhandle, she, her dad and Steph were going to Cody and Kenzie's house for Christmas. The ever present north wind cooled the openings that the door handle and armrest demanded and resting her head against the sunlit window warmed her face.

The events three weeks ago at Thanksgiving were becoming a memory as were the initially frequent discussions about what had really transpired. Within her family, it was inconceivable that the well was a portal into time and even more so, that Chanel could transform into anything but the pretty twelve year-old that she was. Her family generally agreed that something out of the ordinary had occurred to direct her to Miss Ireland's salvation, but what role Jacob and the Indian elders played was uncertain.

It was accepted reasoning that it must have been Chanel in Wonderland or Chanel and Toto in the Land of Oz. A blow to the head confused all the real explanations. But questions lingered. They lingered in her dad and Steph's mind as well as in Chanel's. The only true compatriot to the events as related by Chanel was Chelsea and possibly Cody.

Chelsea was a rational person and had been part of the detective process. And while Cody was more practical and sometimes found that Chelsea could be a drama queen, he knew the story needed more than rationale to have occurred as it did. He wasn't sure about wishing wells and shape-shifting but his faith and beliefs confirmed the world to sometimes be a mystical arena for events.

But in the true realm of things, Tabitha Cross-Huffman

was a greedy child of her father. She incorporated all the manipulations that she could to get her hands on the property that had been stolen by her family from Jacob's parents. Trying to force Jacob into signing mineral rights over to her by drugging a poor eighty year-old woman was desperate beyond merit.

Ms. Tabitha Cross-Huffman and her never-do-well nephew could look forward to counting miserable days in confinement. And while the confined area wouldn't be a dark and damp well, it would offer only a little more freedom. They were charged with assaulting Ms. Ireland and Jacob as well as extortion and attempted murder. Their trial was pending but the evidence was stacked to the ceiling.

The end result in Jacob and Blair's happy reunification after all these years was harlequin romance material. All the energy consumed in hating a boy for his actions were to be magnified to endearment when his true generous nature as was discovered. And with the farm and mineral rights restored to Jacob, he could pursue a more relaxed and prosperous retirement. He had confided in Chanel that, if she was of a mind to, he would be sharing those golden years with Ms. Blair Ireland at his side.

Chanel had reflected on these as they drove west into Texas but mostly she wondered about her gift and the things that the elders and her beloved Guapakah had shared. Since the rescue from the cellar, she has never again attempted to change into the little fox but her mind raced with the possibilities.

She felt the pickup slow drastically and sat up to see what was happening.

"Are we here?" she stretched and yawned.

Her father was slowing to turn down an old gravel road.

"Not yet, we are still about forty five miles from Pampa."
He went on, "I was telling mom about the old Wheeler
county courthouse at Mobeetie. Would you guys like to get
out and stretch our legs?"

"Sure," Steph agreed. "Are you sure that we can still go
inside the courthouse. It is kinda cold to be walking around a
locked building."

"Yeah, Dad," Chanel began, "this wind blows all the time
up here."

"Sissies," he challenged.

The road wound down through ancient cottonwoods and
over a couple of dry creek beds. The Texas panhandle was
part of what had been known as the Great American Desert
in the seventeen and eighteen hundreds and while it was not
a real desert, it was certainly dry and sparsely vegetated. The
cottonwoods indicated a source of surface water nearby such
as a natural spring or maybe even a high water table
underground. This could explain why the old courthouse had
been built here in the 1880's.

Soon, the tall, two-story structure appeared. It had been
maintained and partially restored for tourists. Square and
simple in its design it nonetheless looked like a skyscraper
out here by itself.

The walls were native stone topped by planked wood at
the gables and eaves. A light gray paint flaked off near
corners and wear areas. Above the main double door
entrance was a window. Two crossed skeleton keys with a
big 18 on one side and a big 86 on the other side
embellished the curved upper portion.

There were life-sized busts of famous Wheeler County
lawmen circling a concrete slab in front of the main door. A
decaying wooden flagpole was surrounded by black

historical markers mounted on silver pipe.

Chanel's dad pulled his truck up to the parking area near the circle.

"When I was a little guy, we would come up here with metal detectors and find bullets, buttons and trinkets from the days this place was booming. Across the highway we just turned off, old fort Elliott stood as the last western garrison before Santa Fe, three hundred miles to the west. That flag pole is the last remnant of the old wooden fort. Lots of activity was here during the 1870's and 1880's."

"Why wasn't the courthouse at the fort?" Steph wondered aloud.

"I think because the fort belonged to the army and the courthouse was run by the citizens of the county," Chanel's dad offered.

"Fort Elliott is gone but Old Mobeetie grew around this courthouse until the City of Wheeler was incorporated near the railroad up the highway. The citizens moved the court to Wheeler's town square but this huge building was left to the coyotes that run up and down these cottonwood lanes." He was doing his usual history lesson because they were a captive audience.

He had no more than mentioned coyotes when Chanel's senses became alert to a hidden audience. She closed her eyes and took in the clues all around her.

"Wanna go inside?" he volunteered a tour. "It is really a neat place."

"I don't know about that," Steph replied skeptically. "There may be a need for a real guide."

"I have been up there many times." Chanel's dad started towards the door. "There is a box for contributions on the first floor and even a jail cell upstairs."

"When was the last time you were here?" Chanel joined Steph's argument.

"Couple years ago when I came to Cherub's birthday," he defended, "I walked around and read the markers out front. They were fairly new."

He opened the door and walked in.

Steph and Chanel looked at each other and shook their heads. An exaggerated sigh and a roll of their eyes, precluded following him just as they had many times before. Sometimes they followed him to keep him out of trouble but most times their curiosity was just as great.

Inside, the courthouse was cool but comfortable. The rock walls were good insulators. The wooden floor was clean and polished from the caretakers' efforts. Several different exhibits lined the walls. Documents from Temple Houston, an attorney and the son of Sam Houston first governor of Texas were displayed under a glass cabinet. Photos of Old Mobeetie and select houses in Wheeler County caught Steph's eye.

Chanel headed straight up the staircase to see the jail. Her instincts were on high alert. Was something waiting for her to discover lurking near the cell?

At the head of the stairs she stopped and listened. The whole upper floor was empty. Nothing stirred and no noises permeated the old building even though the wind outside was ferocious.

Chanel walked slowly towards the jail cell that held presence in the far corner of the floor. It was a free standing cell with flat strapped bars on all four sides and a roof of the same material. It was rusty but smooth. Unlike the polished floors on the first floor and in front of the jail door, the floor within the cell was layered in fine white caliche dust. Two footprints in the dust were pointed away from the metal bunk that hung from the side by chains. It was as if someone had been sitting there with both feet flat on the floor.

Chanel reached forward to try the door. She pulled lightly and it swung free from the latch. It was open and she couldn't resist. She walked in and turned slowly around surveying the confines of the metal structure. Then, backing up to the bunk, she placed her feet in the footprints and sat down slowly. She closed her eyes to enhance her other senses. Initially, the room was quiet and without odors.

Suddenly, the aroma of sweat and dust filled her senses. It was the odor of a working man. Leather and old cotton comingled with the sweat to bring an image indelible to her mind. Chanel could feel the warmth of another body next to her. She opened her eyes and was not surprised to find a young cowboy sitting next to her. His head was in his rough and dirty hands. Chanel's heart was in her throat!

Fearing to move or to even breath aloud; she simply watched the cowboy struggling with his confinement. Should she get up and run or should she let him know she was there beside him?

The question was absurd! She was not sitting beside a cowboy imprisoned in a jail cell! She must be asleep in her daddy's car and headed to Pampa, Texas. Her dreams were getting to be a little too intense these days!

She rubbed her hands together. She could feel them both. She put her hand on the cold steel bench. She could feel it also. She extended her arm ever so slowly towards the cowboy's hat. Lightly gliding her finger tip along the dusty brim, Chanel could feel the stiff felt and knew she was not in her daddy's car driving to a Christmas visit. Chanel was in jail with a cowboy. Most importantly, she wasn't completely shocked!

Entering the jail cell had given her the same feelings that walking through the tunnel at the well had given her. She had sensed the existence of another dimension. Subconsciously, she knew to place her feet into the caliche dust footprints. The cell was a portal just as the well had been!

Abruptly, the cowboy stood and walked to the other side of the cell. Banging the heels of his hands against the flat bars he yelled at the jailer.

"You have to let me out!" he called out in frustration. "It will be too late to make me wait for the circuit judge!"

No one answered his plea.

"Son of a ..." he started as he turned back towards the bench. Seeing Chanel, he froze in his tracks.

"Wha... how ...who are you and how did you get in here?" he demanded. His attention went from Chanel to the door. Stepping quickly he reached it and tried to open heavy jail door. It wouldn't budge.

Panic broke Chanel's complacent observation of his actions. The door was open when she came in. She jumped up off the bench and pushed hard against the rusty old door. It didn't move. She was incarcerated with an angry cowboy.

"Wake up, Chanel!" she closed her eyes and chanted, "Wake up, Chanel. Wake up, Chanel!" Her voice rose with each repeated command.

"Wake up, Chanel!" She clinched the flat iron on the door until her knuckles were white.

The cowboy watched her crazy antics with awe. Instinctively, he was reaching his hands out to keep her at bay.

"Hey jailer!" he called out. "I'm saddled with a wild cat

in here. You better git yourself in here quick!"

Chanel stopped her chanting and stared wide-eyed at the cowboy.

"You might want to bring your lariat!" his voice trailed off at lariat.

"You can still see me?" she asked the stupefied cowboy.

"Uh, yes, ma'am, I can." he began. "I can also hear you if that'll make you less loco."

Chanel let go of the door and turned to face him. She isn't dreaming.

"Who are you?" she quizzed.

"Johnny."

"And what are you in here for?" Chanel was desperately hoping it was not for anything mean or ugly.

"I knocked a man off his horse." Johnny answered, never taking his eyes off Chanel's.

"Because?" she dug deeper.

"He was flaying his bullwhip at some injun children." Johnny's tone was calm. He didn't want to rile the wild cat.

Chanel exhaled at his reply. He obviously wasn't a murderer... maybe.

"What did you do to the man after you knocked him off his horse?"

"Why?" Johnny asked.

"I am trying to decide if I should give you my best tae-bow round-house kick or go sit back down on the bench and figure out where I am." Chanel explained.

"Well," he paused, "I don't know what a tee-bow round house kick is but I reckon I'd choose going and sittin down.

"Cause you see ma'am." Johnny reasoned, "I know how I got here, but I'm thinking you're not from around these parts. I think this is like one of them mirages. Only, I aint really sure who is seeing what."

Johnny placed his palm ever so light against Chanel's elbow. He motioned with his other hand to guide her over to the bench.

She followed his direction and moved to be reseated. Their gazes never left each other.

Chanel sat and placed her hands on the edge of the bench on each side of her legs. She wanted to be able to bolt if necessary.

"Okay, ma'am, I answered a bushel of your questions. I got some if you'll allow?"

"Okay," Chanel obliged.

"Who are you and how in blazes did you get in here?" Johnny sat down at the far end of the bench.

"I came in through that door," she related. "It was open and you weren't in here when I sat down. Oh, and my name is Chanel Lane from Elk City, Oklahoma."

"My pleasure to meet you Miss Lane. But, you see, I've been in here since early morning and you weren't. I didn't hear you come in because that door has been locked tighter than a keg of molasses at a honey harvest."

"Johnny, tell me again why you are here. I think that might explain why I'm here." Chanel tried to relax but the abrupt events were disconcerting.

Johnny loosened his posture and shook his head softly in agreement.

"Alright." he began. "I found that some fellas were running rough shod over a group of Kiowa near the old salt seep in Oklahoma Territory. I had been watching this go on for weeks now but they were getting pretty mean to them injuns. Most were women and children. I rode here to speak with Captain Arrington about what I saw. The Captain was

282

in court so I waited outside the courthouse. Directly, the head of them fellas come riding into town leading a freight wagon full of Kiowa women and children. When they pulled over near the livery stable three of the children jumped from the wagon and tried to run. The head fella turned his big roan on them and pulled out his whip. He popped it within inches of one of them children's ears. When the boy fell, the head fella lashed out again and drew blood on the back of the boy's shirt with his whip."

"And so you...?"

"I jumped from the water trough onto the fella and we tumbled to the dirt." Johnny let out an exasperated breath. "I woke up in this here jail." He turned to look away from his embarrassment.

"Why were they being that way to the Kiowa?" Chanel broke the silence.

"The Kiowa were drying the salt and trading it for necessities. The head fella and his gang of no goods were taking over."

"Who owns the salt seep?" Chanel asked.

"Well, Oklahoma is Indian Territory. I reckon the Kiowa own it." Johnny defended.

Chanel remembered the white school men and the way the head of that group acted towards the Kiowa mothers and children. She could not understand the cruel nature of bigotry.

"So, ma'am," Johnny interrupted, "now, do you know why you are here?"

Chanel didn't know much more than she knew before the telling of his crime. Was she to always be destined to rescue someone? Was her gift that kind of curse? And was her Kiowa relation to her previous adventure a binding tie to their culture?

"Ma'am, I don't mean to interrupt but you see I heard these men saying they were going to be taking over that salt seep operation really quick. I don't think those poor injuns can take much more of the hard licks those men are dishing out." Johnny continued, "So, if you have some sort of spook power to get in and out of here, would you mind using it to go fetch Captain Arrington? I think we are running out of time."

Chanel could feel the humor in his words even if he couldn't. Little did he know that…

"Chanel, did you find the jail?" echoed her father's voice from down the staircase.

She turned to see the staircase and saw that the jail cell door was ajar. She pushed lightly on it and it swung open.

"Well, there we are Johnny. Now I guess you can…"

When she turned she was alone. The cell was empty. Two footprints in the caliche dust marked where Johnny had sat.

"Whoa, look at you! Busted!" her dad exclaimed as he topped the stairs and found her standing in the cell. "Cattle rustling or was it giving liquor to the Indians?"

"Dad that's not funny." Chanel chastised sternly.

"What, sweetheart? What is the matter?" he soothed as he reached the stark metal enclosure that surrounded his daughter.

She thought for a moment, shook her head and smiled.

"Nothing, Dad." She opened the door and walked out. Looking over her shoulder at the empty bench she wrapped her arm in his. "What else did you find in this old building?"

Sadness lurked beneath her waves and she didn't want it to surface.

They walked down the stairs to catch up with Steph.

"You guys had enough history lessons?" she offered.

"Yeah, we are ready to go," her dad agreed.

As they started out Chanel stopped short of the door.

"Oh, wait," she said, "I left my camera in the jail cell. You go ahead I'll be right back."

"Okay, see you in the car." Her dad was walking away from the building towards the car.

Steph hesitated. Something in the air was ominous. Something was not right.

"Honey?" he asked.

Steph shook her head to dismiss her thoughts and joined him in his walk.

When they got to the car he opened the backdoor to get a cold soda from the cooler in the backseat floorboard. He stopped and stared at the seat.

"What is it, Honey?" Steph asked as she saw his posture.

"Come with me," he directed, "Chanel's camera is on the seat!"

With quick steps into the courthouse, he bolted up the staircase.

By the time Steph caught up with him she found him squatted down by the cell door. It was empty except for two sets of prints. An adult sized set of boot-prints at the bunk and a trail of small paw prints leading to them.

About the Author

Royal Lantz is an avid history, geography and social science buff. He believes there is a story behind every name, date, location or event that is worth repeating. Sometimes he will have to put on his digging clothes to find the story, but he will find the story…no matter how cleverly you hide it.